wu

Books should be returned on or before the
last date stamped below

HEADQUARTERS 2009    24 AUG 2006    26 JUN 2007

1 2 MAY 2006    2006

27 JUL 2006    2 0 NOV 2006    1 9 NOV 2007  6 SEP 2007

- 2 APR 2007  HEADQUARTERS

2 8 MAY 2007

2 3 APR 2008

1 6 JUL 2008

3 1 JUL

1 2 MAY 2009

D1433372

# PASSING GO

*Also by Libby Purves*

*Fiction*

CASTING OFF (1995)
A LONG WALK IN WINTERTIME (1996)
HOME LEAVE (1997)
MORE LIVES THAN ONE (1998)
REGATTA (1999)

*Non-Fiction*

THE HAPPY UNICORNS (ed) (1971)
ADVENTURES UNDER SAIL, H. W. TILMAN (ed) (1928)

BRITAIN AT PLAY (1982)
ALL AT SEA (ed) (1984)
SAILING WEEKEND BOOK (1985) (with Paul Heiney)
HOW NOT TO BE A PERFECT MOTHER (1986)
WHERE DID YOU LEAVE THE ADMIRAL? (1987)
HOW TO FIND THE PERFECT BOAT (1987)
THE ENGLISH AND THEIR HORSES (1988) (jointly
with Paul Heiney)
ONE SUMMER'S GRACE (1989)
HOW NOT TO RAISE A PERFECT CHILD (1991)
WORKING TIMES (1993)
HOW NOT TO BE A PERFECT FAMILY (1994)
NATURE'S MASTERPIECE (2000)

*Children's books*

THE HURRICANE TREE (1988)
THE FARMING YOUNG PUFFIN FACT BOOK (1992)
GETTING THE STORY (1993)

# PASSING GO

# Libby Purves

Hodder & Stoughton

Copyright © 2000 Libby Purves

First published in Great Britain in 2000 by Hodder & Stoughton
A division of Hodder Headline

10 9 8 7 6 5 4 3 2 1

A CIP catalogue record for this title is available
from the British Library.

ISBN 0 340 71882 X

Typeset by Palimpsest Book Production Limited,
Polmont, Stirlingshire
Printed and bound in Great Britain by
Clays Ltd, St Ives plc

Hodder & Stoughton
A division of Hodder Headline
338 Euston Road
London NW1 3BH

To Kerry Hood, in memory of Skipton

# Chapter One

The tenth of January, 2000, began as an ordinary day. In fact Roy Keaney, shaving his dark stubble with short vicious strokes, reflected with mild disgust that the very ordinariness of everything was a kind of insult. The dull plastic sky, the school run traffic hooting in the road outside, the bathroom mirror itself – Helen's choice, with its irritatingly artful overpriced driftwood frame – were exactly the same as they had been before the millennium night. Nothing twenty-first century about them, nothing at all.

Well, obviously not! An irritated upward flick propelled foam into his eye, and Roy grabbed blindly for the towel. Obviously! If you wanted to be picky you could say that it wasn't even really a new century yet, not for another year. Why should things change?

His eye clear, he looked with disfavour at the pale fluffy towel – Helen's taste again, with a maddeningly priggish, New Agey label bragging about unbleached cotton and natural dyes. Deliberately, he dropped it on the floor. Nothing was different.

Yet, childishly, he had wanted things to change. He had expected some sort of present, some omen that the world and he were moving on together. Judging by the fretfulness of the press over the last few days of the unbearable Christmas holiday, this irrational hope was not unique. A tone of sullen carping pervaded the media in that season: beneath the superficial grousing about the national New Year celebrations Roy sensed another, less rational plaint. What was the point of a new year, muttered a million voices, what was the point of entering a magnificent fruit-machine of a year with three fine zeros all lined up like a jackpot row of oranges, what was the point of having passed the green light to enter a new century – what was the bloody point, if the sky was still grey and the news still depressing and public life still dominated by such whining creeps? What was the point when middle-aged life was a tawdry stained compromise, a premature shameful deal with age and decay?

He should not, perhaps, have dawdled over the newspapers before washing and shaving. There had been a New Year resolution about that, forgotten within a day. He had resolved to begin the day with a brisk walk up to the Heath, a healthy herbal tea and a chapter of Bertrand Russell or, at the very least, Pascal.

Roy blinked, rinsed his smooth chin, reached for the second towel and tried to recapture the brief euphoria of New Year's night, when fleetingly all things had seemed possible.

They had gone to Parliament Hill to watch the fireworks. It was Suzy Darling's idea, bubbling to Helen in the kitchen in the days after Christmas.

'There'll be the most *appalling* crowds down by the river, vomiting and peeing in Trafalgar Square. But the main thing's going to be the fireworks, isn't it? So – how about the view from the Heath? Let's all go. Let's wrap up and take midnight picnics and a backpack of bubbly. Like a street party out on the road. We can take our own fireworks. Remember the Jubilee?'

Helen had concurred in her usual lacklustre way while Roy, silently pouring another whisky for James Darling in the far corner of the big basement kitchen, had raised his eyebrows in masculine deprecation. Behind the jocose pretended despair, he had been remembering the 1977 Jubilee with a surprisingly sharp pang of loss. He could see Marcus saucer-eyed, joyful at being allowed to hold the unlit rockets for his daddy; could conjure up in a moment the picture of fat chortling twins in the buggy, grabbing at the Union Jack cloths draped across the trestle tables in the middle of Ferris Hill Road. At the time, he had longed for his rabble of children just to grow up a bit and not need carrying or wiping or ferrying. Now ... well, perhaps you never spotted the good times while they were on you.

James Darling showed no sign of such introspection, but merely quaffed the whisky and said, 'Another bloody bun fight! Cheers. Onward and upward, if the girls insist.'

In fact both men were quite glad to be forced out that night. You couldn't just stay at home watching berks on the television and getting smashed, could you? Not on millennium night. The night of the three big zeros. And the alternatives – struggling southward to the river, or fleeing like many of their richer London friends to country cottages – were even less appealing. Half an hour would get them to the top of Parliament Hill, the stronghold and symbol of their kind; they could be home by one o'clock if they wanted, duty done. They need not involve themselves in the dense sticky revelries of downhill London; they could look down from their green eminence as the world rolled into a new phase.

So ten of them from the street had gone up the hill together; and among the crowds they had met other neighbours and familiar faces so that Zack, that solitary enigmatic afterthought child, had schoolfriends to talk to. Helen had never really made contact with the younger generation of mothers since his birth, so her friends were women like Suzy who had brought their children round to play with Marcus, Shona and Danny in the 1980s. But those long-vanished childhoods had not haunted the party too badly; enough of their own contemporaries were spending New Year's night without their adult offspring to make the absence of the three elder Keaneys unremarkable. The Darlings had talked about their precious Helena and Dougie, of course, vaunting Dougie's night shift at the hospital and Helena's smart party at Greenwich; but plenty of others had tacitly avoided the subject of their vanished families. Even during the retrospective chatter about Christmas, the question had been easily avoidable.

Roy mostly stood aside a little from the clutch of old friends and neighbours, watching them. Mellowed by champagne in the hour before midnight he experienced a rare flash of universal sympathy. It must be an awkward stage, he thought, especially for the mothers, during the season of high sentimental expectations. Their offspring were old enough to avoid of their parents' parties, and not yet burdened with their own babies and wanting the old folks back as babysitters. At the same time the older generation – his generation – were not yet willing to be old folks anyway. For the past ten years Zack, for all his self-contained detachment, had been a kind of badge of youth for Roy and Helen, a proof that they still had life in them. 'So brilliant, a late baby! Lucky you!' Suzy Darling used to coo into the carrycot, and Roy had winced theatrically to amuse James Darling, but secretly concurred. At the time, the sheer simplicity of Zack's baby needs seemed not a burden but a blessed relief from the dour, scornful, troublesome teenagers.

Yet looking at his last child now, as he stood like his father, alone and aside from the group to stare down through the darkness at the lights of London, Roy could see the beginnings of a familiar distance, hostility and estrangement. It would not take much to turn him into a Marcus, a Shona, a . . .

Well, maybe not a Danny. Lightning didn't strike twice, did it?

He swigged his champagne, from the bottle this time, and waited for the midnight moment. Together, squealing happily, the Ferris Hill party saw the distant fireworks diffused romantically through thin cloud, and the elusive 'River of Fire' as sharp tongues of flame shot upward like bright needles from the bending river. As the lights faded, Roy almost staggered under a moment of elation; as if something inside him had briefly struggled into life, blooming warm and florid from the hard dead earth of his heart. He felt thirty years younger, nineteen again, passionate and optimistic, ready to seize anything. *It will start again now*, said a voice. *A new beginning. The other stuff belongs to the old century. Another chance now. Freedom and light . . .*

Freedom and light! he thought now, pulling on his shirt so viciously that a faint ripping sound came from beneath his left arm. There wouldn't be a clean shirt, probably, so he let it be. Freedom and bloody light! Must have been pissed. Nine days of the new century – so-called – had passed, each of them more dull and irritating than the last. Shona had showed up, pins and studs in her nose as usual and hair like a hedgehog, and talked tactlessly of Danny, until Helen had to tell her sharply to stop it before Zack heard. Marcus deigned to look in, offensively slim and brown from a fortnight off-piste in the Rockies, his foul hair gelled back. He bore a magnum of champagne from the duty free, a vac-packed pair of pashmina slippers for Helen and a too-young toy for Zachary. Roy had been short with him; there was nothing new about that. In the end Marcus didn't stay for supper, pleading a 'meeting with some blokes' down in the riverside warehouse which served him for both home and office. 'Big doings,' he said. 'Came up while I was in Aspen. Tell you sometime.'

Not, Roy thought, that he would. Marcus' business was too electronic, too much a chimera of a new and baffling age, for his father to follow with much enthusiasm. How could his shimmering nothings, cobweb accumulations of empty pixels, be worth the kind of money that was talked of? In a newspaper over the holiday Roy had idly read of new millionaires, of big forthcoming deals, of killings in the weirdly insubstantial world of 'e-commerce'. One sum paid for a web company struck him particularly, as it was precisely five times the June takeover figure for Handfast Books with its modest but honourable backlist and two decades of goodwill and experience.

Marcus, he supposed, was doing deals in this excitable e-world. Good for him. Even better if he had not turned out to be such an insufferable prick. Roy grinned, and yanked in the belt of his trousers with a sharp tug. He liked saying dreadful things about his children to himself; it reassured him that it was not only they who could turn away, shrug and get on with their own lives. Yes, Marcus was a ghastly little turd. Shona was a grotesque, and a pretentious madam as well, with her horrible gallery installations of female detritus and widdled-on sand trays. Ghastly! The current Shona, frankly, had nothing whatsoever to do with Daddy's Shona, the forgotten old cuddly baby Shonie. Not a single body cell was the same after – was it five years? Even less so after fifteen, surely.

Zack at least was normal. So far. Not the brightest, perhaps, and turning surlier by the day, clearly off down the same route of rebellion as the rest . . .

Roy reined in his thoughts, sharply. They worried even him sometimes. Was he an unnatural father? No, natural, surely. It was nature's way that you should stop worrying about your children when they grew. No animal in the world paid any attention to its offspring once they could hunt or graze for themselves. Why should humans be any different? Bloody Marcus. Roy wriggled irritably. Often he did not think of his three older children from one week's end to the next; he was good at forgetting them. But Christmas, New Year, stirred up treacherous memories.

Aside from those unsettling visits, there had been nothing to alleviate the ordinary, dull, dyspeptic post-Christmas doldrum. Roy had decided at one stage that he had the flu, and retired to bed with due ceremony; the following day he got up again, bored, and declared himself cured by zinc tablets. All in all, it would be a relief to get back to work, even at bloody Eden Corp., and submit to the anaesthesia of the humdrum.

✡     ✡     ✡

Helen was in the kitchen when he got downstairs, tutting over the newspapers. She glanced up at her husband, bright-eyed, birdlike beneath her careful, glossy black crop.

'Hi.' She looked back down at the paper, but no onlooker would have guessed that she felt even more glumly anticlimactic than her husband. Roy certainly didn't guess, or bother to try. She was just Helen; another ordinary thing in his life. Once, this woman before him had been the fount and the centre of momentous and thrilling events. She had starred in the dramatic birth of Marcus in the January snows, with the emergency midwife abandoning her car in the blizzard to run up the impassable road. Then later there had been the more decorous hospital birth of the twins, and the long incubator fight for poor little Shona's life while Danny gurgled in smug health, half resented, at Helen's bedside. During the romping, rumbustious childhood of the three small children, it was Helen who presided over a polyglot series of au pairs and nannies, who ran the house and worked at a series of typewriters and keyboards to provide steady income while Roy helped Harry build up Handfast Books from nowhere. Once, this wife of his had been overstretched, exhausted, needed, vital, central.

Now there was only Zack for her to manage. Roy sometimes thought that Helen was bored; but if she was, what the hell. It was up to her to do something about it. Nobody had forced her to give up work; he, frankly, had not expected it. She went back after the first three children, so what was so damn special about Zack?

'I went back for the money,' she had said, tightly, when he put this to her. 'This time I want to be a full-time mother, all right?' Roy had shruggingly agreed; eleven years ago Handfast Books had been doing reasonably well, and they were lucky enough to have a fixed rent on the little house they had lived in ever since they were married. It was always too small, especially with all four children living at home, and the plumbing was atrocious; but it provided a foothold in a far richer, calmer street than they could have afforded otherwise. Two years ago things had looked so prosperous that they had felt able to leave it, and take out a mortgage on No. 33, seven doors down from the Darlings. Helen had seemed very happy with this, and had taken an unprecedented interest in new bathrooms and ethically correct towels and unbleached loose covers and special wallpaper; Roy had shrugged, only sometimes reiterating the suggestion that now Zack was growing up she might like to go back to work to support this frenzy of nest-building. It was never a welcome suggestion.

'I've got another life now,' she said. 'Not paid work but gift work, charities, my art classes, my own friends. I worked for eighteen years, right through three children. OK?'

Once or twice, in an unwontedly perceptive moment, it occurred to Roy that Helen might actually be afraid of going back to work. Certainly she did not seem to be made particularly happy by her wallpapers and charity work and coffee-drinking with Suzy Darling. But the Keaneys talked less and less as the months went by; there was something threatening about Helen in those days, an atmosphere of that weird power that comes with a hidden and unexplained grievance. His own mother, he remembered, had gone rather the same way in his teens. It was not worth protesting about; Helen handled the finances and their costs were presumably not as high these days. After all, Marcus was light years away, and probably richer than they were; the twins had vanished into smoky alien worlds in the London valley far beneath the tranquillity of Ferris Hill; and Zack seemed happy enough at the comprehensive. So why should Helen work? Roy understood none of his family now, and turned away from the attempt with relief, gaining mild but sufficient interest from his own work, the latest books, and increasingly the whisky bottle.

✻     ✻     ✻

Besides, in the final months of the old century the work had taken a new turn: not welcome, but at least intriguing. Back in June, Harry Foster, founder and major shareholder of Handfast Books, had astonished his oldest friend and historically loyal staff by agreeing to sell Handfast to the massive Eden Corporation.

'I don't want to be a publisher any more,' he had said, grinning.

'But you're a good publisher!' Roy protested. 'Think what you've achieved!'

'All the better time to sell out. The future is big, Roy. Big and cruel and corporate. It's no time to be a minnow.'

Roy had come by a meagre ten thousand pounds from his shares, hardly enough to dent the great mortgage on No.33, and had turned his pension into a private one rather than entrust it to the gigantic Eden Corporation's scheme when he moved across there with his authors.

But as Harry had said, before he took off for France with his new young wife, 'You wouldn't like retirement, anyway. You'd drink yourself silly. Eric Manderill at Eden will see you right. Another thirty K a year on top of what you get now, and the sky's the limit. They're really moving in on the whole publishing front – e-books, DVD, tie-ins. That department's going to grow and grow.'

'I don't know anything about e-bloody-books and DVD,' said Roy, 'or much care.' But the extra money was a godsend, and he was luckier than most of the Handfast staff who had no option but to depart in maudlin tears towards early retirement or face-saving pretences at 'consultancy'.

'All right then,' he said to Harry. 'You piss off to France and leave me in the Eden Gulag. See if I care.'

At Eden headquarters Roy continued doing much the same job with much the same authors as before. Sometimes Eric Manderill or one of his team would bounce into the office where he had settled, look with disfavour at the Verney prints and untidy piles of books and talk some gibberish about the New Publishing, but Roy largely ignored them. It was not so bad. Not like the early days of Handfast when work had been more fun than fun; but he was getting older, wasn't he?

Helen broke into these thoughts.

'Zacky went off to school happy enough,' she said as Roy poured himself the last cup of coffee, the one which would make his hand shake by midmorning. Something in her tone conveyed a reproof that Roy had not inquired about his son's happiness that day. He could not, however, bring himself to respond to the reproof.

'Uh.'

'I think he's going to be OK at that school, you know.'

'Mm-huh,' said Roy. 'Good.'

Helen gave up, and swept the newspapers off the table with a masterful movement.

'Shall I ask the Darlings and someone else for tomorrow night?' she asked as Roy shrugged on his coat. 'Or shall we go out? Take Zack with us, maybe. Family outing?'

Fleetingly, Roy thought that she sounded like an actress in some television play about a bright devoted wife and mother. Not the most convincing of actresses, rather one who was copying another actress's performance of the same role. Family outing! He yawned ostentatiously.

'What's tomorrow night anyway?'

'Your fiftieth birthday! Don't do the denial thing, it's boring.'

'Nothing special about fifty,' grunted Roy. 'Like there's nothing special about year two thousand. It's all just numbers. Not worth building bloody domes and letting off sparklers about.'

'Round numbers,' said Helen. 'It's satisfying. Anyway, I wasn't going to build a dome. I just thought we'd have dinner. You're going to be fifty. It's a milestone.'

Milestone, thought Roy. Another cliché. How strangely

similar that word was to millstone. Or gravestone. He was at the door, but turned to say ungraciously, 'Oh, ask who you want.'

When he had gone, Helen's bright mask crumbled and she sat for a long time, shivering. Then she shook her head violently, crossed to the small mirror and practised smiley grins. Later, dressed in jeans and a sweater, she met Suzy Darling outside the dry-cleaners'.

'Look at us! Ladies of leisure!' said Suzy playfully.

'Housewives,' said Helen with a brittle pretence of a laugh. Then soberly: 'It was all right while Zacky was at Ferris Junior and I could pop in and out and be mummyish, but I've gone right off it. Roy goes off to Eden every morning and I kick around the house waiting for Zack to come home, and when he does get back he's straight off to his room or out with his mates.'

'Do you ever feel like going back to work?'

'No', said Helen. 'That's the trouble. Can't face that, either. I'm not just *in* a rut, I *am* a rut.'

'Shall we have some coffee in Starbucks?' said Suzy, knowing the mood.

'Yeah. And a mocha frosted brownie.' The two fell into step.

'Fattening!' warned Suzy, whose grasp of the obvious was renowned throughout the neighbourhood.

'Good,' said Helen. 'Who cares? Which reminds me, Roy's fifty tomorrow, though he's refusing to discuss it. Do you fancy supper?'

'Lovely. But are you sure you want outsiders? Bit of a family night?'

Helen glanced at her friend with slight dislike. Suzy knew perfectly well how it was with the Keaney family. Just because her own perfect pigeon-pair organized James's fiftieth celebration right down to the jazz band in the garden, there was no need to rub it in.

'Nah,' said Helen. 'Family's busy elsewhere. Just a quiet dinner. Rod and Amy are coming, and Zack will light the candles and pour the wine. He likes buttling.'

'All righty,' said her friend cheerfully. 'We'll find Roy a silly present. And don't worry about the denial. They do go a bit funny at fifty. James got that awful haircut, remember. It's only just grown out.'

Suzy Darling wished she had not mentioned family. It was not kind. She had caught sight of Shona on Boxing Day for a minute, which was enough – poor Helen! – and rumours about Marcus reached her often through James's work in the City ('If he's not shooting a line he's sniffing one'). And everyone had known for years that Shona's twin Danny lived somewhere abroad and was never seen. Suzy shivered. How dreadful, how really dreadful if Helena or Dougie moved abroad. How could anybody bear to lose touch with their own children?

# Chapter Two

———————●————————

The headquarters of Eden Corporation lay north of Oxford Circus, east of Madame Tussaud's and the Planetarium, west of King's Cross. Young tourists flowed constantly past it, earnest and heavy with their backpacks, searching for hostel rooms. One or two would hesitate at the Eden portals, confused by the name (there was, apparently, an Australasian chain of cheap hotels called Edenia). Others used its scoop-shaped modern portico as temporary shelter from the rain while they checked their maps.

Then, resolutely, they would trudge on down the unpre-possessing ravines of Portland-stone streets in search of Soho, or Bond Street, or Chinatown, or Theatreland or, in the case of the more geographically incompetent, Harrods. The more sophisticated of the laden travellers would negotiate these streets unmolested, stepping with efficient briskness past the habitual beggars in the doorways and ignoring even the most importunate pavement artists. The less wary, or those from more communicative cultures, would be seduced into eye contact and end up several pounds of 'spare change' the poorer before they reached the comparative sanctuary of Oxford Street.

Roy had not given anything to a beggar in years. Once, as a left-wing student, he had worked shifts in the Cyrenean hostel and harangued meetings about the disgrace of homelessness.

Quoted Lear to them: 'Poor naked wretches, wheresoe'er you are, that bide the pelting of this pitiless storm.' Nowadays his contribution to the struggle against selfish capitalism was confined entirely to printing occasional books by discarded Labour Party traditionalists. He no longer saw the buskers and the sleeping-bag people. You didn't, if you worked locally. You couldn't.

Briskly, he stepped past a grimy doorway where two young men slept through a drugged private dawn, walked unseeingly past a crumpled figure so old that the hair spread over the stone step was pure white, and crossed the side street to the wider portals of his office. Peter Morden and Alan Barton were there, laughing together in the echoing tiled hallway.

'Hello, Roy. Good break?'

'Yeah, fairly. You?'

'Champion, champion. Hey, have you heard about Intaglio-dot-com?'

'Whatdotcom?'

'Our starry new acquisition. It's in the *FT*, this morning.' Peter Morden, a stout, snouty young man, waved a *Financial Times* at him.

Roy shuddered, theatrically. 'I don't pollute my mind with that stuff. I'm a publisher. It's not what I'm for.'

The two men looked at him with what – if there had been the slightest reason for it – he might have taken for pity.

'Look, it's here,' said Alan Barton. 'Whiz kid. Made himself a bomb. You ought to have a fellow feeling, you share a name.'

They were in the lift by now, Morden's fat finger prodding at the fifteenth floor button. Roy glanced down at the newspaper and saw, looking insolently at him from the pink page, his son Marcus. Luckily it was a bad picture. It looked nothing like Roy.

*Big doings. Came up in Aspen.* So that was it. Intaglio-dot-com. He had always thought it was called Interglow. Marcus's illiterate rendering of the word made it sound quite different from Alan Barton's's cultured, Tuscany holidaymaker's pronunciation. Whatever it was, Intaglio-dot-com had been bought by Eden for – yes, five times what Harry got for Handfast.

'Is this kid going to come on the staff, then?' asked Peter Morden. 'Is that in the deal? Twenty-five, isn't he, or something like that?'

'Christ knows,' said Alan. 'I'll go to the smoking room later and see what we can find out.' No smoker ever rose to the very top levels at Eden: Eric Manderill disliked the habit. The unintended result was that the smokers' room, a cheerless chilly space on the seventeenth floor with orange plastic chairs, had become the most efficient information exchange in the building. Here, under a brown-stained ceiling, the pariah caste of nicotine addicts from every division of the company clung together and defiantly exchanged their superiors' secrets.

The lift pinged suddenly, and stopped at the twelfth floor. A thin woman dressed from head to foot in lime green stepped in, and in turn glanced down at the newspaper.

'Do you know, Marcia?' asked Peter. 'Is this Marcus Keaney going to take a hands-on job?'

The woman flared her nostrils and paused. Roy knew her slightly and disliked her intensely. If any of them was going to make the connection between him and Marcus, it would be her. But not yet. She looked, he thought with an edge of disgust, as if she were permanently torn between the desire to show off knowledge and a fear of sharing it.

'Well,' she said, 'I can tell you that he was *here*, on Friday. During the holiday closure. Talking to Sean Lucas and going through files.' Marcia glanced sharply at Roy, and he knew in that moment that she recognized the lines of his face from Marcus's. She gave a small, unpleasant smile but only said, 'Security were grumbling downstairs about having to open up specially.'

The lift arrived at the fifteenth floor and Roy was first out, breathing hard. Marcus had left on Thursday evening, refusing Helen's offer of spaghetti to retire to Docklands and talk 'big doings'. By Friday he had been here – *here* – in the same building his father worked in, having sold his company and, apparently, his services, to the same ogre which had swallowed Handfast. But Marcus had not thought even to mention that such an eventuality was even possible.

*Big doings!* The little turd. Roy pushed open his office door and, once inside, leaned on it, his teeth clenched uncomfortably together. The little *turd.*


'*Excrement,*' said Shona Keaney. 'Despised, distrusted, its very existence disguised, neutralized by water and pipework. But glistening, solid, sculptable, *real.*' She reached out a hand towards the tray in front of her. 'It holds power. It comes alike from male and female. I can break a taboo, make you recoil irrationally from an act which is victimless and harmless. See.'

Three art students watched her, two of them rapt, nodding. They were paying for this masterclass, and valued it accordingly. The third, newly down from Salford, got up precipitately.

'Sorry. Feel sick. Must have ate something . . .'

'Do it here! Vomit *here!*' commanded Shona Keaney. 'Let us see the reality, waste producing waste, taboo confounded, and a terrible beauty is born.'

Disobediently, the boy ran from the room. Shona looked at the others, holding up a sticky unspeakable hand to challenge them.

'Bourgeois,' she said. 'But remember, what has happened here in the last minute is, in a truer sense than any dead gallery, a moment of art.'

The two remaining students nodded wanly, and Shona smiled until the pin at the end of her upper lip almost vanished into the deep, fat creases of her cheek.

\* \* \*

By the end of the day everyone in the Eden building knew about the sensational deal with Intaglio-dot-com, about the phenomenal Marcus Keaney who had wheeled and dealed and parlayed glimmering nothings into his first million-plus share option, and who in addition was joining the Eden board to launch and temporarily head up a new, aggressive, media acquisition department. Those on the inner ring knew, from Eric Manderill himself, that this department would last no longer than two years and that within that time its goal was to make Eden into a serious global force in media. 'Shops and hotels and financial services,' Manderill had told them, 'are no longer enough. The twenty-first century will be the media century. We are looking at an information overclass.'

Roy did not hear this speech directly, but relayed through snouty Peter Morden.

'You're well positioned,' Peter had said admiringly. 'They were obviously just limbering up when they bought Hand-fast. You'll be right in the middle of this media acquisitions firestorm.'

'Firestorm!' said Roy. He had drunk too much coffee, and returned from his lunch break with a full bottle of whisky, which stood now on the desk half full and reeking fruitily, its cork on the floor under the desk. He had done no useful work at all. 'Bollocks!'

Morden looked at him with curiosity. 'I did hear a rumour,' he said, 'that this Marcus Keaney is not unknown to you, old fruit.'

'I cannot tell a lie,' said Roy. 'I sired the monster. He is my son.'

'Has he been in to share the triumph yet?' Morden asked it without a scintilla of malice; his own son, seventeen years old, went fishing with him in a Berkshire reservoir every weekend and told him the details of each new girlfriend with infant guilelessness. He thought that this was how sons were.

'He has not,' said Roy. 'It would hardly be right, would it? To share anything at all with his mere father. Favouritism.' He picked up the whisky bottle, looked around for the coffee mug and poured himself another slug.

He was still drinking an hour later when Alan Barton in turn popped in to verify the astonishing news of the two Keaneys' blood relationship. Roy waved the bottle at him.

'Manderill really doesn't like drink in the office,' said Alan Barton apologetically, backing away as though the whisky might bite him. 'A bit prim, Eden. Obviously, not like what you're used to, Bohemian style.' He gave a short, nervous laugh, anxious not to cause offence; he too was a kind man, more attached to the sea scout troop he ran at weekends than to the hungrier sort of corporate ambition. Nonetheless he valued his job, and the smell of disaster hung around Roy Keaney this afternoon as rank as cordite on a battlefield.

'Manderill,' said Roy stoutly, 'doesn't have to like it. He doesn't have to drink it. And he can fuck off out of my office!' The last words rose to something near a shriek.

Alan Barton turned round and saw the neat, slight figure of Eric Manderill himself, UKCEO of Eden Plc, in Roy's doorway. Horrified at being caught with Roy, then horrified at himself for the ignobility of the emotion, Alan smiled, made a helpless fluttering gesture with his hands, and fled back down the corridor to his own office.

In the event, though, it was not Manderill who made the decision to sack Roy Keaney. Eric Manderill found Roy uncouth, uncorporate, unmotivated and uncomfortably alien to the Eden ethos, but acknowledged that within the small pond of Handfast-style publishing, the man knew his job. When he had agreed with Harry Foster to take his editorial director on to the Eden staff along with the imprint, he had fully intended to give the man a good run, two years perhaps, and then pay him off with a handsome redundancy settlement.

By that time Eden would have grown its own younger

executives and formulated a strategy to turn their publishing arm into something rather more lucrative and modern. Manderill, for all his creepy bearing and robotic delivery, was neither vindictive nor whimsical in his sackings; the very sight of scruffbags like Roy Keaney in his building irritated him, but he was a big enough man – so he told himself – to put up with a bit of abrasion to his finer feelings. Come to that, young Marcus Keaney irritated him too, in a different way, with all that finger-snapping and sly, pale-eyed grinning; and he was on the board and therefore would be more visible.

No; for all Roy's failings, it would not have been Manderill who plunged in the knife. It was his new HMA, or head of media acquisitions, who said, just before the day's running meetings broke up into working lunches, 'I want to put a new A-team in, right through the media sections. I want it seamless. I want it young. I want it on-message.'

'You want to put someone in over Roy Keaney in the books section, then?' said Manderill, thinking with a twinge of irritation that this would mean another executive salary. These kids always wanted their mates in. Old flatmates and leggy girls, usually.

'Nah,' said Marcus with studied carelessness. 'Not *over* him, *instead* of him. I'm afraid the old man'll have to go. I mean, it's obvious – won't he?'

'We were planning to give him two years,' said Manderill. 'I told Harry Foster that we valued a certain stability. Roy Keaney deals with writers, and they can be quite difficult, I'm told.'

Marcus had a sudden, untypically whimsical impression that the CEO said 'writers' in much the same tone that a nervous safari customer might say 'hippopotami'. Reassuringly he said, 'There's plenty of hipp— of writers out there, and the only one we'd really hate to lose is Lucilla Steer, and I met her last week at the Groucho and she told me the old man had been really rude to her. She was thinking of moving if she had to keep dealing with him – I happen to know she slept with old Harry for about fifteen years, so it must have been a blow when he pissed off to France. But shit, if you promised the guy two years, give him two years' money.' A petulant tone crept into his voice. 'If you keep him, he'll resist every frigging thing I try to do, you know that?'

Manderill picked up the telephone and spoke to the company accountant. He listened carefully for a few moments, then said, 'Fine,' and put the phone down. Turning to the lounging figure of Marcus, suppressing his dislike of the wet red lips, pale eyes and leather trousers of his new colleague, he said, 'Two years is more than we usually offer. But if you say so, fine. The company has a lot riding on the work you're going to do for us.'

Marcus nodded in his offhand way, and made as if to leave. But Manderill then added in a different voice, 'One thing, though – listen to me.' The thin little man raised a white finger, and even Marcus was chilled into stillness by the cold snake eye. Awkward, half-risen from the chair, conscious of his leather trousers riding uncomfortably off centre at the crotch, he listened as Eric Manderill said, 'One thing we can do without is bad PR. He is your father, though your family feelings are your own business. But if he goes, we put a gag on him, and his whole redundo is going to hang one hundred per cent on him keeping stumm. You can do the same. As far as the trade press is concerned it's his decision, a hundred per cent, and we are very nice guys indeed. And you personally had nothing to do with it. OK?'

Marcus, wriggling imperceptibly to bring his unruly trousers under control, nodded and said, 'When you gonna do it? I need to get going, shake it about a bit, put out some feelers for the best people.'

'Tomorrow,' said Manderill.

The morning meetings had gone on longer than planned. As the CEO and Marcus stepped out of the faux marble lift at the ground floor, they saw Roy Keaney on his way back from lunch, his bottle of whisky held naked, undisguised, by the neck.

'Hi,' said Roy to Marcus, in a nasty voice, thickened by alcohol.

'Hi and 'bye', said Marcus, blithely, and waved, for all the world as if he was only saying goodbye for the duration of lunch.

# Chapter Three

Zack Keaney paused his computer game, and regarded with detached interest the way that the figure with the gun shimmered surreally, the spurt of flame frozen in the barrel.

Like a flower growing sideways. Why, he wondered, did the screen throb like that. Throb? No, that sounded like something that hurt. Pulse? Yes, *pulse* was a good word. Sort of wet and alive. He liked taking pulses at his St John Ambulance group in school. Perhaps he would be a paramedic, like on telly on Saturday nights. No, a nurse would be better. You got to talk to people more, not just shout, 'What's your name? Right, can you hear me, Lily?' to people stuck in crashed trains.

He had once told Mum that he wanted to be a nurse, but she had just said, 'Don't tell your father, he won't like that,' and laughed, but not with her eyes. It was a bit like the Danny look she had, which he knew of old: a look that meant that it was wise to change the subject.

He considered re-starting the game, but the man with the gun bored him. Zack did not, in point of fact, get nearly as much satisfaction out of these games as most of his schoolmates. You had to play them, obviously, so that you had stuff to talk about. You had to borrow them and swap them and ask for them at Christmas, or you weren't a proper boy. But right now what he fancied was a walk in the damp secret dusk, up to the edge of the Heath.

On his own he was only allowed as far as the street light by the last house, but he liked to stand at the edge of his territory and look outwards. He could look far into the Heath's darkness and pretend it was the sea, or the desert. Sometimes men and girls came past him and went on into that darkness, following the thin line of lights along the path; sometimes men with other men. But if he said he was going for a walk, then Mum would come with him, and try to chat about embarrassing stuff like 'growing up'. She had this fixation about puberty and stuff, and Zack was a boy who preferred to think things out for himself while he walked.

Ah well, homework, then. He turned the screen off and reached reluctantly for this schoolbag. Half of it was geography, which was nearly all colouring in and copying and drawing. Kids' work. He had thought that the colouring would stop when he was at secondary school, but no such luck. Resignedly pulling the folder towards him and starting to shade in a patch of steppe, he wished – not for the first time – that he had brothers and sisters to do homework with. His brother and sister were so *old*, and actually not much fun at all, even as grown-ups went. He had hardly seen Marcus – six, seven times that he could remember, always near Christmas – but for as long as he could remember Mum had talked about him, making comparisons.

'When Marcus was your age I had to chase him out for walks, he hated fresh air.'

'Marcus and his computers – when he was your age he never stopped fooling around with them. Did you know he won a competition for designing games? He sold his first when he was only fifteen, just after you were born . . .'

Shona, on the other hand, he could remember living with at home. She definitely used to live with him and Dad and Mum, in the old house up the road. Right up till he was about six she used to come home from her art school for the whole holidays.

He liked her then; when he was really small she used to paint with him nearly every night, sitting with him at the kitchen table and making him laugh with mad suggestions.

'Why don't you grow some hair out of his ears? Or between his toes? He's not hairy enough. Is that a tomato he's standing on? Tell you a good idea, Zacky – sometimes when you can't finish a painting you should turn it upside down and carry on that way.' She had given him a set of oil paints and told him not to bother with brushes but to squeeze it straight on. Mum had been furious at the mess.

It was hard to remember, he thought, just when Shona stopped being fun. In the end bit of his memories she was still there, had a bedroom in the house, but went out a lot and was starey and stroppy and picking fights with Mum. And – this part he remembered with reluctance – she seemed to stop noticing him at all.

The fights were always about Danny, only by that time Danny was just a name and not a person with a bedroom. Zack's memories of Danny were hazy; there was definitely sometimes Danny in the background of the painting memories from when he was very little. But he was pretty sure that by the time he started school when he was nearly five, there was no Danny at all. But the name hung on in phone calls, the ones Zack wasn't meant to overhear; it was always a sobbing kind of name, he thought, a name associated with people being furious and blaming other people. He had asked questions for a while, but got no answers, so he had grown into the habit of avoiding it. Perhaps Danny was dead, or in prison, or a junkie. The thought made Zack feel odd and cold inside, as if he had stumbled out of real life into a film. Once there had been a boy at school called Daniel. Zack really liked him, but had never asked him home for tea out of an obscure sense that the very name was unsafe.

It had been strange, at Christmas, to hear Shona talking openly and loudly about Danny again. He had been passing the kitchen doorway.

'You really, really ought to give Danny a chance!' his sister was saying, clearly and angrily. 'I can understand Dad – just about – it's the testosterone talking there – but this hole-and-corner stuff you do, pretending – it hurts, you know. People hurt. Just go public! Stand up for what you believe in! And if you don't believe it, try and get real!'

Zack had watched her from the hall, fascinated. Not so much by the row – he blanked out Danny rows from old, efficient habit – but by the fact that as she spoke, Shona seemed to change and become someone he recognized from long ago. She was angry, but not sneerily; angry in a wanting-to-help-someone, serious kind of way. With a shock he had a vivid memory of the old Shona, who painted with him; she had been round-faced but ordinarily sort of nice-looking, with floppy brown hair, kind and laughing and not cross or weird.

For years now he had seen only the new Shona, with funny stubbly knots of hair, and sometimes green make-up and pins through painful bits of her face, and angry sort of clothes. She came round three or four times a year, no more, and he hated it if his friends were there to see her. A lot of them had cool, in-yer-face sisters who wore funky street clothes and weird hair, but the weirdness of Shona was something else. Different, and seriously embarrassing. Now, slagging off Mum in the kitchen on Boxing Day, in spite of all the funny clothes and hair and the disguising fatness of her face, she looked like his big sister again.

He put the finishing touches to 'Africa – main crops' and looked, with disfavour, at 'Africa – climate'. One day, work and life would not be this boring. He had to believe that.

One day, thought Roy, he would get the hell out of Eden and find a way to earn a living that was not frustrating, humiliating and altogether more than enough to drive you to the bottle. Amazing that he had lasted six months of trying to be an honest publisher, mewed up in the money-grubbing, jargon-fuelled sewer that was Eden Corp. Amazing that he had come to think of it as routine, just another place you had to go by day if you wanted the salary cheque to arrive every month.

He pushed his chair back, balancing it perilously on its back legs. Having worked for years at Handfast on an old dining chair with a moulting cushion, he had sentimentally brought it with him to Eden HQ as a gesture of protest against the cool contemporary black leather swivel-chair culture of creeps like Eric Manderill The truth was that the old chair was uncomfortable; but like the other truth – that Eden actually funded and produced some perfectly good books, distinguishable only from Handfast's old output by the fact that they were more cheaply printed and aggressively sold – it was one which Roy in this mood preferred to ignore.

Bloody corporate Philistines, bloody Conran chairs, it was all part of the same conspiracy against honest men like him. He took a long pull at the whisky bottle, savouring the breach of taboo and the breaking down of his own long dammed-up fury.

He thought, with fuzzy anger, of weaselly little bloody Marcus, that cold selfish bastard son of his, scampering around the building preening his whiskers like the rat he was. Roy blanked out the work he had enjoyed, even at Eden, and focused his thoughts passionately on the one book he had championed since June which had not been automatically agreed by the finance department. It was a scholarly tome on Thomas Tompion the clockmaker. Roy consciously stoked up his righteous indignation on the subject. Vetoed! Ha! On grounds of the large advance demanded, the cost of illustration and the small potential market. It would have sold enough to wash its face, thought Roy, and graced every library for decades, and that would have been good enough for him and Harry in the old days, but now . . .

Now he was drunk. Too drunk to let himself remember that Harry had actually turned Tompion down six months earlier, that the world was not black and white but pearlized, ever-turning, changing shades of grey. He considered throwing the whisky bottle through the plate-glass window, but cowardice got the better of him and he placed it instead in the corridor waste bin outside Alan Barton's room, sprinkling the last drops on the carpet to give an air of dissipation to the blameless Alan's office.

Peering in through the glazed door he saw a stack of faded blue quilted sleeping bags neatly rolled in the gap between the stationery cupboard and the wall. Sea scouts! Christ! At least he was not a a hobbyist. He was an adult, a scholar, a man of letters, unfairly imprisoned in this tower of Philistines.

Then Roy went home, and Zack heard his father clashing around in the kitchen, swearing as he searched for bread and cheese. The boy decided, on balance, to stay up in his bedroom with his own television rather than join his parents. When Helen came up to see him, he said that he had already had two sandwiches and wanted to see a film. She looked quite relieved, he thought.

# Chapter Four

The sack can come in many forms: direct and manly, *faux* caring, shrouded in jargon, confusingly disguised or brutally frank. Sometimes there is lunch involved, with consequent digestive difficulties and memorable social embarrassment. Eden eschewed such sticky, personal encounters. It was a very large corporation, its authority stretching over hotels and shops and increasingly over magazines, radio stations and books. Its lawyers and human resources staff had evolved standard routines for delivering the sack, and indeed its stated policy on 'outplacement counselling' frequently drew admiring comment from members of the press who had never actually encountered the process at first hand.

For as numerous former employees observed, the company's offer of supportive counselling about what to do with the rest of your life would have felt warmer, somehow, if the initial bad news itself had been delivered by a human being rather than a buff envelope in the internal post. Roy, for instance, hungover, sullen and half an hour late on Tuesday morning, entirely failed to recognize the presence of the sack in his in-tray at all, and might well have left it there all day unopened.

This had often happened to the duller-looking items in Roy's post in the good old days when he was working with Harry and their temperamental, foul-mouthed joint secretary

Elisa. Now it was his efficient Eden secretary, Marie, who tripped in and smilingly pointed out the envelope. Marie did everything smilingly. Goodwill and sweet nature shone from her pale golden hair and scrubbed innocent smile. Some mornings, Roy could hardly bear to look at her.

'That one's marked strictly personal,' she said. 'And it didn't come with the rest of the post, but on its own. So I haven't opened it.' Then she produced a white envelope of her own and put it on his desk. 'And happy birthday!' she added, with a giggle. Catching Roy's nonplussed expression, she added, 'It was on the file.'

Roy had a fleeting memory of Elisa, cursing round the dank old office with her flapping shawls and cigarillos. The only anniversaries Elisa bothered with were those of her own three abortions and four divorces. A birthday card from her would have been a nine days' wonder. Whereas Marie, he thought unkindly, was the sort of saccharine creature who probably gave birthday cards to her cats.

When she had withdrawn, Roy looked down at the card, an inspidly tasteful watercolour sketch of an Oxford library, and felt a twinge of self-reproach, aware that he had not thanked the child properly. She knew nothing of him, Marie, beyond his lifetime's work with books; so she had taken the trouble to find a picture of some books. Nice girl. She hadn't been tactless enough to mention the fifty thing, either.

When he had looked at the card for a while, his mind straying treacherously towards his own *farouche* daughter, he shook his head as if to clear it. Then he pulled the bigger envelope towards him and ripped it open so carelessly that he had to hold the top few lines of the second page together to read them. He was still holding it, still staring at it, when Marie smiled her way back into the room.

'Did you know anything about this?' he asked, unfairly. Then, seeing that she clearly didn't, 'I've been sacked. Made redundant.'

The shock on her face calmed him a little, and he remembered that this was her first job out of college. He said awkwardly, 'You'll be fine, I'm sure of it. Your job will still be there. It seems to be a bit of restructuring, but not downsizing.' Jeez, thought Roy, I'm talking like them now.

'But you run all the old Handfast stuff,' said Marie. 'Will it all be changing, then? Is it the e-book and electronics thing that was in the papers? Won't there be books any more? Why's it suddenly happened now?'

Roy looked down at the papers again. He had not had time to consider why. Oddly, it was not the first question that sprang to mind; the first one was more like a long exhalation of 'Wha-a-a-t?' He had not welcomed the shift to Eden when Harry sold up; he had expected tedium, frustration, a long slow attrition that would eventually drive him to angle for early retirement. But for some reason he had never expected the sack. Why? He considered the question now, came very rapidly to the correct answer, and felt bile rising in his throat.

'I don't quite know,' he said after a moment. 'Not for sure. I'm going to see Manderill now. Ring him, tell him I'm coming.'

He rose to his feet, pleased to find that his legs worked. Marie backed out, horrified at the thought of telling – rather than asking – Mr Manderill's formidable assistant about a visit from her own boss. Erika belonged to the defensive school of thought, and considered that part of an Eden PA's job was to keep her unruly charge from causing trouble to the CEO. But it was too late anyway. By the time Marie had composed herself enough to dial Erika's number, Roy Keaney was upstairs at Erika's door, wrenching the door open without a knock to present his shaking, sweating form in person.

'Where is he?' he demanded.

'In a meeting,' said the small stocky figure at the desk, unruffled. Her rigid bouffant of coal-black hair was silhouetted against an impressive curving sheet of glass and a vast misty view of London roofs, which continued into the famous semicircular lighthouse view from Manderill's own office.

'Did you want an appointment?' She glanced at the smaller of the two computer screens on her desk.

'What use will that be,' asked Roy, 'when I only have three hours? It says here that "it is suggested" that I clear my desk by lunchtime so that I can have "an uninterrupted meeting" over lunch bloody miles away at some outplacement agency in sodding *Clapham*.'

'That *is* normal Eden practice,' agreed Erika. 'The appointment is for thirteen fifteen, your taxi is booked for twelve forty-five and will go on, at the company's expense, from Clapham to deliver any personal effects you may not want to keep with you. It's company policy. Generally people have their broader outplacement discussions over lunch and then go back to the agency's office to discuss arrangements.'

'What arrangements?' said Roy belligerently. 'And why am I discussing this with the monkey instead of the organ-grinder?'

'As you see in the documentation,' said Erika smoothly, 'the arrangement is that you have the right to use a dedicated office space at the outplacement consultancy, with telephone and Internet jobsearch facility for one month at existing salary. Thereafter you will receive a form from Accounts so that you can opt to have redundancy emoluments paid either in two lump sums at a six-month interval, or monthly as before until December two thousand and one. It helps people who plan to capitalize their own business.'

'You've done this before, darling, haven't you?' said Roy nastily. Then, cracking into rage again, he howled, 'Where's *Manderill*? I do have a right to some explanation—'

The inner door opened. Marcus came out, and looked at his father.

'New pastures, I gather,' he said. 'Exciting, yah? Thought you'd be pleased.'

'You little ...' Roy lunged at him, but his elbow struck

against a filing tray, lifted with impressive speed by Erika to parry the blow. He pulled his forearm back, numb, and was still rubbing away the subsequent sharp agony as Marcus vanished into the corridor and Eric Manderill emerged in turn from his sanctum.

'Don't make a thing of it, Roy,' he advised. 'It's a good deal, and you've a lot of good work left in you. Somewhere.'

With which double-edged compliment he, too, was gone, leaving Roy and Erika to glare at one another in front of the wide bent view of the city.

'Of course, he never went to Clapham,' said Helen to Suzy Darling some hours later. 'He sent the cab home with his spare suit and a few books, which puzzled me a bit, you can imagine.'

Suzy clucked comfortingly. 'Worse than teenagers, when they send these weird visitations. James once sent a bike round with a salmon, and I spent all afternoon ringing his poor secretary trying to find out if I was supposed to cook it for a short-notice dinner party or not.'

'At least James came *home*,' said Helen. 'Do you know where Roy is now? After I'd puzzled for a while over the stuff in the cab, he rang up to tell me about the redundancy, and the Clapham thing, and what he proposed to do. He sounded pissed. I could kill him.'

'So where is he? Did he go straight round to a tribunal, or a headhunter, or something?'

'He stayed at Eden,' said Helen. She had been brittle until now, telling her story to her friend in a dry, almost joking little voice. Now her voice cracked and ran up an octave. 'In another capacity, he said. So I asked what capacity.'

Suzy leaned forward, her hand on Helen's arm, trying to convey sympathy but only managing to exude burning, excited curiosity. 'What capacity? I mean, another job? In the company?'

'No,' said Helen, her breathing rapid. 'He says he is staying in the capacity of a picket line.'

'Is there a strike, then?'

'No. Just Roy. On the doorstep. "A very short picket line, but righteous" is what he said. And then he said "day and night". Someone's secretary rang this afternoon, something about him having stolen a sleeping bag from someone's office.'

The kitchen door opened. 'Mum,' said Zack, 'when's Dad home? I've done his birthday card on the computer.'

'Birthday!' shrieked his mother unaccountably. The boy stepped back in mild alarm. His mother was staring, not at him but at Mrs Darling. 'Oh God, the party – Rod and Amy are coming, and you and James . . .'

In small matters Suzy was a swift and effective woman. The entire contents of her freezer passed briefly before her inner eye as she said, 'No problem. Suppose I feed Rod and Amy? Then you can go into town and bring him home. Then we'll all have a drink and laugh it off.'

She was, Helen thought with a rush of gratitude, a good friend to have. That was the dinner party embarrassment solved. But a small aggrieved voice at her elbow said, 'So when's the birthday party supper, Ma? You said I could pour the drinks, OK?'

'Be quiet!' she shouted, and the shrill sound of it seemed to echo back over too many years of motherhood, of failure and frustration. 'Just be quiet!'

'I only *asked*,' said Zack, aggrieved. 'What *is* your *problem?*'


Roy thought long afterwards that during the Tuesday morning when he became fifty years old, he briefly rolled time back and became twenty again. Leaving Manderill's office with the memory of his son's stubbled, shuttered face burnt into his memory, he had gone into the nineteenth floor gents' lavatory and stared into the mirror. Blurred by loose wrinkled skin, devoid of the usual slicked-back dark hair, his eldest son's face stared back at him.

He narrowed his eyes and tried to remember whether, in his distant student years, he had looked like Marcus. Yup, certainly had. Without the sneer or the waxed-back hair, obviously. One reflection led to another, and sitting precariously on the lid of the pedal bin for a while, Roy thought back to the end of the 1960s, to the ORSS, the Oxford Revolutionary Socialist Students, and how different they had been to these sneering acquisitive little beasts of his son's coterie. They had fought the system, and enjoyed it; howled at Enoch Powell at the Union and staged a massive sit-in at the Examination Schools in protest at—

At what, exactly? A moment's frowning thought recaptured it: that particular occupation was a protest against the university keeping personal files on students. Why on earth, he wondered, had they minded so much? These days every official bastard knew every damn thing about everyone, instantly and electronically, and the students seemed to care not at all. Why had the class of 1969 been so worried about a few manila folders?

Never mind. The point was that they had. They had believed enough in their cause to sit in the historic building overnight with guitars, singing 'We shall not be moved' and – for less obvious reasons – 'Long Black Veil' and 'Banks of the Ohio'. He mouthed the words, experimentally. *And only say-ee, that you'll be mi-yeen* . . .

He had been there. He had fought the cause, oh yes he had, and sat down to be counted. He could feel that freezing marble floor beneath his bum now, and hear the dislikeable huffing sound of luckier revolutionaries getting a grope in the small hours.

The germ of an idea came to him. He could not do it sober, but then he was weary of sobriety. Where had it got him, his hard-working life, his reading of typescripts late into the night, his painstaking negotiation with agents and printers, his bringing home of bacon, humouring of a wife's obsession with bloody power showers, his supporting of ungrateful and graceless children who then betrayed and despised him? What had he earned, for all his loyalty to Harry and to Handfast and to the gods of middle-class righteousness? Nothing. Only the right to be sold like a serf to a careless new master, then thrown on the tip six months later with his own son's close connivance.

Of that last fact he was sure, as sure as the glint in Marcus's eyes that morning could make him. A seven-year-old dialogue flashed into his mind.

'Dad, for the last time, I'm not staying at Balliol. I'm fixed up. Stay cool.'

'While you wreck your life? You don't know how lucky you are.'

'What, lucky like you? Look at you. Dad, it's over, all your snuffly old Oxford world. Totally over. You are such a loser not to see it.'

'Get out! You useless little tosser. And don't come to me when you're on the scrapheap without a degree.'

'Don't come to me when you're on the scrapheap with two of them, dude.'

There must be conversations like that flaring up and dying every day between the generations, thought Roy. The difference in their family was that he and Marcus had both meant it. Something had gone wrong between them long, long before – God knew when, sometime in the years of computer-gaming and overwork, sometime between the twins' demands and Helen's withdrawal into vague depression. The last row had been during the *annus horribilis*, the year when Danny left.

The other difference from normal families, he supposed, was that Marcus had been efficient enough to take him literally and get out when he was told to. He had never slept a single night under his parents' roof again. And if they didn't come near you for more than an hour once a year, thought Roy, how did you change things? By bloody e-mail?

And now these insufferable Eden bastards, egged on by his own son, wanted him to go and be outplaced in Clapham and then shipped home, with the contents of his office drawers. Go straight to Jail. Do not pass Go. Hah!

So Roy went to the boardroom, broke the lock on the drinks cupboard and took a bottle of Famous Grouse to his office. Then with Marie's clean beige folder and a black felt pen he devised a placard to tack to the blade of a canoe paddle which, fortuitously, he found lying around in Alan Barton's empty office while he was helping himself to an East London Sea Cadet Corps sleeping bag.

Helen found him at seven. It was not difficult. Walking up from the Underground it was only minutes before she saw that a knot of curious passers-by had formed around the curved stone portico of the Eden Corporation HQ. Her heart began to hammer unpleasantly, for she was a woman who had grown to dislike scenes. She hoped he would come quietly. As she grew closer she could hear a horrid rhythm which extinguished that hope.

'*Wee — shallnot — weshallnotbe — moved — wee — shallnot —*'

Her instinct was to turn round and walk sharply back to the Tube station. A dismal sense of duty drove her on. If a woman's role was to civilize her men and children and cement the tribe together, than she had failed; failed entirely with Marcus, done less than well with Shona and poor Danny, and was at this very moment neglecting a sullen Zack, who had not been at all mollified by the suggestion that he rent a video and warm himself some beans. The least she could do was stop Roy making a cake of himself.

She shouldered her way through the curious little knot of people, and saw her husband sitting on the step, his back against the side of the porch and his lower half a quilted blue caterpillar in a nylon sleeping bag. At his side a scrawled placard tacked to some kind of wooden oar read, 'Eden IS The Serpent'.

Between snatches of song he was extrapolating on this theme aloud, which explained the audience.

'— *shall not be moved!* Do you know what Eden is? It is a cancer. It is a company that eats companies and turns them into shit. It is a vampire that sucks you dry and then outplaces you, like putting the bins out. It is sucking the nation dry. *Just like a tree that's standing by the waterside* ... Comrades, we stand against Eden and the rotten culture that it stands for!'

When he caught sight of his wife in her familiar red parka jacket, Roy's ranting tailed off and he stared for a moment in silence. A few of the audience shuffled away, glancing back as they moved down the road. Three youngish men and a Japanese woman with a carrier bag remained, their curiosity open and frank. How the streets had changed, even in her adult lifetime, thought Helen. London 2000 felt nothing at all like the mellow, still civilized, still almost Ealing-comedy city of the seventies.

She approached Roy's step and said, 'Come on. Let's go home.'

The warmth of the whisky was draining out of Roy now, and his back was cold against the marble veneer of the porch. Looking down at the sleeping bag he had pulled to his waist, he felt suddenly ridiculous and vulnerable. Helen came closer, standing on the step; now he had to crane his neck to look up at her from the perspective of a beggar.

It was a perspective to which he been gradually growing accustomed, throughout the afternoon. Bad feelings about this enterprise had come over him in waves, but each time less strongly. Earlier, in the middle of the afternoon, someone had thrown him a fifty pence piece. He had seriously faltered in his resolve then, but when Manderill came out and hissed at him not to be a fool, it had hardened again. The man was clearly upset, which was in itself almost as invigorating as the drink. *They thought they had me on their rails*, he said to himself then. *Thought they could flick me with a finger and I'd coast round the curve out of sight. But I jumped the track. Blocked the track!*

When his colleagues had crossed the threshold beside him to go home, with scared glances and mutters of 'You all right?' he had again felt the treacherous pull of reason. He could get up, dust himself off, plead shock, be shipped off to some corporate psychiatric service ...

No. Instead he had barracked the retreating wage slaves with cries of 'You next! Don't think they bloody care about any of you! Those days are passed. There's nothing to be loyal to!'

Helen, however, was another matter. Roy had been so confusedly enraged all day about his working world and the disgusting Marcus that he had all but forgotten his home, wife and remaining son. He looked up, blinking.

'Come on,' she said again. 'Come on. Suzy's cooking supper.' Then she paused and added, 'We can talk about all this later.'

Roy found it very hard, in after days, to explain to anybody what happened at that moment. It was an unseasonably warm evening, and across the road, through the stream of shashing traffic, he could see the lighted windows of other offices, a coffee-bar with steam coming from the vent in the pavement, and the legs and feet of people hurrying past. It was indeed a new perspective. Although his back was cold, his legs were warm, almost sweating, in the padded bag. Above him the portico stuck out enough to give a sense of shelter. He was neither hungry nor thirsty, although he would soon have to think very seriously about having a pee.

Altogether, there was something appealingly simple about just sitting there. People did it all the time, after all; London was full of sitters, and nobody stood over them clucking disapproval. They just got stepped over, and thrown the odd coin. It was, thought Roy, like a very simple, very obvious open door leading down into another world. It was a wonder that everybody didn't take it.

Helen's words, falling from above the broad red parka jacket, were a summons from the far side of the trap door, a populous, complicated, demanding region of fuss and duties and constant testing.

'We can talk it all out later,' she repeated, fatally.

Oh God. A great weariness pressed him down to the simple step and the smooth unquestioning wall. Talking was the last thing, the *last* thing ... It had been a life of talking: talking about money and bathrooms and marketing plans and bonuses and holiday arrangements and schedules and – once, long ago, when they had still thought there was an answer – about where they had gone wrong with the children. Always talking things through, always going round in great meandering circles of words to end up where you began.

The voice above the red jacket spoke again, a third crowing of the cock. The young men had gone away sniggering, but the Japanese shopper still stood there smiling politely, waiting for the show to go on.

'Roy,' said Helen, her voice squeaky with pleading. 'Come *on*. This is no place to talk.'

That's right, thought Roy. No place to talk. That was the best bit about it. From the pavement you could declaim, or rant, or defy the constabulary, or maintain a sullen sleepy silence. But you didn't have to talk. He wriggled into a more comfortable position.

'Sorry,' he said, without much air of apology. 'But I'm staying here.'

'All *night*?' said Helen. Fear crackled through her suddenly; she had, after all, lived twenty-six years with him. They were attuned. Not always pleasantly *in* tune, but reverberating help-lessly to one another's discords. It was not the thought of just one night that made her afraid. Roy confirmed her fears almost instantly.

'Why not all night?' he said. 'People live for years on the streets.'

'Not people like you.' Helen gathered all her firmness, all her years of handling children and adolescents. Badly, she thought, but handling them nonetheless. 'You can't live on the street. Come home.'

'Who knows?' said Roy. 'Who knows what I can do? Anyway, Eric Manderill really hates me sitting here, which is a good reason not to move. If you knew Eric Manderill you'd understand.' He stopped, abruptly. This was bad: he was starting to talk things through, to go into the quagmire of motive and justification. Sod it. No more talking. He smiled up at Helen with a gaiety that shocked her more than anything else had done. 'See you around, anyway.'

'You can't just ...' Helen began, and then was mercifully saved from tears by a rush of anger. 'Oh, do as you like. Happy bloody birthday.'

He watched without emotion as his wife dissolved into the hurrying winter crowds. Then he pulled up the sleeping bag to his shoulders, buried his head in his knees and closed his eyes.

He never saw her hesitate, turn and come back towards him. When something dropped lightly onto his head he merely huddled for a few moments before pulling it off and opening his eyes to look at it. It was the red fur-lined parka jacket, but of Helen herself there was no sign.

# Chapter Five

Amy Partlett was a lawyer in a big City practice, her husband Rod a teacher of singing in three north London schools. They made an odd couple, her brisk precision of speech and sharp little features contrasting with his tumbling grey curls, baggy corduroys and leather-patched jackets. Their mating made more sense when you knew that both her previous husbands had been bankers, Dutch and American, who had fled back to their own countries with women of their own cultures. Rod, too, was marked by a failed cosmopolitanism, having raised three children with a Spanish opera singer who was back in Andalucia now with two of them.

All differences between the Partletts, therefore, faded into insignificance compared with the relaxing blanket of Englishness that enwrapped them both. They listened to the omnibus edition of *The Archers* on Sunday morning in bed, sometimes while eating anchovy toast. Only the presence of Rod's 25-year-old son Juan, a permanent fixture in the top-floor bedroom, threatened this idyll. Juan, who was technically supposed to be improving his English, had come up in conversation during the hour that Suzy and James Darling entertained the Partletts in lieu of the aborted birthday party.

'It's the thing these days. They don't move *out* any more,' said Amy. 'You'd think he'd want his privacy and all that.'

'Helena's talking of giving up her flat,' said Suzy, her blue eyes misting a little as they always did when the subject of her beloved daughter came up. 'Of course, it's bliss when she's home, and lovely that she still feels it *is* home, but if you think of the way we were as students, and how keen we were to leave home ... yes, it is strange.'

'It's because there aren't any rules any more,' said James. 'We don't police their lives, so why shouldn't they have the free laundry service and the run of the fridge, and keep their own earnings for clubbing?'

'What *is* clubbing, actually?' asked Rod, who liked to act out small fogeyish fantasies. 'Juan doesn't *club*. He just borrows money and takes girls to dinner. And then,' he grimaced, 'home.'

The company ignored his question, staring into their drinks for a moment in silence as each thought of their adult children.

After the pause, Rod continued, 'Anyway, I like it. Secretly. It makes me feel like a patriarch. Leader of the tribe. I rather fancy Juan moving his wife in and having grandchildren laughing at my knee.'

'What's so funny about your knee?' asked James. 'Anyway, you wouldn't like it really. Bet *you* wouldn't, Amy.'

'Well, Juan's fine, I suppose. But I still think it's odd these young adults even wanting to live with their parents,' said Amy. 'After I went to Cambridge I never really lived at home again, and Mummy and Daddy certainly didn't expect it. I can just imagine how their little faces would have crumpled up with shock if I'd turned up at twenty-three.'

Zack, who had been sitting on the floor of the Darlings' living room, flicking through a book, got up and said abruptly, 'S'cuse me, Mrs Darling. When do we have supper? Only I want to go home for something.'

'Half an hour at least,' said Suzy. 'Will you be OK? Got a key?' She had swept Zack up with her when Helen left, unable to bear the idea of the boy making his own supper when a birthday, however adult, had been promised. His silent presence had kept the conversation off the subject of his father's aberration, a piece of self-denial which required great fortitude from the four adults. Now they perceptibly brightened as the front door slammed, only Suzy looking uneasy for a moment as she said, 'I suppose he'll be OK ... it's only a few doors along.'

'Course he will,' said Amy scornfully. 'He's a big boy now.' She finished her wine, held her glass out absent-mindedly for more, and as James poured it said eagerly, 'Right, Suzy, while he's gone, tell us *precisely* what Helen said.'

When the gist of the Keaney situation had been summarized for them, the three adults sat wrapped in thought for a moment. Then Amy said, 'Wasn't it Eden which just bought up Intaglio-dot-com? Marcus Keaney's e-media company?'

'Yup,' said James. 'It was all round the office today. The Keaney boy's going to join them and brainstorm a whole new division. It's like a bloody great python, that company. Swallows a whole goat, burps, and looks for the next one.'

Rod Partlett said, '*Do* pythons burp?' but nobody paid any attention. His wife was off on a far more interesting trail.

'Do you suppose,' said Amy Partlett, 'that Marcus being in the division has anything to do with Roy being made redundant?'

A shocked silence fell over the four.

'Surely not,' said James uncertainly. 'I mean, rather the opposite. You don't make your father redundant on your first day ...'

'Don't you believe it,' said Rod. 'I've seen things, in Spanish companies ... Nanda's southern relatives. Old stag, young stag, you know.' He shook his head sagely, and this time the others gave some thought to what he said.

'Well, that might explain him being in a strange state,' said Amy. 'Poor bastard. Eased out by your own son on your own birthday.'

'Marcus is hardly ever round at their house, is he?' Rod

Partlett, accustomed to the constant soap opera of a school staff room, was as feline a gossip as any of the women in the street. 'I always think it's rather hard on little Zack, no brothers and sisters taking an interest.'

'Helen does very well with him!' protested Suzy, but she too could not resist the lure of analysing the Keaney household. Helen was her friend, yet there were curious areas of silence in their relationship; light-hearted and solipsistic as she was, Suzy nonetheless felt flickers of awkwardness when she chattered about Helena and Dougie and their grown-up lives, and met with only silence from Helen, and an unwillingness even to look back at the childhoods their children had all shared.

Now she said, 'It's true, though, she doesn't really talk about the others. Shona had that exhibition at the Hemroyd Gallery, and none of us knew anything about it till the Sunday papers.'

'Can't blame her. The sort of stuff their Shona exhibits would be bloody hard to describe over the dinner table,' said James.

'Even over coffee she didn't talk about it,' said Suzy, whose mind was a literal one. 'And she doesn't mention Marcus really, and as for Danny, well, you'd forget most of the time that there had ever been another twin.'

'We never knew Danny,' said Amy. 'We only really met them just after Marcus had gone. I remember the row about Marcus leaving Oxford in his first term, but I can't remember who it was who told us that the little brother had just gone as well. It certainly wasn't Helen or Roy. I do remember thinking it was a bit early for the brother to take off, since the twin was Shona and she was still at school.'

'I knew Danny,' said Suzy. 'Since he was a little boy. He was lovely – very polite, very precise, very intense about things. Didn't look a bit like Shona. There was some kind of trouble with him at school, though. Helen never said what. Then James and I did that year in the Frankfurt office, and when we got back, there was no Danny and I heard about him leaving home, but Helen's never said anything. By the time we got back she was as clammed-up about the whole thing as Roy. Just said he was in a hostel and everything was fine.'

'Anna Durant said she thought he had a row with his father about – you know – sexuality,' said Rod. 'She reckoned he came out as gay, perhaps. She taught him French for GCSE, but he never sat the exam. Don't know why. Durant says she always wondered if he *was* gay. But then, she thinks everyone's gay. Lesbians always do.'

'She's not, is she?' Suzy grasped the opportunity to change the subject. 'Miss Durant who does the modern languages?' Unease was filling her now on Helen's behalf, and she felt disloyal to be encouraging speculation about one of Helen's children, however long-vanished.

After a few moments of spirited argument over Miss Durant's orientation ('Bloody waste if she is,' said James incautiously), Suzy excused herself and went down to the basement kitchen to look at the lasagne in the oven.

When she looked up, she saw the white face of Helen, who was tapping cautiously on the window over the sink. Stifling a small scream of alarm, Suzy went to the back door and pulled the bolts. It was a rarely used door, and scraped awkwardly on the tiles.

'Sorry,' said Helen. 'I couldn't face ringing the front doorbell and meeting everyone. Look, I can't go through with tonight. I'm sorry, I've landed you with our party. The thing is, Roy isn't coming home. He says he's sleeping on the street.'

'For a sort of demo, you mean? Like national sleep-out week for the homeless?'

Helen shuddered. 'Christ, I don't know. When I was coming up on the Tube, I was really convinced that he means it. That he wants to drop out, for good.'

'In a woolly hat, you mean? Crisis hostels, selling the *Big Issue*?' Suzy looked wildly around at her kitchen, as if the Aga and the shining pans and the bunch of onions were talismans against the catastrophe of such an awful world snatching away one of their own kind.

'I would be quite glad,' said Helen bleakly, 'if I thought he had anything so focused on his mind as being a *Big Issue* seller. They're people who are on the way back up, aren't they? Roy's nose was pointing downhill.'

'Come by the radiator. You're freezing. Your hair's wet. Where's your coat, anyway?'

In the end Helen was persuaded to join the group for dinner for Zack's sake, armed with a cover story about Roy having come down with the flu and being advised to bed down in a friend's flat in Great Portland Street rather than travel home. The company politely pretended to believe this and animatedly talked of other things, with the hearty optimism that befits adults in whose midst is a child not yet eleven years old.

Zack, making ridges and turrets with his lasagne, was not fooled. His slams of the Darlings' front door had been purely theatrical, both going and coming. He had in point of fact travelled no further than their dining room, whose serving hatch had a most conveniently thin and smooth ply surface to put a tumbler, and an ear, against. Hearing his mother in the kitchen had been harder, but when she moved towards the radiator, shivering, she had said something about giving Dad her coat to sleep in if he was spending the night on the pavement, and something else about him starting to sell the *Big Issue*.

Now Zack watched his mother with practised eyes. She was lit up, giggling a little, drinking wine, pretending everything was all right apart from the flu. He would demand the truth about Dad later.

Or the truth about Danny. Perhaps that should come first. The Danny stuff, which troubled him in parts of his mind and body he was only newly, dimly aware of, had been the front line of his family research ever since Christmas. He had to find out about that. So the Dad thing might have to wait its turn; grown-ups, in Zack's experience, could not bear telling children very much truth all in one go. It could take weeks to solve the Danny problem even if he wasn't nagging about Dad as well.

It had taken him a whole fortnight, after all, just to find out about Shona putting poos in an art gallery, which was actually quite funny and not seriously worrying at all when you thought about it. He had had a bad time over it at school, yeah, because the Ron Hill gang had seen it in the papers before he knew about it. But even then, a year ago, he could see that it was a sort of joke of Shona's, to shock people and stop them just drifting around in art galleries yakking, like they usually did. Mum probably thought that he, Zack, would drop dead of shock if he found out that he had a gay brother *and* a father who slept on pavements *and* a sister who did sculptures out of piles of poo.

It was hard work, he thought not unresentfully, when people thought that the best thing they could do for you was never to tell you anything.

# Chapter Six

It was three in the morning when Roy woke with a stiff, shooting pain in his neck. The twisted sharpness distracted him momentarily from his aching back and the pins and needles in his hands, which had been resting uphill on his chest, clutching the quilted sleeping bag. He had put the red coat on, glad of the nylon fur in its hood as he fell asleep. The furriness made him remember, between sleeping and waking, the black cat of his childhood. Nellie, she was called; an idle amiable beast who used to hide under his bed while his mother tucked him up and then creep out conspiratorially to his soft summons, and sleep all night on his pillow, warm fur against his cheek. Involuntarily, with numb fingers, he stroked the edge of the hood.

In the darkness he shifted against the cold stone of the Eden portico and wriggled his hands inside the sleeves of the coat to warm them. He must have slept for four hours, because it had been eleven by his watch when he cautiously crept round the side of the building for a pee, and then returned to his bag. Near the entrance to the alley was a bale of newspapers, resting against a side door he had never noticed. They were the next day's, which filled him with wonder: he had never known you could get tomorrow's news so early. With difficulty, Roy ripped off the plastic strap that bound them and took six or seven thick broadsheets to insulate him from below as he settled back to sleep. Cardboard would have been better. No wonder street sleepers used cardboard boxes; a wonderful material.

Looking around, he saw that he was not alone. Near him, a few doors down, an elderly man slept, dead-looking, his white hair trailing on the stained concrete of a fashion wholesaler's doorstep. Next to the old man, as if on guard, a tough-looking boy with a bleached streak in his hair sat upright, hunched over a polystyrene cup which, Roy saw to his envious amazement, was steaming.

He stared for a moment until the boy, feeling his gaze, turned and said, 'Hi.'

'Hi', said Roy. The boy went on regarding him.

'You the guy who was making all the noise, yeah?'

'Er, yes. It was a demonstration.'

'We don't like that. It brings the Old Bill round. Gets them moving everybody on. I'm just telling you because you're new on this pitch. You don't shout at people, right? If you do, the pigs reckon you're a junkie and there's trouble for everyone.'

Roy did not feel equal to arguing, but a wave of irritation passed through him. Even here, then, even here in the gutter there were rules and social conventions. The hell with it! He huddled crossly in his sleeping bag for a moment and then, unwillingly, asked, 'Where'd you get the coffee?'

'Over there.' The boy pointed at a van Roy had not noticed. Roy shook his hands out of the sleeves of the parka and began fumbling in his suit jacket pocket for coins.

''S free', said the boy, with an edge of contempt for Roy's naivety. 'They come every night, right? Coffee, soup.'

Roy felt increasingly uncomfortable. If he got up, and left his bag and newspaper, would the boy steal them? If he took the sleeping bag with him, would it be construed as an insult to the other street people? His mouth was foul and dry, though, and after a few moments the longing for coffee overtook him and he pulled himself awkwardly to his feet and stepped out of the sleeping bag.

At the van, a fair-haired girl in her twenties looked at him with curiosity. He was still wearing a work suit and tie, crumpled as they were. She would have taken him for the last remnant of an ordinary office party or middle-aged spree, if she had not just seen him emerging from a sleeping bag in a doorway like any other dosser on her beat. She had been doing soup runs for long enough not to express much curiosity straightaway.

'Coffee?' she said. And, as he took it, half turned away and asked casually over her shoulder, 'You staying out the night?'

'Yes', said Roy. And, surprising himself, 'I live here, now.'

She turned back to him, genuinely startled. Nobody *ever* said that. People said 'for the moment' or went into rambling accusations about their wives throwing them out, or the hostel being full of dirty junkies. Few people ever claimed to live, deliberately, on the streets. Even in London, even in winter 2000.

'If you want a bed,' she said, 'there's a hostel five minutes from here. I can get Degsy,' she jerked her head to the interior of the van, where a bald-headed young man sat yawning, 'to show you, if you like. You can turn up any time. It's warm.'

'I like it here. For now,' said Roy, and took his coffee away. The girl looked after him, uneasily, and turned to her companion.

He yawned again and said, 'He's making a point. He's one of those that are out here to show somebody and make them sorry. You get them, sometimes. Leave him alone.'

Back at his pitch, Roy looked around him at the dull night landscape and shivered. The heat of the drink made a small, warm focus of comfort which somehow underlined the bleakness all around. The darkest hour, he thought. Darkest before the dawn. But dawn would not be for hours yet. He could see the girl and the bald young man silhouetted in the lighted window of the van opposite, and a lonely car squishing down the damp street. Otherwise nothing moved. The boy who had spoken to him sat, eyes open, arms round his knees, staring into blankness with wide dark pupils.

Just as sleep was creeping over Roy, with again a faint comforting memory of the cat Nellie, a tremendous eructation from close by made him start. In his sleep, the white-haired tramp in the next doorway had farted.

Helen had drunk enough to send her to sleep, but enough also to wake her up in the dark hours before the dawn. Lying on her back, hot-eyed and unhappy, she stared up at the shadowy outlines of the plaster ceiling rose ('Many period features,' the estate agent had gloated, watching the price float up day after day in the year they bought it). The faint glimmer of a street lamp filtered through the curtain, giving the room a ghostly, mournful memory of light.

She had lain awake thus through many nights, quiet in the darkness, trying not to disturb Roy's noisy, flailing, sighing sleep or to envy him his oblivion. She thought tonight, as she had thought often in these grey night hours, that if it had not been for Zack's late, inexplicable birth she would almost certainly have gone under by now. What 'going under' meant, Helen was never quite clear; but surely some mental nemesis must await a woman who faced middle age without rewarding work or a noticeably rewarding marriage, whose friends were familiar without being close, and who inarticulately mourned too many people, both alive and dead.

Perhaps she would have taken to shoplifting, or left Roy to his grumpy self-pity and his drinking while she embarked on some series of humiliating affairs (somehow, Helen always imagined them as humiliating rather than thrilling). Perhaps she would have found a new office job and developed a middle-aged pash for the boss. Perhaps she would have badgered her doctor for successive generations of feelgood pills, or taken to secret sherry-drinking.

Instead there had been Zack; a merry new baby, a way to wind the clock back. There were nappies and night waking again, for which her contemporaries pretended to pity her; but there was gurgling laughter too, and slow walks to see the ducks, and a small confiding hand in hers, and paintings of rainbows and huge happy suns, and endless, sticky hugs. Coming during the worst years with the older children, these little comforts had softened the abrasion of family life. Helen thought of Marcus at that period, a boy in black with hair gelled flat; of his casual academic brilliance, his computers and his smart insolent contempt for parents and teachers. She thought of Roy's answering spurts of petulance towards his eldest son, and the way that every attempt she made to reconcile them only seemed to mire the warring males deeper in mutual antipathy. She thought of Shona's running battles with the school art department ('She has real talent, Mrs Keaney, but she has to learn that perversity is not always the same as originality' – 'Mum, I am not staying at that fuckwit school'). She thought of Danny, shouting tearful horrors, slamming out, coming home defiant and shuttered and then one day not coming home at all. From all these things Helen had at least been able to turn gratefully back to Zacky in his highchair or on his tricycle, sunny and uncomplicated, always up for a cuddle and a chapter of *Thomas the Tank Engine*.

Helen's thoughts and memories curled away from her into the darkness of the silent bedroom. Perhaps it was the seduction of Zack's happy babyhood which had made her miss cues and lose contact with the teenagers. Perhaps if she had not been so distracted she could have reined in Shona's perversity, bridged the growing chasm between Marcus and his father, and even headed off Danny's disasters and desertion.

But again, perhaps she could not have done anything about any of it. Perhaps, without baby Zack, it would simply have destroyed her. When Helen heard or read about women who 'held the whole family together', it filled her with dismay. Who were these women, where did their strength come from? The centrifugal force of her family during those years seemed irresistible, far greater than one woman could resist. Especially without Roy. He would never talk about the elder children, never make suggestions, never guide them. When the first three were small, she thought with tired, detached wonder, he was an interested father, a perfect New Man envied by her friends for his deftness with nappies and generosity with his time after work. To some extent he was the same with baby Zack. Yet once the unquestioning trust of childhood faded from each child's eyes, to be replaced by the critical gaze of adolescence, Roy withdrew from them with a sharpness which surprised Helen. And hurt her, too.

'This computer's seriously crap. I need more memory. I need a better machine for the stuff I'm working on.'

'You've only had that one six months.'

'Stuff moves on, Dad. For fuck's sake, even you can see that.'

A father should listen and argue at such a point, thought Helen; he should ignore the rudeness, talk sensibly about costs, take an interest in the reasons for the boy's urgency, and try to appreciate his vivid new computer world. But Roy had either shouted back with flaying insults or simply got up, silently, and left the room. It was the same with Shona and with Danny.

Well, worse with Danny. Obviously. Three different people, different children escaping from childhood dependency in different directions, yet they all had the same contemptuous flame of energy in them, and when they showed it they all met with the same angry coldness from their father. And all Helen could do was watch, and cuddle Zack, and pretend that the change was not happening. One week, it would seem, Roy was playing dominoes with a child and reading translations of *Beowulf* aloud; the next week that child had taken a step too far beyond his authority and met the sudden blank wall of his disapproval. There would be brief reconciliations, but before long the child's defiance would flare up even more brightly, in even more terrifying a form, and Roy would turn away and feign indifference.

It would happen with Zack, any day now.

At least, it would if Roy ever came home. Helen shivered, and rolled the duvet tighter round her shoulders.

After a while her shivering eased, and an odd sensation overtook her. It was as if the soft quilt hardened, thickened, set around her like concrete. It became a shell, a carapace, an unpierceable armour. Slipping in and out of dreams, Helen retreated ever further into the safety that it offered. Something wailed in the distance - a police car perhaps, or a distraught cat - but deep in her fastness, thought Helen confusedly, she need no longer hear the high, sad music of the world's complaint.

# Chapter Seven

It was almost light when Roy woke again. This time he had lain down properly flat on the pavement, curled up, and the fur hood was still comfortingly round his head. What woke him was the toe of the young man with the white streak in his hair who had told him off for ranting.

'You got money, right?' said the figure towering above him.

Roy squinted up. So this was it: he was going to be mugged. He moved his head slightly, away from the direction of the boy's foot.

'Not a lot,' he said.

The boy heard the tone of his voice and said irritably, 'I'm not a fucking mugger, mate. I was only telling you that the caff,' he jerked his head towards the café across the road, 'does full English, two ninety-nine, but no dossers after half-pass seven, right? So if you want to eat, you better go now.'

Roy was discomfited, and wanted to apologize without knowing how to do so. He sat up and cocked his head on one side in a donnish, interrogative way. It was an old trick for placating writers who were feeling insulted or otherwise hard done by; ask them a question and seem fascinated by the answer. Everybody loves to be consulted.

'Goodness,' he said. 'How do they know which customers *are* dossers?'

'Because you got a sleeping bag,' said the boy, with the air of one dealing with an imbecile. 'An' if you don't take your sleeping bag in wiv you you'll get it nicked. Plus, it ain't hard to spot us, is it? We're not exactly Men in Black.'

'Well, thank you for the advice,' said Roy. 'May I buy you breakfast, perhaps?' Again, his publisher's instinct: buy them lunch, leave them happy.

'Fought you'd never ask,' said the boy. When he grinned, he showed a mouthful of the most terrible teeth Roy had ever seen in a Western country: black and brown, gappy and broken.

Roy was not a hiker or an outdoorsman; breakfast to him was normally a dyspeptic, fretful business of half-eaten toast and black coffee. Not since his student days at rock festivals and demonstrations had he experienced the heady effect of a hot meal after a cold night out. He had forgotten how invincibly happy and strong a man feels after a brave yellow egg with greasy bacon, sausage, fried bread and toast; how magical limp toast could be rendered by the laying of lurid marmalade on cheap margarine and the lubrication of hot milky tea. His companion wolfed his meal down quickly with minimal conversation, muttered 'Cheers!' and left.

Roy idly watched him down the street, for the boy did not return to his doorway but vanished from sight in a southerly direction, his bundle of bedding under his arm. Then he sat basking in the warmth with his third mug of tea until the shelving bosom of the Italian proprietress blocked out the light, and he looked up to see her uncompromising folded arms and challenging stance. Time to go.

'You have-a to move your things,' she said. 'Bed things. No street-sleep people now. Soon I have many customers for the coffee. There is no room.' She swept an expressive arm in an arc above his head, and Roy saw that she was right. When the only two tables were occupied – his and the one where an old man sat bowed over a cup of coffee – there was barely room for anybody to reach the counter for a take-out cappuccino. She had turned away from him now and was shaking the shoulder of the old man with the flowing, dirty white hair.

'OK, Misery. You go now.'

In one of his terse comments over breakfast, the boy with the bleached streak in his hair had told Roy that the old man's name was Misery. Or at least that if it was not, this was the only word he uttered when asked it. 'Care in the community, like,' the boy said. ''E's not dangerous.'

'Are a lot of people you meet on the pavement – sleeping out, I mean – are they mental patients?'

'Few,' said the boy.

'But not you?'

'Council care,' said the boy. 'From when I was ten. Well, on and off.'

That was just before he left the café without further conversation.

Roy noticed that the old man Misery had not been asked to pay for his coffee; also that the Italian woman had, unasked, put down a bowl of baked beans and a spoon in front of him. He marvelled that all these things had been happening day after day within yards of his workplace and that he had known about none of them.

Now, standing up, he gathered his possessions and out of old habit slapped his jacket pocket. There was no wallet. Nor was it in the parka, or anywhere to be seen. As he bent to look under the table, without much hope, he was aware of the proprietress's renewed attention.

'He steal your money?' she asked. 'This is bad thing. Now he will buy drugs, enough drugs to sell again. He is not your son?'

'No,' said Roy emphatically. 'No relation.'

'When you come in, you have money, I think he was your son. I think good! Now he go home with his papa, no more drugs.'

'I am not,' said Roy, 'the kind of papa who has that sort of influence. Sorry.'

Leaving the café, he felt strangely light-hearted in spite of the theft. He still had his bank card in an inside pocket, and the comfort of breakfast was strong within him. Across the road near the Eden doorway he glanced at his watch, and saw to his surprise that this, too, had disappeared. Clever little bastard! As he considered his next move he saw a familiar car approaching, with a uniformed driver at the wheel.

Eric Manderill. Big corporate cheeses get in early: it could barely be eight o'clock yet. Quick as a flash Roy was on the doorstep, the bag pulled round his raised knees. By the time Manderill's car had pulled up and the CEO's door opened, he was ready.

'Morning, Eric!' he roared. 'Getting down to work early, then, are you? Busy-busy-busy, things to do, people to sack!'

Manderill halted, white-faced. For a moment Roy thought that he was going to jump back into the car and slam the door.

Seeing a knot of girls and a young man, presumably from the Eden postroom team, walking into earshot, Roy raised his voice even more and continued, 'Which division gets the benefit of your managerial nous today, Eric? Now you've ensured a brain-dead future for the publishing division by hiring my dear son Marcus, who's next? Going to wreck another decent little country town with a bypass supermarket, are we? Or authorize a new line in pornographic lingerie for the under-tens? Or is your great brain focused on screwing down the price of peas from some poor bloody African plantation? What's to modernize today, Eric?'

Manderill glanced back; his driver was moving smoothly on, bound for the awkward little car park at the back. There was a door into the building from there but Eden executives rarely used it, preferring to be dropped off at their impressive portico and greeted by respectful commissionaires. For a moment, hearing

Roy, Manderill considered running after the car, banging on the roof and reclaiming it for a dive to safety. Then he squared his thin shoulders and marched towards the door, and the shouting Roy. He could see spittle coming from the man's mouth; every fastidious inch of his skin cried out in disgust. He must not speak; he must not reply.

'Manderill! King of the apes!' yelled Roy. 'Hello, girls. Do you know how the mandrill is defined, in the Oxford English Dictionary? Mandrill – the largest, most ferocious and most hideous of the baboons. It has blue cheeks, the mandrill, and a most excellent red bum. Come on, Eric! Show the girls your fine red bum! Then get in there and get on with the job of degrading and dumbing and downsizing anybody with half a brain! Mandy, Mandy, sweet as sugar candy!'

Nobody ever – *ever* – joked about Eric Manderill's name. Not since school, when his sufferings had been immense. He was in the building now, but the electric doors had not slid shut behind him because some of the postroom girls were still standing in the range of the control beam, looking down amazedly at Roy in his sleeping bag. Pursued by invective, the chief executive bolted for the lift, noting as its doors mercifully closed that the two security men on the desk were failing to stifle their mirth. They would not, he silently resolved, be on that desk for many more mornings.

As Manderill's lift carried him upward away from danger, Roy's ranting ceased as abruptly as it began. He smiled up at the girls, sunny and assured, and began to rattle on with an eloquence which would have amazed his wife and family if they had been there to hear it.

'Sorry about that,' he said. 'It's my new job. Did you hear that they sacked me from my old one? Now I'm playing a very important role, dating back to Ancient Rome, indeed. You remember from school that there used to be a slave hired to ride behind conquering generals on their chariots when they had a triumph through the streets of the city. The slave had to keep whispering, "Remember you are a man!" in case the general decided he was a god. That's me, that's my new job. I say to our revered leader, remember you are a Manderill!'

The spell of his shouting broken, the girls hurried past him, round the end of the desk and into the ladies' next to the postroom for their morning brush-up and informal conference.

'It's Mr Keaney, innit?' said one, awed. 'I go to judo with Marie, from his office. She was ever so upset when he said he was going to sit on the step.'

'I think it's good,' said her friend, grimacing in the mirror. 'People think they can sack people and just get away with it. When my dad lost his job—'

'Yeah, but he's going on like a loony,' objected the first. 'They'll get the police to take him away, this rate. What good's he going to do himself?'

Outside, however, Roy had reverted to the role of a meek homeless bundle, silent and vacant as Misery and the bleached boy had been the night before. He correctly guessed that Manderill's first move would be to call the police. Large and impressively uniformed though the security men at the desk were, it was common knowledge that they had virtually no power of coercion, least of all over the space outside the sliding doors.

The process of summoning the police, however, took longer than either of the foes might have expected. Erika was not yet at her post and Manderill – who retained enough self-control not to dial 999 – was unaccustomed to looking up telephone numbers, particularly in an outer office so sleekly minimalist that finding the doors and drawers of Erika's desk was a problem in itself. At last he got them.

'There's a man on the step,' he began, 'who may represent a danger to my staff . . .'

So a young policeman was diverted by his pocket radio from strolling watchfully through Berwick Street market looking for early morning drug deals, and came to investigate. He found Roy apparently asleep, huddled to one side of the porch. Two doors down old Misery – a very familiar figure to the force – sat outside the fashion house, mumbling to himself; and at the end of the road the black pavement artist began his morning's exhibition.

In Manderill's office, the constable said, 'There's no disturbance, sir. You'll appreciate that with the situation as it is, regarding police-public relations and government policy on rough sleeping, it would be difficult for us to do anything more than advise the gentleman to move on.'

'So do that!' spat Manderill. 'And make sure he does it!'

'The thing is, sir,' said the policeman, 'the gentleman appears to be asleep. We don't generally—'

'Oh, get back to your station,' said the CEO angrily, 'and bring some reinforcements. I'll ring your chief up myself and make it clear that he absolutely *has to go!*'

While the policeman was upstairs engaging in this unsatisfactory conversation, Roy took the opportunity to stop feigning sleep and greet some of his colleagues.

'Hello, Peter! Hello, Marcia! Enjoy your day. It could be your last. It was my last day yesterday, did you know? A little birthday present, an outplacement package. Because they don't give a bugger, you know, they don't give a toss. I had a diary full of appointments, books halfway through production, things which only I know how best to handle professionally. None of that mattered once my son swanned in and asked for my head on a plate, like some sort of Salomé in leather trousers. There isn't any dignity or meaning in work, for these people, you know. As far as Eden is concerned, you're just cogs in the mechanism. COGS!' He raised his voice because Marcia, unlike Peter, had hurried through the doors to get out of earshot.

Peter Morden stood wretchedly by his former colleague, hearing him out, then said, 'Roy, old man, a word in your ear – don't do this. Please. It's for your own good I'm saying it.'

'And for *your* own good I'm saying, get out of Eden! They're vicious, pointless, amoral, heartless, dangerous—'

'So why did you stay till they sacked you?' Morden was nettled. 'I never heard you say any of this while you were on the payroll.'

'That,' said Roy, 'is because I am a coward. Probably through never eating proper breakfasts. I have had breakfast now and I feel terrific and I see clearly. And what I see is that this is a disgusting—'

At this point he saw the policeman getting out of the lift, slumped forward and began snoring. Peter Morden – who was quick – assessed the situation and wondered whether to tell the copper that Roy was faking it and had just been haranguing staff. Then he laughed to himself, shook his head, and went on into the building, passing the policeman with an innocent and untroubled air. Onwards and upwards. What larks to tell his son about at the weekend!

The morning wore on. As he greeted each arriving member of staff with his new eloquence, Roy's mood swung between elation and cold fear. He had never thought of himself as a brave man or a fighter, and his outbursts of defiance scared him, so that each surge of defiance was followed by a hollow coldness in his stomach, which in turn could only be warmed by another bout of rage. Shouting at senior managers was a strange new kind of fun, and found him at his best. Remonstrating with colleagues was harder; the worst moment was when Alan Barton marched up to him and cut right through the rambling Roy rhetoric with a grievance of his own.

'Where's the paddle?' he demanded. 'I can just about stand you pinching the sleeping bag, because I had two spares for the weekend and they're pretty old. I don't think I'd issue it to a scout after you've slept in it, frankly. But where's the paddle?'

Dimly, Roy remembered his drunken manufacture of a placard the day before. He looked around; the paddle was nowhere to be seen.

'That was a brand-new bloody paddle, twenty-two quids' worth from Albemarle Street, for the Indian canoe team in the Docklands rally. Where is it?'

'It must have been nicked,' said Roy.

'Nicked *again*, you mean,' said Alan, nastily, 'seeing that you nicked it in the first place. Look, Roy, I don't know what you're doing here—'

'Protesting,' said Roy with weak defiance.

'But whatever it is, it's your business, and the sea scouts are mine. I want twenty-two quid. Now! Even then I don't know whether they'll have any more of them in stock.'

Roy fished in his pocket, remembered the theft of his wallet, and said, 'My wallet's gone too. I'll give you a cheque.'

There were no cheques left in his book.

'I've got a cash card.'

Alan stood silently, waiting.

'I can go and get some money out of a hole-in-the-wall, but not yet. Later, when it's quiet. Tomorrow I'll bring the money, I swear. And something for the sleeping bag.'

'Keep the bloody bag,' said Alan, moving away. 'But for Christ's sake, don't keep this charade up much longer. It's embarrassing and it won't do you a smidgen of good.'

Roy was shaken by this interlude; there was too much aggrieved sensibleness in Alan Barton for comfort. Far better was the moment when one of his own diary appointments – a director of a major bookshop chain and noted puritan – descended from a black cab and walked purposefully towards the doors. He would have ignored Roy as an unexceptional piece of modern London street furniture but as he came into earshot the huddled bundle on the step began shouting his name.

'Alec! Alec Devereux! Good to see you!'

Devereux halted, puzzled, and looked around for some vertical figure, some fellow denizen of the upper pavement level. None of the scuttling lunch-hour shoppers seemed to have spoken his name.

'Grand to see you, Alec!' said the voice at his feet. 'Delighted you could make it. I'm afraid I can't offer you the usual tea or coffee ...'

At last the bookseller stopped and looked down, with dawning horror, at the apparition on the pavement. For a man who had only been on the streets for twenty-four hours, Roy was looking convincingly rough. His stubble had grown, uneven and challengingly ginger; his hair, which had been due for a cut anyway, blew in uncontrollable wisps; he was wearing a red fur-collared woman's anorak and beneath it his shirt was far from fresh, and decorated with spodges of sausage grease from his breakfast. Yet what frightened Alec Devereux more than any of this was the glimpse of a grey suit jacket and – under the casually thrown sleeping bag – trousers which still, despite everything, had a crease down the front. Roy had become something worse than the average street sleeper. He had become a dreadful caricature of white-collar man; a memento mori among suits.

'Roy? Roy Keaney?' stammered the visitor. He stepped back, an unwise manoeuvre since he was standing on the lower of the two stone steps. Half falling, he cannoned backwards into a large woman in a padded jacket, who saved him by clutching at his jacket and causing the seam to jerk most unpleasantly under his armpits. Apologizing, wriggling his way back to comfort, he stared at Roy, who had begun to talk with a worrying, jerky eloquence.

'Yea, even the righteous may stumble if the Lord guide not their foot, Alec. Carry on, carry on. In the doors and up in the lift. You'll no doubt be looked after in there by my successor. I'm sorry I can't give you his or her name, I have no idea which particular nose-rotted, square-eyed, strangle-crotched seventeen-year-old they've put in charge of Handfast titles since they sacked me yesterday. Don't look so worried, Alec. Rejoice, rejoice, rather! For Eden has brought our shabby old world of mere books into the twenty-first century of fluttering pixels and decaff lo-cal online literature cobbled up by cokeheads. My son's in charge, you know. Marcus Keaney. You'll love Marcus. He'll make you welcome and lay you out a line of the finest white Colombian to sniff in the new millennium. Beats the old dry sherry down at the Publishers Association, hey, Alec?'

Devereux gaped. He remembered Roy Keaney as a pleasantly spoken, charmingly diffident, acute but unthreateningly donnish publisher of the old school; a bit resistant to certain aspects of the necessary modern market ethos, certainly, but well within the desirable range of professional contacts for a man in the book trade. This wild pavement creature shocked him at a level of his being that he rarely explored. There was a desperate treachery in his descent; Roy at this moment affected him like a rip in the fabric of the universe. As for the allegations about young Keaney's drug habit, that was deplorable, quite deplorable. One heard things about these younger media types but, well ...

Alec Devereux felt unsafe. He looked behind him, and all around, as if searching for an escape route. Then, glancing through the doors, he saw approaching the sweet calm vision of Marie, Roy's familiar secretary. The electric doors opened before her and she came towards him, smiling. He could, at that moment, have run into her arms. Roy watched sardonically from the pavement as she greeted him.

'Mr Devereux, I tried to contact your secretary. I'm so sorry, we'll have to ask you to reschedule the appointment, as Mr Keaney has—' She was going to say 'left the company unexpectedly', but as the figure at her feet bore eloquent witness, Mr Keaney was only too close to the company headquarters.

Roy took over, fixing Devereux all the while with light wild eyes. 'As Mr Keaney has been sacked, and is currently conducting all negotiations from the front doorstep, where he has been put out, like all the other rubbish.'

'I'll go,' said Devereux. 'I'll telephone from my office. Thank you, Marlene.'

'Marie!' cackled Roy. 'Not Marlene, or Mavis, or Minnehaha.

"Sweet Marie, who waits for me," cha-cha-cha.' He executed a horrid little dance with his fingers on his knees, looking as he did so more demented than at any time that day. Then he raised his fist in a victory gesture at a young man, some tourist presumably, who was flashing at him with a small camera.

Marie, hot-cheeked with embarrassed indignation, hesitated for a moment when Devereux had gone, then clutching to her chest the folder she was carrying, she knelt down on the step by her former boss, hunkering back so that her eyes were level with his. It was the first level encounter that Roy had had since he sat in the café at dawn with the boy who robbed him. He did not like the sensation, and looked slantwise away from her.

Marie spoke. 'Mr Keaney. Roy.' He had always told her to call him Roy, and she sometimes complied. 'Please.' Her pale hair swung forward as she leaned in towards him, and she flicked it back, unselfconscious, concentrated, with a kind of childlike intensity. '*Please* listen.'

'Don't please, don't plead,' said Roy, but his voice was weaker and more uncertain. 'Go back in, get on with your life, child. Leave me alone.'

'Please, really, Mr Keaney. They're saying awful things in there, about what Mr Manderill's going to do about you. It really, really might be best if you just go home now, and then they might not do it.'

'Do what?' sneered Roy, regaining composure. 'Bring in a fork-lift and sweep me away? Have me arrested – me and all the other poor naked wretches who sleep on the pavement in London West One? Take me to court? Do *what?*'

'Mr Keaney,' Marie felt, after all, happier with the formal term of address, 'it's none of my business really, but your terms-of-redundancy notice, the bits you left on the floor and in the lift—'

'You mean my one-way ticket to the Clapham Outplacement and Extermination Camp. I didn't bloody need it, so I didn't bloody take it.'

'I read it,' said Marie. 'So when Erika was talking in the canteen at lunchtime, I knew what she was going on about. Mr Keaney, they've got the right to not give you *any* money.'

Roy was silent.

Taking his silence for abashed attention, Marie continued, 'They're getting a lawyer. There was a thing in it about unfavourable publicity and you not causing it. And the cleaners brought me up more bits, and there was a copy of your old contract you signed when you came, with a yellow highlighter on the bit about bringing the company into public disrepute.'

Roy gave a small crazy laugh. 'I'd forgotten,' he said, 'that I ever did promise to bring the company into public disrepute. Isn't it lucky that I've finally got round to doing it? All debts paid, hey?'

Marie looked at him with big, blue, puzzled eyes for a few moments as he grinned at her and then again abruptly looked down in that odd slantwise fashion. Then she put her hand on the doorway to steady herself and rose stiffly to her feet.

Looking down on his slumped street presence now, like the rest of the upper world, she said, 'I'm going to ring a doctor, Mr Keaney. And I'm going to ring your wife.'

# Chapter Eight

On Wednesdays Helen helped out at the Ferris Residential and Day Centre for the Retired. It was a red-brick, Victorian-Gothic edifice, not large but somehow looming; it dominated the upper end of the road, but in her early busy days as a working mother she had scarcely given it a thought when she hurried past towards the bus stop. Few of its residents were able to walk as far as its front gate unassisted, so there was little evidence of them on the street. The small back garden was hidden, and only the council minibus bringing in the day attenders gave a hint of the lives which drifted aimlessly towards their close behind the patterned brick façade.

There was an ambulance parked there on that Wednesday morning. As Mrs Beazeley, who called herself the 'matron manager', was prone to explain with a little *moue* of resigned distaste, 'We don't allow hearses to park outside, even when death has been certified. It depresses the residents.' Other things which might depress them, thought Helen, were the gloomy laurel bushes outside the window, the never-silent television, and the cook's conviction that old people are so fond of rice pudding that they will not mind having it as an accompaniment to a main course of boiled rice and chicken.

Helen had first come to help out during a flu epidemic shortly after Zack started full-time school. Suzy – who was flirtatiously variable in her charity work – was trying to start a singing group in the dayroom with unwilling help from Rod Partlett, and told Helen how three of the five full-time staff were off sick, and the residents living on sandwiches and doing without cups of tea. Helen never intended to volunteer for more than a week or two, but long after Suzy had moved on to other good works, the place had remained a habit; almost, she sometimes thought, an addiction.

She still gave sporadic assistance with the tea trays, but the real purpose of her Wednesday was to indulge any of the elderly clients who so wished with a day of games. Together they played backgammon and Chinese chequers, picquet and Ludo and Mah-jongg and Halma and other dear dead family pastimes all but forgotten in the age of the computer and the television screen. Helen knew them all, better than most of her generation, because she came of a military family serving around the world through the fifties and sixties in the hearty, bookish, faintly Edwardian atmosphere of British expatriate communities. She and her sister Molly had played Fox and Geese with chess pieces while bullets whanged off embassy compound walls outside, and been taught the elements of bridge by a masterful major-general's wife desperate to make up a four in barren Bahrain. They had triumphantly thrown double sixes onto wobbling bamboo tables high above Kowloon, and – briefly back home for some dull winter holiday – escaped the boredom of long Scottish evenings in vicious Scrabble tournaments.

Molly was dead now, taken by a rogue tumour in her twenties; their parents both went not long afterwards. But among the more shabby-genteel of the Ferris Home denizens, week after week Helen was comforted by the ghosts of those childhood evenings and by the way that dull old eyes would quicken into competitive, mischievous fire as the old familiar gambits and chances made them once more nimble of wit and ruthless in strategy.

They were a minority, her games players; only six or seven

of them at any time, and they had their work cut out to find a quiet corner away from the wide blaring television which immobilized the majority. The adversity drew them together, cosy conspirators against the screen.

'What have you brought us this time, dear lady?' the old gentlemen would inquire, and the old ladies would peer from wheelchairs or lean frail spines forward from the carefully placed cushions, anxious to see what the canvas carrier bag held. Helen had tried leaving games for them to play between her visits, but the brisk, clumsy young care assistants swept them up too cavalierly, muddled the pieces and lost the play currency, dumping the boxes carelessly in the cupboard. It upset the players, and Helen herself, and finally a consensus arose that it was better to make a proper event of Wednesday and look forward to it in between times. So Helen would select from the old family collection each week, bringing a choice of games and always the chessboard in case any pair – usually of men – wanted to sit apart in a private intellectual duel. This week she had, among other treats, an ancient but complete Cluedo and, for the first time, a set of spillikins.

'I don't know how we'll get on,' she said. 'Perhaps we won't bother actually to play the game. But I wanted to show you these spillikins, because they really are special. Molly and I had them as children. My father's Indian cook carved them. Look.'

It was only in this company that she ever mentioned Molly or her parents. Only the old, she thought, entirely understand bereavement, because it is usually only they who have lived long enough to know how it works. The old know that after the first raw year, and the few years after when the grief decreases, the process of fading seems abruptly to stop. The dead one does fade to a bearable memory, but then the memory intensifies again in a new way. It becomes a coloured, vivid, benign ghost always at your side. It comforts, but at the same time acts as a shield or curtain between you and the careless world of the living.

The spillikins were indeed a marvel: fashioned from shards

and sticks of ivory, each one beautiful yet ingeniously, fiendishly hard to disentangle and twist free from the heap without catching on another. On the end of each was a carving: there were medieval-looking axes and halberds, intricate birds, heraldic beasts, pine trees with saw-edged branches. The old players exclaimed in wonder.

'Beautiful work!'

'Like doll's house carvings! When I was little we were taken to see Queen Mary's doll's house . . .'

'Gracious, that's a standard British Army bayonet he's made there, in among all the picture-book Tower-of-London stuff. Must have modelled it on something in your father's regimental stores!'

'I remember that bayonet,' said Helen, smiling. 'I can actually remember one game – on Christmas evening, in Scotland, when we were home on leave. I must have been about ten, and I got in a rage with Molly when I caught the bayonet on the griffon's leg and made the whole stack move just when I was winning. She laughed at me and I was so furious that I swept the lot off onto the floor. I remember, because I was sent to bed and never got my mince pie and mulled wine that we were promised.' She paused, almost going on to tell the old people how it was that night; how, standing by her bedroom window hot-eyed and indignant, she had seen a shooting star fly impossibly long and bright over the hills of Galloway.

'I think,' said George, the old man who had noticed the bayonet shape, 'that we're all a bit too tremblish in the hand area to get much of a game with spillikins any more. I could go in for some Cluedo, though. I used to play it with my son.'

His son was dead too, thought Helen. Dead in his thirties, hardly older than Molly. George had spoken of it once, which was enough: the bond was there now between them and did not need reaffirming. They were not maudlin, this aged generation of decayed gentry; not even the saddest of them. They knew that fate was fate, and that the only thing for it was to soldier on regardless, waiting for the relief column of pneumonia, emphysema, a stopping heart or some swift cancer. She smiled at George now, and reached for the Cluedo box. In the background the television chattered bright and patronizing in front of the half-circle of chairs and their dozing or staring occupants; intent, alive, defiant, the games players reached out tremulous old hands for dice and counters.

All through the morning, until the lunch trays were cleared away and the second session was starting, Helen did not allow her thoughts to stray to her living family, and especially not to Roy on his pavement. She had decided, in the bleak unhappy hours before dawn, that he would be back by the time she got home, expecting some kind of display of sympathy and understanding.

She had also decided that he was going to be disappointed.


While Helen played Cluedo, and Mrs Beazeley drifted through the dayroom grumbling genteelly about her staff shortages and the ungratefulness of These Modern Young Girls for residential jobs, some miles to the south a very modern young man was perched on an upturned bucket in Shona Keaney's Brixton studio. Julian Hemroyd, of the Hemroyd Gallery, was a dapper 31-year-old who affected black suits with black open-necked shirts; he had made a great deal of money in public relations and ran his Islington gallery mainly as a teasing operation to keep the world guessing. Ideally, he liked to be referred to as 'the new Saatchi', or 'the latest Britart Svengali'. It was his mission to generate as much outrage as possible in the more conventional newspapers and to be condemned by at least two church leaders per year on Radio 4.

However, his natural instinct for making money had served the gallery well, and if his artists could ever bring themselves to supplement their various crumbling, putrescing, visionary heaps with something which lasted more than a few months he was always grateful. He had been pressing Shona Keaney to diversify into video installations, but this she resisted, only once allowing herself to be filmed rolling naked in mixed human and animal excrement under the title *oursandtheirs, whatdoesitmatter, indirtI growclean.*

Now he said, 'Ooh, *that's* new – tell me about it.' The object was a large old-fashioned gilt frame, a junk shop item by the look of it, lying flat on the table. It seemed to be filled with melted white candlewax, oddly pitted with indentations of various sizes.

'Spit flowers,' said Shona. 'A homage to "Piss Flowers", but taking the concept onwards, with ecclesiastical echoes. "Spit Sermons" is the working title of the whole series. I spit at the wax while it's warm and malleable, then the result hardens into a cartoon – a parable about fossilized dogma. Then I let it get even colder, and the dogma cracks and crazes, and I write REVERE ME across the corner. There are,' she concluded, 'some wonderful nubbly textures. It isn't just intellectual satire.'

Hemroyd cocked his head to one side and said, 'That's *interesting*, Shona, that is astonishingly interesting. Have you considered supplementing the spit with, say, ejaculate?'

'That is *so* patriarchal,' said Shona. 'As if it was needed. *So* Gilbert and George. You are last century's man at heart, aren't you, ducks?'

Hemroyd roared with laughter. 'Touché,' he said. 'No, seriously, it's going to be tremendous. May I?' He had leapt lightly up from the pail and put his hands on the frame. 'Is it hard enough yet to hold upright?'

'Yup,' said Shona. Hands in her overall pockets, a massive but oddly graceful figure beneath the fright wig of her spiky plaits, she watched the dealer as he held up the picture, pirouetted round to let the light fall on its surface, stretched his arms to hold it out as far as possible, frowned, cocked his head, pursed his lips and generally went through the pantomime of his trade. She knew what he was thinking. He was thinking that it was nice and durable, and therefore saleable at a large commission; he was thinking that the overtones of blasphemy would go down very well indeed in his galleries in London and Glasgow but less well in Cheltenham; but that on the other hand, spit and candlewax were not quite as lucratively shocking as Shona's usual raw materials. Perhaps if he were to suggest a joint exhibition with Martin Chunt, who did the crucified roadkill foxes and pheasants with motor-tyre haloes? Chunt had earned the gallery half-page articles in all four Sunday broadsheets when the Bishop of St Leonard's condemned him. Astonishing that he had not thought of pairing him with Shona Keaney before.

As she read the gist of his thoughts, the artist was thinking her own. One more exhibition for this pretentious popinjay, said Shona to herself, one more big shocking splash, and she would have enough saved capital to go back to drawing. She loved drawing more than anything; paint had never made her particularly happy, and indeed a lot of her sensationalist daubing with body fluids was intended as a light-hearted satire on the cult of paint. Ugh, those oils, those thick old Bratby canvases, those cruddy linseedy mountain ranges of coloured muck! Drawing, simply with a pencil and simply what she saw, was what nourished her. Stored away, never to be shown to Hemroyd, was a growing portfolio of small, exquisite, often resonantly sad landscapes and streetscapes recording the England of the century's end: its building sites and underpasses, grimy parks and nettled dereliction and gallant little gardens by railway sidings. One day she would show these. Perhaps under another name entirely.

Meanwhile, cheque by cheque, scandal by scandal, Hemroyd was building her the financial independence to do so. She did not yet waste money on a home of her own, although one day she felt she might; for the present she slept on an old mattress in the studio, or sometimes round at Danny's or –

rarely — with a boyfriend. She ate at cafés or filled up on apples and ginger biscuits; she drank herbal tea to avoid the bother of fresh milk and the expense of a fridge. There was an element of conscious protest in this domestic discomfort; on her rare visits to Ferris Hill Road, Shona's permanent streak of sadness was intensified by the arid homeliness of the new house, by her mother's pointless refurbishments of bathrooms and joyless home-making and her little brother's lonely, over-tidied bedroom. To the world they looked fine, Helen and Roy and Zack. To their daughter they just looked desperate.

Julian Hemroyd had put the picture down and begun to roam around the studio, as was his custom. It was a profitable habit. More than once he had found something broken or rejected, or even once a pile of discarded rags which his accustomed eye recognized as a potential exhibit in its own right.

From the far corner he said casually, 'I met your brother the other night.'

Something in the silence troubled him, and he turned, surprised to see Shona frozen, staring at him with alarm in her eyes. Her face was so white that he noticed for the first time the slight roseate inflammation round her lip stud. He filed the image away, and continued easily, 'At the Limehouse Club. I think he was celebrating his deal with Eden. Quite a coup.'

Shona suddenly seemed to relax, the tension flowing out of her strong body. 'Oh yeah, brother *Marcus*,' she said. 'Sold up big, hasn't he? We're not a family that shares news every night on the phone, but I read it in the Standard.'

'Well, he's done extraordinarily well for himself, in his world, hasn't he? As you have in yours. There's a talent for seriously original thinking in your family, I suspect.'

Shona looked at the flattering smiler before her with renewed wariness. 'Yeah,' she said. 'I suppose. We do what we have to do.'

Hemroyd had come to take her out to lunch; he liked to look after his artists, and had a careful repertoire of restaurants to suit them. Some, for all their loucheness, liked the high life of the Ivy and the Mirabelle; others liked to eat gefilte fish in the East End or egg and chips in workmen's cafés. Many had violently left-wing views and would misbehave if fed expensively. For Shona, who teetered on the edge of this category but liked her hot dinners, he had targeted a modest Italian trattoria near Waterloo station.

Outside in the street, they fell into step together amicably enough, talking about his recent visit to New York galleries. Shona was in the middle of expressing a salty view of the £30,000 paid for Aaron Felupta's papier-mâché-coated rotting whale when Julian spotted a newspaper seller ahead of them.

'Sorry, do you mind? I think they're doing the review today for Maurizio Greer.' He dived for the paper and opened it as they walked, anxious to riffle his way to his review. At page two, however, he stopped dead, so that Shona, a pace behind nearly cannoned into him.

'Speak of the *devil!*' he said, his voice rising to an effete squeak. Shona, irritated, reflected to herself again that the day when she severed her links with the Hemroyd Gallery would be a good day.

Julian turned to show her the picture. 'And there *is* Marcus,' he said. 'And that must be his – must be your father.'

Shona took the newspaper from him; so intent was he on the story that he resisted for a moment, but she was taller and had a firmer grip with her big hands. Not for the first time, Julian shrank from his client.

Standing in the street, together they looked at the picture of Roy with his arm raised in full rant, snapped that morning by an alert trainee in the Eden Hotels HQ division and sold, in strict confidence, to the evening paper.

The picture of Marcus was inset and a brief late story bore

the headline: 'SACKED REBEL DAD SLATES E-MILLION "COKEHEAD".'

'Wow,' said Julian, with boyish admiration. '*Is* that your father? He's certainly going out with a bang. Wish he was my client.'

Shona read the story through then said, 'I should probably go up there. Should I?'

Julian had never known her ask advice before. He considered, then said, 'You have a certain profile yourself, of course. The follow-ups . . .'

Shona looked at him now in genuine dismay, suddenly years younger, a bewildered fifteen-year-old.

'Oh *shit*,' she said. 'You mean that if I go, there'll be press, and they'll make the connection, that I'm Marcus's sister?'

Julian thought of her coming exhibition, of the press coverage, of the days and days of columns and features that would follow her intervention – of the stories that could be spun about the fashionable Web whiz kid and the shocking crown princess of Britart, against the background of a generation battle fought out in the boardrooms of the immense Eden Corporation between this ragged defiant Old Testament father and his treacherous electronic child. It was mouth-watering, irresistible. Aloud he said, 'Well, why not? No harm.'

Shona went on looking at the paper.

'No,' she said finally. 'I'm not going near it. It'd be the wrong kind of publicity for all of us. They can sort themselves out. And Julian, listen to me now,' she laid a heavy hand on his shoulder, 'if I find out that you've done any leaky stuff that connects me with this shenanigan, I will hack your nuts off with a blunt knife.'

'Darling! Would I?' Hemroyd managed to look affronted.

'Yes,' said Shona. 'But you won't, because you rightly suspect that I am not a very well-controlled person when it comes to unpleasant physical violence.' She tightened her grip on his smooth black-clad shoulder and pressed down, so that Julian winced. Then she let go. 'I'm afraid I've got to skip lunch. I need to talk to someone quite urgently, someone who's easiest to get at lunchtimes.'

# Chapter Nine

By late afternoon Roy was desperately sleepy. He remembered the feeling from student sit-ins, when the adrenaline of revolt would suddenly ebb, leaving only a sense of vulnerable silliness. But in those days there had been hundreds of them to huddle together and reinforce one another's confidence. Well, dozens anyway. Today he was alone. Two photographers had come from daily newspapers to take pictures of him, flanked by reporters holding out absurdly tiny tape recorders. He had treated them to versions of his rant on Eden, Marcus, Manderill and the state of the world, but when they had left he felt disinclined to further communication. Another policeman had come and suggested that he go home; when he had gone, Marie had come back and said that the company doctor was out of the building but that she was definitely going to ring Helen.

He had a sense that things were closing in, that the upper world was shining a bright cold light down on him and preparing grapnels and cranes to haul him up, dank and dripping, into its power. He must wriggle away, deeper into the fusty comforting dimness of the winter streets. He should not have spoken to the newspaper people; they were, he now saw, enemies of the darkness that he needed. Their flashlights hurt his eyes. He had a nagging sense that something he expected, something he had summoned with all his power, had failed to materialize.

Closing his eyes, drifting towards sleep, it came to him that he had expected Marcus to come out and speak to him.

What a stupid, stupid thought! Roy woke with a jerk as his head fell back onto the hard stone. He needed to get away from here for a while. He pulled himself upright, turned towards the sliding doors of Eden and looked up at the towering building, window after window climbing towards the distant parapet. For a moment it seemed to him that everything was the other way up, and that he could throw himself the height of the building this very minute, to die crushed against the blue sky floor. Teetering on his high pavement, he leaned forward, imagining the upward fall.

Then he wrapped his sleeping bag round his shoulders and shuffled off along the street, like any other tramp in search of quieter, warmer rest. As he went he saw the old man Misery waking from some ancient dream to stare around him at the darkening street.

'He's gone,' said Marie tearfully to Helen. 'I tried to fix the company doctor to come but it was no good, and I couldn't get through to you. Then I thought he might come to my doctor, 'cos I only live in Pimlico and it's a walk-in Wellness Centre, I thought they might help him. But by the time I got back he was gone.'

'Did anyone see where he went?' Helen was standing with the telephone in the bright hallway at Ferris Hill Road, fiddling with a potted fern. Zack was, she hoped, upstairs and out of earshot.

'There's an old man sleeps in the other doorway sometimes, the Fashionista wholesale place. I asked him, but he just mumbles stuff.'

'Well, thanks for ringing and for trying. Why did you think he was ill, rather than just angry?'

'Mrs Keaney, I just was so worried.' Marie had been nervous

of ringing Helen; the wisdom of the ladies' cloakroom was that unless you were a complete dog your boss's wife *always* thought you were after him, especially if you rang the home. She had needed all her nerve to ring Helen, and reaction against that previous terror made her emotional now.

'The thing is, if you'll 'scuse me saying it, he looks so wild. I thought it might be, you know, one of those nerve storms.'

Helen smiled to herself. Marie must, she thought, have had a lovely old-fashioned upbringing to know that particular expression. Raised by grandparents, perhaps; it was the sort of thing her old people at Ferris Home said. A nerve storm!

The telephone relayed the high cheeping little voice again, saying something about contracts and Eric Manderill. Lost in her own reflections Helen hardly listened, merely reassuring Marie that everything necessary would be done. But as she put the phone down, she doubted it.

She was finding a curious difficulty in responding to Roy's revolt; it was as if, at the moment when she dropped the red parka to keep him warm, she had dropped also the duty of caring about what he did. He did it for himself, she thought. And, with a brief flash of rage, that's why he does everything. For his bloody self.

Then numbness descended again; she could manage neither anger nor anxiety for Roy, only a queer detachment. It was over; it had, she seemed to see now, been over for years.

The numbness was not unwelcome to Helen. She turned, and looked at her reflection in the hall mirror: pale, unsmiling, under a shock of feathery dark hair which should be grey. She had done her best by this damn family, she thought; earned and cooked and cleaned and organized the holidays and read the baby books and turned up at every parents' evening and dealt with Roy's moods and mediated between him and his atrocious children. She had believed in the family once, worried about it, planned for it, built nests for it out of her own feathers. Even as the elder children faded into an unsuccessful past and Zack grew up and prepared to elude them in turn, she had refurbished and tidied and chosen paint to reflect optimistic moods which neither of them felt.

She had done her best for the family, yes; and yet one by one its adult members had stubbornly gone off down their own roads, eccentric, self-willed, and totally indifferent to her feelings. First Marcus – cold boy! – then Danny, then Shona, now Roy. He would be in some pub, staying with some friend, drinking all night in Soho. The hell with him.

Yes, they had all gone their own road. Now there was just her and for the moment, Zack. And he would rebel any day now and leave her, too. Even as she thought of him Helen yawned, and contemplated a very early bed. Zack claimed to have eaten a sandwich at his friend's, and she herself had no heart for making supper. As she climbed up the stairs she called out goodnight to the boy more from duty than desire.

A small noise reached her, and for a fraction of a second she hesitated before turning away from his door towards her own. Once, years ago with the first children, she would naturally have gone in to attempt a bedtime hug and pick up a few dirty clothes from the floor with a loving cluck of reproof. But maybe, she thought, the maternal instinct just wore out if it never met a welcome in return. This child never seemed to mind, anyway, whether his mother fussed over him or not.


Zack, in his bedroom, was busy rehearsing a question: 'Mum, I want to know something. Is my brother Danny gay?' He said it to his Star Wars mirror, a little frightened at the temerity of even saying Danny's name aloud inside the house. He had made an attempt, that day, to get some information out of Miss Durant at school. At the end of French he had offered to carry her books down the corridor. With her, at least, it seemed to be fine to say the name.

'Miss, did you know my brother Danny?'

'Yes, indeed I did. He was rather good at French, like you.'
Anna Durant smiled down at the boy, rather mechanically. Had
Daniel Keaney been good at French? She hardly remembered.
There were so many children.

'What did you think he was like, when he was at school?'
Zack had framed the question with great care and thought; he
could not ask 'What *is* he like?' because that would give away the
fact that he, Zack, never saw his big brother and was therefore
weird and out of line.

The teacher considered. A vision of Danny came back to
her, clearer even than when she had been asked about him by
that old gossip Rod Partlett.

'He was very – passionate,' she said, then glanced nervously
at the child in case he had misinterpreted her. But there was
no other way to put it. 'He knew what he wanted, and he
was restless.'

'What did he want?' Zack was a mercilessly blunt interro-
gator.

'I don't know,' the teacher said lamely. 'He never told me.
I only had him for a couple of periods a week.'

Zack had given up. Asking teachers was not going to be
much use; they changed over so often that not many would
have known Dan. For a moment, practising his question about
gayness again to the mirror, he wondered how he would feel if
the answer was yes.

Being gay was a puzzle to him. At school they were told
that homophobia was bad and that gays shouldn't be bullied,
which was a bit obvious. But it was also in the papers that being
gay shouldn't be 'promoted' to schoolkids, and there were rows
about it all the time in the news.

Mr Partlett had said that he reckoned there was a row
between Danny and Dad about being gay; but was that likely?
Zack frowned judicially. In his experience Dad and Mum seemed
to be pretty cool about gays. On New Year's night with the
Darlings they had both been laughing and joking with Peter

and Martin from No. 29, and everyone knew that they were sort of married.

Yet something about Danny had made Danny have to leave. To leave and never, ever to come home again, even at Christmas; to leave and never even be talked about. Zack shivered, and jumped into his bed, pulling the quilt up round him. What yawning unspeakable desert had claimed his brother? How could he vanish so far into oblivion?

There was one other obvious avenue: Shona, he thought, would certainly know. She had been talking about Danny in the kitchen at Christmas, and although she was weird these days, quite a stranger to him, he had an instinct that she would not have normal adult views about what children should be told. The idea of asking Shona bothered him rather, because he was not sure what she would think of him. Sometimes he caught her looking at him with a kind of pity, which he disliked very much indeed. She would probably feel very sorry indeed for him if she knew that he didn't know anything about his own *family* without listening at doors.

Maybe he should write her a letter – on the computer, so she saw he was not a little kid.

He curled up, flicked off his light and switched to considering his father. Calling goodnight on the stairs, his mother had not sounded particularly worried, so presumably Dad was OK and just off sulking somewhere. This had been known before, and if he was in trouble with Mum about his pavement joke, he might not come home till she cooled down. Zack quite liked the idea of the pavement-sitting, what he had overheard about it anyway. It sounded like the sort of thing you might do if you got really, really fed up with school. Years ago, Dad had told him about student demos in 1968, big fights in Paris and all of them coming to London on buses and shouting at the American Embassy and being chased by police horses. Mum had told Dad to stop putting revolutionary ideas in his head, but Zack had really liked the ideas. If Dad was having a revolution, that was actually quite cool. Dad had once explained what a 'refusenik' was, and Zack had liked that too. Obviously if the pavement-sitting got found out about, his friends would give him a hard time again, like they had about Shona's exhibition, but so what?

Something stirred, stretched and settled in Zack, warm and complacent as a cat. It was a feeling he sometimes had: an immense sense of comfort which stilled any nervous shiverings, a warm conviction of his own solid, central rightness. He was entitled to be whatever he was, and to know whatever concerned him. So he had a weird family — so what?

But he did wish he knew what it was about Danny. As he fell asleep, he was still thinking of different ways to phrase the question.


Eric Manderill did not waste time. It was next morning that Helen was roused from her bed by a firm knocking at the door.

'Mrs Keaney?' said the man, who did not look terribly like a postman or a parcel man. 'Is your husband Mr R.J. Keaney of this address?'

'Yes', she said sleepily, standing on the mat in a torn old cotton nightdress. She reached out for the envelope he held.

'Can I give this to Mr Keaney himself?' said the un-postman.

'No. He's away. You can give it to me.' Fuddled, she added unnecessarily, 'I handle all the bills and things anyway. Always have.'

'And you are prepared to sign for this and undertake to deliver it to Mr Keaney without delay?'

'When I can. What is this, anyway? You're not the post, are you?'

'Caprini,' said the man obscurely. 'Sign here, then, if you would, madam.'

Helen signed, shut the door on his retreating back – which was, she noticed, exceptionally broad and well-muscled – and stared down at the envelope. It was white, long, and legal in appearance, with a handwritten address and in the corner the faint familiar outline of the Eden Corp. logo, an asymmetric sunburst. Her stomach twisted. She took it into the kitchen and, still staring at it, flicked the switch on the kettle. It hissed for a moment and flicked off: dry. Helen did not want to put the envelope down; it felt an unsafe thing to have touching any part of the house, as if it might ignite. Eventually she tucked it under her chin while she filled the kettle and snapped the switch again. She did not open it until she was sitting at the table, coffee before her, with the kitchen door shut.

When Zack came down ten minutes later and started crashing around with cereal bowls and spilling cornflakes, she was still reading and reading it, trying to take it in.

Dear Mr Keaney,

*Our Clients Eden Corporation*

As you may be aware we act for your above former employers. We are instructed to write to you following the regrettable events on Tuesday 11 and Wednesday 12 January 2000 when you saw fit to beset the Company's London office in an obstructive and derogatory manner and made a number of assertions to Company employees, customers, suppliers and others concerning our Clients which were untrue and pejorative.

All this behaviour, which was recorded on our Clients' security equipment, constitutes a series of clear breaches of your employment contract, entered into on 16.6.99 after you had been separately advised on its terms by your own solicitors at our Clients' expense.

The provisions breached include Clause 11.1–10, Clause 12 and Clauses 14–17. Under the related provisions you are accordingly no longer entitled to the benefits specified at Clause 18, in particular your severance payment, two years' salary commencing on 10th inst., outplacement advice and the transfer to you of the Company's car.

To sum up, our Clients will not be making any payment to your account on 11th inst. or thereafter, and require the immediate return of the car in good condition. You may achieve this by causing it to be delivered to McCrimmons BMW of Edgware Road, with the appropriate documents and keys – they will clean and valet it as necessary.

Further, our Clients are considering their options and actively taking advice on the possibility of an action founded in defamation, to seek damages and costs and in particular an injunction restraining you from further such comment, and will only refrain from pursuing these remedies if you cease all contact with the Company, its employees and business contacts, and immediately acknowledge this letter with an open letter to us retracting the things you have said, and worded in a manner suitable for publication at our Clients' discretion.

If you are in the slightest doubt as to your position you should immediately seek legal advice, as these are matters which gravely affect your rights. To assist your advisers, a further copy of your contract with our Clients is enclosed, though we understand one was handed to you at the time of termination of your employment. It appears to have found its way with other papers into a water dispenser in the lobby of our Clients' office, causing damage to plumbing and electrical equipment valued provisionally at £87:25 plus VAT, but so long as the other issues are promptly dealt with our Clients are minded to overlook that aspect.

We are taking steps to have this letter served upon

you personally by Mr Caprini of I-Ball Services, to ensure safe delivery, and his affidavit will be relied upon in any future proceedings.

Yours faithfully,

F.W.G. Minge

Senior Partner, Minge, Haddon & Minge

Go straight to jail, do not pass Go, do not collect £200 . . . Helen started as Zack sat down heavily at the table opposite her, his bowl of cereal slopped before him, and began peeling a banana with his teeth and simultaneously scribbling extra lines on some piece of homework with a Biro.

'Morning,' she said, and went on staring at the letter.

'Mum,' said Zack after a moment. 'Why did my brother Danny leave home? Was it because he's gay?'

Helen stared at him, unfocused, as if she was wondering who he was. 'No,' she said absently. 'Christ, no. Gay would have been fine. Your father could have lived with gay.'

Then her brain clicked back into a more accustomed state and she heard herself rushing to say, 'It was all a long time ago, darling. Best forgotten.'

Zack had never needed such resolution.

'Well, why then?' he persisted. ''Cos he was only about sixteen, I worked it out. People don't usually go away when they're sixteen. And if they do, they come back in the holidays, right?'

Helen looked down at the letter, and up at her implacable son, and screamed.

# Chapter Ten

'He's not there,' said Erika to Manderill. The chief executive was sitting at her desk, which unnerved her, doodling with her private pen upon her private stock of paper. He had scattered newspapers, open and untidy, across the virgin surface. That morning he had come up by the back stairs from the car park entrance, and peremptorily ordered her to go downstairs and check the front entrance for 'the Keaney man'.

'No sign of him,' she reiterated, moving closer to her desk to try and reclaim the territory.

'Good,' said the chief executive, ignoring his personal assistant's urgent body language and tapping on her polished desk with her best pen. After a moment he got up, threw the pen down carelessly, and began walking up and down. Erika slid into her chair, blushing to feel the warmth of an alien bottom on it. She found herself thinking, disgracefully, that it was odd for Mr Manderill's thin bottom actually to have any warmth in it. Eventually he turned back to her, silhouetted against the brightness of the curved window.

'Now I want Marcus Keaney up here, straightaway.'

Erika picked up the telephone, pushed two buttons, spoke briefly, listened, then turned back to her master. 'He's not here. Sent a message that he's ill.'

'Get him on the phone.'

Two more buttons, and a longer period of listening. Manderill still paced restlessly up and down the outer office. This was almost unheard of; normally when he was not prowling the corridors on his soft soles, giving his employees salutary shocks, he operated entirely from his own desk, summoning Erika into his physical presence only when absolutely necessary.

Eventually Erika spoke down the telephone. 'Mr Keaney, I have Mr Manderill for you.'

To her astonishment Manderill reached across her desk for her own handset rather than retreating to the privacy of his desk. Everything was wrong today. She would have a headache later. She had been tense ever since yesterday, fearing that Manderill somehow blamed her for not making Roy Keaney sufficiently aware of the legal risk of harassing the company. Manderill, she knew, had an almost superstitious faith in the invincibility of those who were legally in the right; Mr Keaney's reckless uncontrolled protest was precisely the kind of thing which upset him most.

Still, by the sound of it, it was not her he was angry with, but the younger Mr Keaney. Which, considering the morning papers she had devoured in the coffee bar, was not entirely surprising.

Manderill, his pointed features screwed up, his nose twitching, was speaking down the telephone to Marcus now. 'I want you in here,' he said in a cold thin voice devoid of even his usual meagre ration of charm. 'You know what we have to discuss.'

At the other end of the line Marcus grimaced at his mobile phone in silence. He was lying in a Soho club bedroom, a tangled sheet across his groin, his dark hair slick with sweat, his head pounding with a mixed hangover. TLC, he thought. Tender loving care, Irena called it; or alternatively tequila-lager-charlie. He had been a bit tense after the *Evening Standard* paragraph, wondering how Manderill would take the bit about the coke. So he had taken a bit of coke himself, to cheer him up, and had a few drinks to discuss it. Mainly with Irena, who had said he was 'a dork' to go and work for Eden anyway.

'Nobody works there, it's mega sad,' she said. 'Nobody with a choice, anyway. You got two million quid, babe, if you dump the shares. If you want an empire, go start one. You're getting like Bristow in the cartoons, wanting to work halfway up a tower and look at the pigeons. Be like – oh, I don't know – Matthew Freud, or Julian Hemroyd.'

Marcus was uncertain about the rest of the evening; he might, just possibly, have slapped someone. Probably Irena, for bracketing him with that little greaseball Hemroyd. Right now the last thing he wanted was to talk to Eric Manderill. Or to anybody. He thought longingly of the cool, welcoming blue swirl of his computer screens back at the flat. He did not even have a laptop at the club to play with. Irena, he thought, had stolen the latest one.

He lay on the bed under the genteelly cracked club ceiling, listening to the quacking mobile. Eventually he said, 'I don't think there's much point, do you? Why don't we call it quits? I'll ring my lawyer.' And he pushed the off button before Manderill could reply. That would show him Marcus Keaney wasn't some kid to be preached at and told off by fathers and headmasters and tight-arsed suits who thought that contracts could buy them souls.

As he rolled onto his side and curled up angrily for more sleep, old words flickered through his head. '. . . *Never hold a job down. Never fit anywhere. Never finish a worthwhile project. As soon as you get started on something you quit. Ever since you were a little boy. Butterfly mind.'*

But I made money, screamed Marcus silently. I made as much money in one go as you did in your whole sad frigging career, Dad.

*'And nobody'll want to work alongside you, with that attitude – work's more than just cleverness, you know. It's a human relationship. Ask Harry,*

*ask anyone who's made a success of their life. And you're not prepared to bother being human.'*

Ah well, fuck it then, thought Marcus. You were talking about old work, Dad, your kind of work. All that a twenty-first-century man needs is a screen and a brain.

He reached out for Irena, before he remembered that she, too, had walked away sometime in the small hours, saying much the same thing as the voice in his head. *Bad attitude.* What the fuck did they mean, with this wittering about attitude? You had to look out for yourself, didn't you? A hollowness opened up inside him, and he flung himself face down on the pillows and told himself that he was not unhappy, not unhappy at all. Just pissed off, right?

Back in the Eden building Eric Manderill slowly put the telephone down and moved towards his inner office door at last.

'Erika,' he said. 'Legal department. Now. Put them through, have Customer Relations on standby, then get me a cup of coffee and liaise with the lawyers about letters for my signature.'

It was not often, thought Erika, that you actioned letters of termination of contract to two members of the same family in two days.

Zack had been slightly unnerved by the scream, even if Mum did explain that she thought she saw a mouse. He did not entirely believe in the mouse, because there had never been one in the house before, so why should one turn up just at the very moment that he managed at last to put the straight question to her? Grown-ups, he reflected, did tell an incredible lot of lies.

He went to school in a bad temper, banging his rucksack against the railings so viciously that he could hear the plastic of his calculator cracking against the iron. At the top of the road he glanced up at the castellations and the stained-glass doors of the Ferris Home. Spooky old heap, full of witches. He was not going on much longer like this, round here, stuck between boring school and an ever weirder family. Not much longer.

Helen read the letter again.

> '... Under the related provisions you are accordingly no longer entitled to the benefits specified at Clause 18, in particular your severance payment, two years' salary commencing on 10th inst., outplacement advice and the transfer to you of the Company's car ...'

She supposed she had better ring the garage and tell them to collect the car. She had all but forgotten that it belonged to Eden; Roy never used it for work, so they had taken the opportunity not to replace the old Citroen back in June. Maybe if she posted them the keys ...

The car was not the point. She was in charge of family finances, always had been, just as she told Caprini on the doorstep. At any given moment she knew, almost without thinking, exactly where they stood. She had learnt caution and frugality during the long years of paying rent, while Handfast Publishing slowly established itself and her menial but reliable earnings supplemented Roy's technically better, but frequently delayed, payments from the struggling Handfast.

Since then relative affluence had come to them, and Helen had abandoned both work and frugality. In the two years since the move, and especially the six months of Eden salary, Helen had lavished money on the new house, on Zack's computer, on clothes for them all and pleasantly wasteful housekeeping. She had an obscure but luxurious sense that after the years of working motherhood and worthy intellectual poverty, she was damn well owed a bit of rich-bitch recklessness. You could hardly be friends with Suzy Darling and not develop envious yearnings in that direction. Roy meanwhile had relaxed his own, never very impressive, attempts at economy and switched from Japanese blends to single malt. All the same, Helen had never quite shaken off the old habit of always knowing to a few pounds exactly where the Keaney finances stood.

She knew it now. They had no savings, prosperity was too new to them and the last building society account had gone into the deposit on the house. They had lately talked, desultorily, of starting some tax-efficient savings scheme, but this had gone no further than a pile of patronizing yet confusing leaflets shoved in a kitchen drawer. Roy's private pension, for what it was worth, had fourteen years to run. The joint account was a mere fifty pounds away from its ultimate overdraft limit.

And why not? thought Helen with guilty anger. Christmas had come on top of paying for the two new bathrooms, and the new towels and blinds and shelves and fitments which their splendour demanded. Why should she feel guilty for letting this happen? There had been, after all, the comforting prospect of the 'payment on the 11th inst.' to which Mr Minge referred. It included – would have included – the New Year bonus promised when Eden shares shot up. For a moment Helen felt flaring indignation that Eden should deny Roy his due payment for December, when he had still been a fairly loyal servant; then she remembered that the 11th inst. money would in fact relate to January, of which he had worked only one day before sitting on the pavement swearing at people. Eden, quite untypically, had the generous habit of paying management salaries in advance rather than arrears; she recalled the flush of ready cash back in June when they switched from Handfast's habit of paying as late as possible.

So they were right; if Roy had indeed kicked a hole in his contract, they owed nothing, and there would never be another penny's income from Eden. Instead of rising on the grateful tide of the salary and bonus, the account would lie where it was, beached. Instead of a credit balance of £4000, it would remain stubbornly at a debit figure of £3950. When the regular mortgage payments and the rest went out that overdraft would rise further, taking it beyond the permitted limit. Nor would any income whatsoever be forthcoming to meet the next standing orders in 26 February, 26 March, 26 April . . .

Helen was good at mental arithmetic and calculations of compound interest. By summer they could owe twenty thousand pounds even without eating. By the end of the year, allowing for interest, they would have wiped out even their theoretical equity on the house. Helen knew what Roy, for all her years of irritated propaganda, had never really grasped: how eerily easy and quick was the process by which a comfortable seeming middle-class household can lose everything and become paupers. She looked around the immaculate kitchen with sudden dislike.

It was a nice house, had seemed like a dream house as well as a source of future security. When they bought it, in an excitable property market, victory in the bidding had felt like something to be grateful for: a new start, a symbol of a more ordered and less precarious life. So they had paid the house grateful tribute ever since, feeding the great thankless maw of the mortgage, cossetting the stupid pile of bricks with painters and builders and plumbers, thinking nothing was too good for it. Helen remembered chattering stupidly to Suzy about how you mustn't spoil the ship for a ha'p'orth of tar, and with a flush of embarrassment recalled how much the wallpaper had cost for the hall and stairs. It would have paid this month's mortgage. If they had stayed in the rented house at No.10, it would have kept them going for two months.

But it was still, Helen savagely thought, not her fault. It was Roy who had, on some drunken whim, pulled down the curtain on his Eden job and lost his redundancy money. One moment – HIS moment – of self-indulgent bravado had ruined them entirely.

Helen looked down and found that she had scribbled the figures on the bottom of the Minge, Haddon & Minge letter with Zack's homework Biro. She tried to think about Zack, and what the coming embarrassments would mean to him; but her mind blurred, and she found herself thinking instead of Marcus at the same age, cool and scornful, and of Danny with his passionate stridency and unthinkable demands. Zack seemed unreal, irrelevant. Was that, perhaps, how she and Zack and the house and the mortgage had seemed to Roy in his moment of revolt?

Dry-eyed and passionless, she read the letter through yet again. Now that the shock had passed, she felt only indifference. So the tide had gone out. That was the way of things. She thought of her earliest reading, the beloved E.Nesbits and Hodgson Burnetts which had travelled round the world in the tea chests of her childhood exile, and become the somewhat unfashionable topic of her final dissertation in 1974. Families in these books were always vaguely losing all their money, or having Father disgraced in some way. Being 'ruined' was all in a book's work to Bastables or Railway Children or Little Princesses.

Ruin was, she had confidently explained in her thesis, a handy authorial device for depicting children facing real challenges while still ensuring that the children themselves were recognizably the cultural equivalents of your affluent target readership. The late Victorian or Edwardian authoress could not expect to attract a respectable nursery readership with tales of real working-class children facing real street poverty and abuse. In those books the notion of Ruin, of being cast on the world without a penny, had an invigorating and even cosy glamour about it. Tumbledown little cottages, lovable old railwaymen to make friends with, rats to tame, all that. But now she reflected that real Ruin was not glamorous at all. It brought only a sense of weary shame, a reflecting on wallpaper and power showers and bygone irretrievable waste and improvidence.

As for Father – always distantly revered in this literature – the figure that he cut in their particular ruin was hardly the stuff of improving fiction for the children of the professional classes. 'Hush now, darlings, we must be brave and do without jam on our bread. Father can't be with us because he's lying on a pavement in Marylebone singing "We shall not be moved".'

These days, the books she read were middling Aga sagas of contemporary life, shared and swapped with Suzy Darling. If she were living in one of those, thought Helen, it would be obvious what a modern heroine would do next. She would rally from the disaster, make plans, confront the bank and demand that it believed in her, and probably start an imaginative small business of her own to redeem the family fortunes. She would stay cheerful and caring with her children, take hard decisions, try to understand her man (although perhaps allowing herself a thrillingly carnal yet tender short-term love affair with a younger model) and generally bustle about the task of rebuilding a safe nest for the family, whatever shape that family ended up by taking. The woman would save the day, and win approbation and sympathy from a vast invisible network of kindly disposed readers.

Since it wasn't in a novel, Helen thought sourly, none of this would happen. If Roy could flip his lid and walk away from his responsibilities, so could she. This family, down the years, had proved that its essential nature was centrifugal, its members spinning off one by one like sparks from a Catherine wheel, leaving the centre dead. Why should she, Helen, play the part of that dead burnt-out heart? She slammed down both hands flat on the table so that her coffee mug jumped, then picked the mug up and threw it, followed by a parabola of black coffee, crashing through the window.

# Chapter Eleven

The day before Helen's rude awakening, after she had abandoned Hemroyd to find a solitary lunch, Shona bought her own copy of the evening paper and took it into a café she knew. Behind the steamy windows, wreathed in smells of bacon and toasted cheese, she rested her elbows on the cracked plastic table and read the story again, trying to tease the hard facts out of it.

This was made more difficult as it was written with a curious thin, curling malice, the prevailing tone of the stressed Londoner's evening paper. Shona, whose nature was free from malice if not from occasional impulses to violence, wondered briefly why the paper's undoubted cleverness took this particular form. Perhaps it was felt that the chance to read snarling insinuation about total strangers served some homeopathic purpose, preventing commuters on the Underground from falling on one another with fists and teeth.

What seemed clear was that her brother had, on selling his maverick cyber empire to take up this exalted new post, made it his business to sack their father as soon as possible. That this should happen did not remotely surprise Shona. Marcus's talent for unbalanced ruthlessness had been perfectly familiar to his sister since they were five and three years old. As for her big brother's relationship with Roy, she had discussed that often enough with Danny through their teenage years.

'Dad always liked Marcus best,' Dan had said once, swinging a skinny leg from a precarious perch on the chest of drawers in the small back bedroom. The two of them were lounging there one Sunday afternoon to avoid a poisonous atmosphere downstairs. 'So he really hates it that Marcus doesn't like him much. It's worse than if it was just us.'

Shona could see that bedroom now, an absurd slice of a room in the little house at No. 10. Once the twins reached thirteen it had been hers, with Danny and Marcus sharing the slightly bigger one across the landing. But she and Dan had been roommates since babyhood, and neither liked the new arrangement. Often enough, her twin would creep in at bedtime, dragging a duvet, and sleep on the floor, curled on the hard matting with the insouciant grace of a cat. Marcus also liked the arrangement; sharing anything was not his strong point.

Shona turned back to the paper. What also seemed clear was that Roy had, to some extent at least, flipped. Ranting, as the newspaper described it, was not his normal style. As a rule, even when drunk her father only became more and more heavily ironic.

Of the content of his rant Shona broadly approved. Eden was a machine for processing mediocrity; its hotels were uniform and tacky, its supermarkets cynical and no doubt exploitative, its staff reputedly tense and unhappy, and no doubt its publishing arm would be just as nasty. She had felt quite sorry for Dad having to go there, part of a package negotiated by that silver-haired old phoney Harry Foster. Also, Shona disapproved of companies diversifying. Eden might have been a perfectly reasonable supermarket chain, before it ballooned to its present grotesque hybrid state. What did grocers know about publishing? They couldn't even run very good hotels. Nonetheless, like Alan Barton, she had a puritanical instinct that those who had taken the Eden shilling were not the best qualified to lie across its doorstep berating it for wickedness just because they got sacked.

She looked closely at the picture of Roy. He was, she observed, wearing a woman's anorak with a fur collar. The colour was poor in the photograph, but she was fairly certain that it was the coat her mother had had hanging up in the hallway when she called on Boxing Day. Shona had a fine eye for detail. She held the picture up close and peered, and was certain. It was not a cheap chainstore coat, which was why she had noticed it. The detail was good, and the front particularly well cut to look tidy whether or not the fur hood was being used. It was the same jacket, definitely Helen's.

Yet the story in the paper said that Roy had been surprised by a sudden sacking, and had walked straight out when he got the redundancy letter ('flounced', it said). It also clearly indicated that he had set up camp immediately on the doorstep without going home. It was unlikely that he would have set off with such a womanish coat that morning, expecting none of this; and anyway she remembered how much he hated taking any kind of coat to work, and always came home wet and cursing when it rained. Therefore Helen must have come down and given it to him.

Did this mean that Mum approved? Shona considered, her big frame slumped over the table, her fingers idly dragging a plastic spoon through the sugar bowl. No, she decided; a wife who approved would have brought Roy down one of his own coats, or a blanket. For all her professional weirdness and the ferocity of her appearance, Shona had a gentle intuitive side to her; in very few moments she came close to the truth of Helen's arrival, hope, horror, retreat, and brief furious moment of compassion. She almost saw the coat drop on Roy, and her mother's stiff lonely figure walking away.

Well, it rang true. Roy and Helen's daughter frowned, more than a little troubled. She knew what it was to live on the streets. She had come close to it, smelt the pavement, understood the laws of the dispossessed, and long ago she had witnessed another rescue. That there must be a rescue now was something else that seemed perfectly clear to her. Possibly Dad had already gone home. Somehow she doubted it. She had his picture, after all, and pictures were what Shona understood best. There was something in his eye, his hair, his heedless wearing of the red furry anorak, the ungoverned line of his raised fist, that she recognized very well. He was a man who had stepped over a line. She knew about these things.

After a while she pulled out the page, folded it with care and thrust it in the pocket of her jacket. The rest of the newspaper she threw carelessly onto an adjoining empty table.

'Ishmael,' she said to the proprietor, who was wiping down the inside of a glass display case and keeping a wary eye on the violently hissing coffee machine, 'has Danny been in yet?'

'No' till one o'clock. There is class today, I think.'

'OK,' said Danny's twin. 'Be a sport and start me up an egg and chips while I wait.'

'OK, OK!' said Ishmael, and yelled a staccato Turkish instruction through the dangling plastic strips across the kitchen door. He liked Shona, all the more since she had had her picture in the papers as a controversial artist. Fame pleased him.

That night, while the solicitor's letter was still locked up, ready for a dawn delivery, in the office of Mr Caprini of I-Ball, Roy found himself walking southward towards the river. He was dog tired, stiff now and hungry again. He kept to the narrow streets and alleys, threading past heaps of rubbish sacks, shiny and glistening like great slugs, breathing in the sharp unclean smells of dank corners, averting his eyes from huddled hooded figures already bedded down for the night. Sometimes a figure would overtake him, scuttling along, talking to itself; once he saw to his surprise that the speaker was not one of the normal population of borderline demented or drugged street dwellers but a clean-cut businessman talking into the almost invisible hands-free wire of his mobile phone. 'Yah, yah. So the flotation is when – April?' It seemed that the line between London's deranged and London's achievers was blurring.

At Oxford Circus, drawn by better smells, Roy stopped and spent the small change from his trouser pockets on a large, aggressive-looking sausage wrapped in a damp roll and a piece of kitchen paper. When he bit into it, the soft interior squirted into his mouth, not pleasantly but with a definite flavour of fish. The skin, he thought, must be plastic. After two bites he threw the rest of the sausage away and crammed the damp bread and onions into his mouth, almost gagging on the greasy stiffness of it. He had stopped to eat, flattening himself against the side of the doorway of a clothes shop; it specialized in big sizes, and as he struggled with the cheerless little meal, a constant flow of stout women came past him, shrinking visibly away from his dishevelled presence. After a few moments the manageress came out, with a determined smile.

'Can't stand 'ere, mate,' she said, not unkindly. 'Bit in the way, right?'

Roy saw that she was wary of him, and managed a placatory smile. It was, he thought, remarkable how quickly people recognized a denizen of the lower world, the universe from below the trap door of respectability. Red anorak apart, he was dressed exactly as he had been the day before, leaving for work; his normal style was less dapper than the Eden hierarchy preferred, to be sure, but he was still quite smart for a publisher. Perhaps it was the stubble that marked him out now so clearly as an alien; that, or the sleeping bag. He had tied a piece of string round it which he found in the anorak pocket, but the effect was not soigné.

He moved away, and the manageress looked after him for a moment before going back into her shop.

'Gave me quite a shock,' she said to the junior behind the counter. 'When I saw the fur hood from the back, right, I thought it was a woman. Then he turns round and there's all this stubble. You get some weird ones, don't you?'

'I feel sorry for them, really,' said the girl. 'It's ever so cold.'

Roy walked on southward down Regent Street, unnoticed in the throng of evening shoppers; but the wealth of the big shops and the brightness of the lights oppressed him, and soon he swerved off to the left, into the edges of Soho. It was scruffier there, and the warm light of cafés and the faded glamour of the Palladium stage door cheered him a little.

Pausing by some shop window, staring blindly ahead with his thoughts freewheeling, he put a hand in the pocket where his bank card lay and felt its reassuring hardness. He transferred it to the depth of his trouser pocket and for a while he stood, hand in pocket, flicking the corner of the card with his finger and considering whether to go back onto Regent Street to find a cash machine. The thought of the brightness and West End bustle daunted him.

He was further daunted when a policeman came up behind him, his uniform forbiddingly reflected in the sex shop window, and suggested that he take his hand out of his trousers and move along there, please. In the end Roy walked, slowly and vaguely but always moving, averting his eyes from the Piccadilly crowds and the theatre queues, until he reached the open space of Trafalgar Square and then the deeper darkness of the Embankment Gardens. In this dank space, with unpractised stealth, he found himself a bush to huddle under.

There he slept until morning brought the next policeman, the beginnings of a feverish cough, and rather later a bad moment at a cash machine on Charing Cross station. Standing there, shivering slightly in the warm smell of coffee and croissants from a nearby kiosk, Roy discovered that Helen must have used her card to withdraw the last fifty pounds of overdraft available from their account.

Helen, to do her justice, had not deliberately emptied the

account. After smashing the window with the coffee mug she felt immediate shame, and with it a return of harrowing, debilitating worry. Around her spread the house, mutely accusing, reminding her that with every passing minute it devoured electricity, oil, insurance, council tax, mortgage interest; that even if you did not eat, modern life cost money hour by hour.

This – not any desire to impoverish Roy – was what drove her down the road to the bank machine to verify the state of the overdraft. While she was there, she drew out the final fifty pounds. She hardly even remembered Roy's existence as she did it, so pressing and primitive, so almost physical, was the urge to have money in her hands as a talisman against the starkness of impending ruin. When it was in her purse she went into a coffee shop and sat at the side counter, drinking black coffee because it was cheaper than latte, looking out at the prosperous Hampstead street and wondering what to do.

She could wait for the bank to open, ask for an interview and explain the family predicament to the manager. She had never met or even seen the current manager although the name, Ms H.V. Habib, was familiar from the correspondence about the mortgage. Times had changed since the financial cliffhanger of their early marriage, when Mr Rendlesham of Barclays used to be as familiar a member of the cast as the family cat.

Putting herself into Ms Habib's place, though, Helen recognized that there would be questions that had to be asked, notably about Roy's strategy for securing fresh employment. Without Roy to answer for himself, this could be awkward. If she said that he was ill, the bank would look beadily at the mortgage and conclude (quite rightly) that the Keaneys had not a cat in hell's chance of paying it. If she claimed that he had abandoned her, and played the poor wife card, the banker would want to know her intentions regarding divorce proceedings, alimony claims and the rest of it. She could ask for mortgage repayments to be frozen for a few months while they sorted themselves out, and for an extension of the overdraft, but with her approaching fifty and Roy now past that bitter landmark, no hard-headed bank would be convinced of their ability to carry on paying £24,000 a year until the year 2015.

A young Asian girl, immaculate in a short-skirted narrow red suit, came over to the counter carrying a calfskin briefcase, a frothing cappuccino and a croissant, which difficult load compelled her to carry her morning paper gripped between her strong white teeth. Wriggling up onto the stool, she took the paper out and made a humorous grimace at Helen, as if apologizing for the absurdity of her approach. Then she turned her attention back to the newspaper, spreading it out on the counter. Helen glanced down, and felt her stomach sink. She clutched at the counter, fearing she might fall off the tall stool. The morning tabloid – with more time at its disposal than the London evening paper – had done Roy's protest proud.

Covertly, she tried to read over the girl's shoulder. 'SACKED? TRY AND GET RID OF ME' ran the headline, over a picture of Roy, rather artistically taken through a forest of commuters' legs. The girl was reading the story and kept obscuring bits of text with her hand or the shadow of her croissant. Fragments were enough:

> ... most of London's homeless choose their doorways at random, but not militant 50-year-old Roy Keaney. He had a good reason for taking up space in the doorway of the giant Eden Corporation – until Wednesday he had a plush executive office of his own inside it ... Keaney, whose accusations against his son and now arch enemy Marcus have set the corporate dovecotes fluttering, was unrepentant as he told our reporter, 'He's a snivelling little cokehead' ... Eden bosses were saying nothing yesterday, but CEO Eric Manderill, close crony of senior government figures and famously jealous of company reputation, may also have something to say about Keaney's description of him as a 'morally bankrupt baboon' ...

The newspaper's owner stirred restlessly, aware of Helen's interest but unwilling to pick a fight, and hunched more closely over the paper. Helen considered pointing at Roy's picture and saying, 'That's my husband!' That would show this neat affluent young madam what pitfalls the next thirty years might have in store for her.

But she said nothing. Slowly, she slid off the stool, tidied away her paper cup, shrugged her bag onto her shoulder and left the coffee bar. The girl in the red suit did not even glance up to see her leave.

As Helen walked back up the street towards Ferris Hill Road, the shock and shame of the newspaper report gradually wearing off, her main thought was that she must go and see Suzy Darling.

In the mornings Suzy was generally home, either cooking or organizing James's and her own clothes for a trip away.

It was not so much Suzy's advice she wanted – when in their lives had the Darlings ever confronted a financial crisis? – but Suzy's presence, her smile, her good coffee. Even the look of her would be comforting. Suzy was always crisp and shining, laundered and happy, as unthreatening and uplifting as a bunch of spring flowers.

They were not really confidantes these days. When they had both been younger and their children at the most demanding ages, they had seemed to talk a great deal about their feelings, but in those days most of the feelings had been straightforward ones: exhaustion, or domestic frustration, or worry about schools. Back then, thought Helen, troubles were easy to share because everyone at the school gate had a pretty similar set. All young mothers, even if their incomes were diverse, lived in an easy enough freemasonry. But as children grew older and more different from one another, it was inevitable that the problems and frustrations also grew apart. With a school-gate friend you can decently discuss a five-year-old's trouble with bullies, but not a fifteen-year-old's trouble with boyfriends, or a troubled boy's relationship with his father. That takes another level of friendship entirely, and somehow in latter years Helen had not managed this. By the time Marcus and Danny left home, there was very little that she and Suzy could share, below the surface of light gossip and domestic detail.

There were things now which were undiscussable. Helen did not feel ready to tell Suzy, that stalwart fundraiser for National Marriage Week, that she was through with Roy for good: that her carapace had hardened for ever. Indeed, that discovery was fresh and startling enough to Helen herself. Amy Partlett, with her trail of discarded bankers stretching across the northern hemisphere, ought to be more understanding, but she was at work. Besides she would tell Rod, and telling Rod anything at all was roughly equivalent to writing it into a song lyric and giving it to Elton John.

Nor did she want to discuss Marcus and what he had done; not with anybody, not ever. Sharper than a serpent's tooth, that boy, the original thankless child. As for the other fatally centrifugal tendencies her family had shown, those too were out of bounds.

On the other hand, there were areas where Suzy's level, literal, practical brain might be of use to her. Suzy might steady her. Helen, unused to rebellion, was not happy with the fact that she had, an hour earlier, thrown one of her best coffee mugs through a closed window. She did not want to be out of control; it was not dignified. It was not something that her games players at the Ferris Home would appreciate her for.

Quickening her step, she hurried up the road to the Darlings' sunny yellow front door.

# Chapter Twelve

———◆———

Half an hour later Suzy spread her elbows on the big kitchen table, noticed a piece of fluff clinging to the cuff of her cashmere sweater, flicked it off, bit her lower lip thoughtfully and said, 'Rent.'

Helen looked back blankly.

Suzy said again, 'Rent it. Let it. The house. Short term. Your main problem is the house and you're absolutely right, they eat money. But if you rent it, you can keep paying the mortgage and rent a little flat yourselves while you get sorted out. Get your post redirected and that leaves the bank in blissful ignorance of everything. The less they know, the better, James always says. If they smell redundancy or any kind of crash they just call in debts and you're doomed.'

'You need permission from the mortgage people to rent things out,' said Helen.

'Fairycakes!' said Suzy. 'Nobody does. For God's sake, ask James. You know how his company's always moving people for six months here and three months there? Like when we went to ghastly Frankfurt. There are rich yet homeless foreign bankers and world troubleshooters roaming London, *begging* for somewhere to lay their heads. Especially if it's up here, where they think they might meet leading British intellectuals and writers in the supermarket, fat chance.'

Helen smiled, almost for the first time since she had arrived white-faced on the doorstep.

Suzy smiled back. 'Now you've done the bathrooms, you and Roy could even rent number thirty-three to *Americans*, and get all sorts of big money. Tell them you're off on a long business trip yourselves.'

*You and Roy*, thought Helen. How tactful, how sweet Suzy was. She had decided to pretend that she didn't know Roy was not home. She had even thrown a cushion down hastily onto the little kitchen sofa to hide the morning newspaper. Helen could see the corner of it peeping out, the great black word SACKED just showing.

'Do you really think I – we – could?' she said.

'If I ring James now,' said Suzy, 'and get him to ask around and see who's coming on secondment to all the banks he does business with, I bet you fifty quid you'll have an offer by tomorrow. Don't take less than five hundred quid a week. No, more.'

'Would I be able to sign things on my own?' she asked.

'Dunno.' Suzy narrowed her eyes, staring down at her neat little hands around the coffee cup. Then she raised her head and looked Helen in the eye, challenging her. 'Would you have to? Wouldn't Roy agree? It's sensible, and it'd only be temporary.'

For a moment Helen returned her look, then dropped her eyes with a sidelong, almost cunning expression. Suzy went on watching her. In the end Helen only said, flatly, 'I'd be grateful if you did ask James, anyway. Keep my – keep our options open.'

And with that, her interlocutor had to be satisfied.


Danny and Shona sat at another table, not of scrubbed French oak like Suzy's but of crazed plastic at Ishmael's café. Outside, the traffic roared and smoked up the road to Waterloo Bridge, rattling the windows and sending up skeins of damp grit from lorry wheels. The twins were bleary-eyed and cast down, having spent much of the night walking through the West End scanning the faces of the street sleepers.

For a while they had separated, Danny to check the hostels and Shona the Embankment. Passing through Trafalgar Square, Shona had suffered an altercation with a pack of late-night drunks who thought her hairstyle amusing. This put her so seriously out of temper that she threw the rudest of them into the fountain, and when the rest turned on her was forced to flee, her big form surprisingly nimble, down to the railway station and into the ladies'.

From here she had walked the length of the Embankment, peering carefully at every sleeping or coughing form. Once she had seen a red jacket and run towards it with a spurt of excitement, but it was an old woman, crazy and confused, whose state so concerned Shona that she spent half an hour escorting her to the crypt of a Wren church for hot coffee. After this she came back to the Embankment but drew a blank; none of the homeless huddled round the Savoy Hotel hot-air vents had noticed a newcomer, nor had any of the volunteers on the soup runs seen a middle-aged, unexpected man in a woman's red fur-hooded jacket and business suit.

The hostels were equally fruitless, but, as Danny said, 'He wouldn't have gone to a hostel, would he? People don't, at first. You don't know how it all works. You don't know who it's safe to talk to. I didn't.'

'I suppose he wouldn't go to a soup van either.'

'He may have gone home. Or gone off to stay with some friend. We may be completely out of order,' said Danny. 'Douglas said that we shouldn't assume he'd stay on the street. People are more scared of it than that. He might have gone to a bed-and-breakfast to chill out.'

'You know what I think about that,' said Shona. 'Look.' She pulled out the folded sheet of evening newspaper and spread it on the table. Danny looked, dark head cocked to one side, then shrugged.

'Yeah, right. See what you mean. He looks out of it.'

'So what do we do? Talk to Mum?'

'You can. I can't, can I?'

'I still think,' said Shona, 'that we have to get them over all this. Christ knows, I'm not in love with the big warm jolly family thing, but it has to get worked out eventually.'

Danny looked bleakly at the table. 'Why?'

'Well, think about it. Why have we just spent half the bloody night wearing our feet out looking for Dad? You haven't even spoken to him for six years, but out you came.'

There was a silence, and when Shona looked up, she saw that there were tears in Danny's eyes. She covered up the moment with practised tact.

'I'll talk to Mum,' she said. 'At least find out whether he's got back.'

'And if not?' Danny was poised again now.

'Some more nice little evening walks for us, I suppose. It's a surprisingly small city, down on the street. If he's there, we'll find him.'

Danny began to laugh and then softly to sing:

> Down among the dead men,
> Down among the dead men,
> Down among the dead men,
> Le-e-et him lie!

\*     \*     \*

Suzy Darling's prediction was not entirely right; in the event it took three working days before James – or rather, James's secretary – came up with the Groschenbergs, on secondment from New York to the Ein-Europa Bank to work between London and Brussels on single currency systems development. George W. Groschenberg himself would rather have made the family base in Brussels, where he would work half the week, or at the very least to have got a house within a short ride of an airport. Tammy Groschenberg, on the other hand, was set on the idea of a Real London Home, either in Kensington (where she could read to her two small children from the original *Mary Poppins*) or in Hampstead (where there could be at least a fighting chance of spotting Glenda Jackson in the street). Tammy Groschenberg usually got what she wanted, and as soon as she saw No.33 the discussion was closed.

'I love it, we'll take it,' she said, with a flash of her threateningly perfect teeth. 'We got six months for sure, perhaps till October at the longest. That OK?'

She was a neat thin woman in blue jeans and a cashmere camel polo-neck sweater, hair cropped and streaked like a very expensive urchin. George W. himself was a small, fiery man with heavy glasses and receding red hair. Impatient at having been made to take two hours out of the office, he was already tapping a number into his mobile phone.

Tammy said again, 'October OK? If we're out early, we pay, it's our risk.'

Helen nodded, stunned by the speed and decisiveness of this alien tribe. It explained a lot about Suzy, she thought; no wonder she had not gone back to work, when in James Darling's working world these moves and changes of earthquake proportions could be imposed with so little ceremony.

Tammy produced a notebook and began to fire questions. 'Schools,' she said. 'You got kids? Where'd they go? We had home tuition in St Petersburg, but never again. Then support systems – you gotta maid we can hire?'

'Business first, honey,' said her husband. 'We generally put our letting arrangement straight through Human Resources at the bank, so—'

'No,' said Helen, well-drilled by James and Suzy. 'We prefer to do a direct cash deal, monthly in advance, with a damage deposit of,' she consulted her own pad, 'four weeks' rent, which is very moderate round here.'

George W. Groschenberg sucked his teeth. 'Yeah, OK,' he said. 'I'll claim it that way. They might not like it too much, though. Might haveta do it on a hotel claim basis—'

'George!' said his wife warningly. 'This is my house, OK? I have just bonded. The kids and I take enough crap from that bank, it can just bend its rules a bit for us or we're outta here.' Then, with a dazzling smile at Helen, 'I didn't mean it was mine, right? It's your house, and it's darling, but if I don't get myself home-wise in a flash I can't handle this life we live. Global nomads, you know?'

'OK, honey, OK. So – tenancy agreement?' said George, looking at his watch with barely disguised dismay. 'Do you wanna fax me something?' He produced a card. 'And hey, I see you maybe got a tax situation here and I'd like you to know we understand that perfectly. That agreement does not go anywhere that your Internal Revenue's light can shine. We were in St Petersburg, and Naples. We know about this stuff.' Disconcertingly, George W. gave a jaunty wink.

'Er, right,' said Helen.

He punched the air in a restrained sort of way, looked at his watch again and mimed throwing a ball to his wife. She was bubbling, flying, in overdrive again.

'And it's OK for the twenty-fourth? Really OK? It would be *so perfect* to be settled before the kids fly over.' Tammy scribbled on her pad, tapping her big teeth with her gold pen, dancing from one foot to the other in excitement. 'You sure that's OK?'

'Yes,' said Helen again. Today was the eighteenth. She remembered, with a jolt, the imminent direct debit for the mortgage.

'The deposit,' she began.

'Gimme bank details,' said George. 'If I get that through by close of business tonight, can we call this a deal?'

'Shake,' said Helen, proffering her hand.

'That is *so British!*' shrilled Tammy happily. 'See, honey? Not a lawyer in sight. Now you know why I wanna live in London not Brussels!'

'I gotta get to the office,' said George with decision. 'Tammy, if I leave you the driver, will you stay and do the girl talk and the closets?'

'Yay!' cried his wife. 'If that's truly OK, er, Helen? Hey,' swinging round, she lit upon Zack's picture, aged two astride a pushalong caterpillar, 'is that your kid? He is to die for. Is he excited about your big trip?'

Helen followed her gaze to the photograph. She had not, as it happened, told Zack anything at all about any of it: not the money, not the rental, not the imaginary business trip to Johannesburg.

'Terrific,' said Suzy later. 'Well, financially terrific anyway. Does it get you out of the wood?'

'Yes,' said Helen. She felt increasingly odd, detached from her own life; she had negotiated with Tammy Groschenberg that she would retain the loft and the smallest bedroom for storage, and leave out books and pictures to be boxed up or in place at the Groschenbergs' discretion. Then she had spent three hours throwing personal possessions into trunks and bin bags before being overwhelmed with horror at the new bare impersonality of the house and fleeing up the road to Suzy's. 'Yes, I can draw about three hundred pounds a month and still have the mortgage paid, and they're taking over all the house bills directly. Till July, anyway.'

Suzy fell silent. Three hundred pounds a month would barely keep the Darlings' drinks cupboard stocked, certainly not if you counted cocktail snacks.

'You know that you and Zachary can stay here as long as you like,' she said. 'There's the top floor with Helena and Dougie's old bedrooms, and their bathroom, and the little kitchen thing the nanny used to use. We'd love to have you.'

'You can't,' said Helen. 'What about when they stay over, or you have guests? We can't squat in your loft like some protected species of bat.'

'Of course you can!'

'And anyway, what about the Groschenbergs down the road? They'll think it's bloody odd, us pretending to go off on a business trip to Johannesburg and then lurking in your attic seven doors away.'

'Mmm.' Suzy was thoughtful. 'Well, for a few days anyway.'

She felt desperately sorry for Helen, but pity was impossible to convey when her friend maintained icy tracts of impassable silence on the subjects which must be of the greatest torment to her. Over the whole weekend and Monday, although they had met for some time every day, she had not been able by hinted questions even to discover what state Zachary was in about the upheaval. Still less could she get near the subject of Roy's return. The newspapers had given up on the story when he left the Eden doorstep, and Helen swerved away from any mention of her husband's name.

It was all very odd and upsetting, and all that poor kind Suzy could do was endlessly to offer food and drink and lodging. *Corporal works of mercy*, she thought with a sigh when Helen had departed to welcome Zack home from school. They were in the catechism they taught her at convent school: '*To feed the hungry, to give drink to the thirsty, to clothe the naked, to harbour the harbourless, to visit the imprisoned, to bury the dead.*'

Fine, thought Suzy, rinsing the teacups. But there was another set – Spiritual works of mercy, were they? – including '*To counsel the doubtful. To comfort the sorrowful . . .*' She had counselled a bit, about the letting, and was duly proud of the result. But how could you comfort the sorrowful when they would not admit the sorrow?

✶   ✶   ✶

Zack stepped into the house, throwing down his schoolbag, and looked around. It had begun, then. There were black plastic dustbin bags blocking the hall, and sounds of heavy things being dragged around upstairs. He climbed slowly up to his bedroom, glanced in and saw that it was untouched. Having established this he went to his mother's room and found Helen flushed and breathless with an armful of sweaters and jackets. She started guiltily when she saw him, and dropped the clothes on the bed.

'Sweetheart, I've got to talk to you,' she began.

Zack hunched his shoulders and kicked the door frame, but not hard. 'Yeah, right,' he said. 'About letting the house, yeah?'

Helen stared. 'Oh ... you knew,' she said lamely. *I am an inadequate mother*, she thought. *Always was. Can't even keep a secret.*

'I was in the hall,' said her son severely, 'when you were telling Shona on the phone.'

'Yes ... she rang on Friday.'

'Did she ring about Dad?'

'Y-yes.' Helen was still panting, less from exertion now than from a kind of panic.

'So does she know what Dad's doing? 'Cos you haven't told me, have you?'

'We don't know,' said Helen. And, regretting it a second later, 'He's just vanished, that's all.'

Zack looked at her, moody and self-contained, not visibly upset. He had very much the look of his father, working out some problem he had brought home from Handfast in the early days. It was a centred, concentrated look, the look of a thinker who needed only information, not encouragement or comfort.

'So why are we moving out? So he can't find us if he does come back?'

'No!' cried Helen, scandalized. 'Of course not, what an awful thing to think!' She was all the more vehement because something inside her had, indeed, been nastily satisfied at the idea of Roy rolling up to his front door one day, thinking he could swan back in and pour a drink, and finding Tammy and George W. Groschenberg in residence. 'No, darling, it's just that he lost his job and we can't pay for the house for a while, so it makes sense for you and me to go somewhere cheaper while we sort it all out. We can leave things here, and just take what we want for the moment.'

Zack frowned, still concentrating on some invisible subtext to all this. 'So what shall I pack?' he asked, with an air of one still avoiding the main question. 'What sort of place are we going to? Do I need my duvet or a sleeping bag? When do we go?'

Helen did not answer for a moment, then she picked up the pile of clothes again and said, 'We move this weekend. Suzy and James have very kindly offered the top floor at their house for a while. It's got its own bathroom and even a place to make tea and toast and stuff if you want to have your own breakfast.'

'Are you going to be there too?'

'Only for a night or two,' said Helen. 'Because of the Groschenbergs. They think I'm going away. They don't know what you look like, so you can stay on the street with Suzy and carry on with school.'

*Madness, madness,* she thought, *I'm making this up as I go along,.*

But the sense of escape grew jubilant within her, stronger than affection, more vigorous than habit. Brief guilt stabbed her as she glanced at the bag, then faded abruptly.

Zack seemed unperturbed by the news. 'So I'm sort of leaving home by myself?' he said after a while. 'Like Danny.' To his mother's amazement, he smiled. 'I'll get my stuff organized, then,' he said.

Later that night, as she pushed some boxes aside in the attic, Helen's attention was caught by a faint, deep, melodious chiming sound. Investigating, she found a dustbin liner filled with children's old soft toys. She must have put it there when they moved to No. 33, unable to discard the faded old friends completely, but unwilling to give them cupboard space in the house.

There were spiders among them now, and a few dead flies and a great deal of dust, but the old faces and paws and ragged ears were bravely recognizable. Here was Marcus's favourite Katie Koala, a Postman Pat with his nose chewed off by Shona's best friend's puppy, Danny's rag doll, half a dozen teddies, a knitted Christmas angel and a curiously sneering plush creature who in games was always formally referred to as Mister Tiger.

Delving, she found at last the thing which had chimed: it was a tightly stuffed fur-fabric cube, about four inches across; it had been home-made by Roy's mother in the year that she died, just before Marcus was born.

Helen knelt there in the dust under the dim attic bulb, and shook it gently. At its centre was some kind of hollow ball with a chinking bell, deep and musical; when a crawling, crowing, exultant infant threw and chased the great soft dice around the room, the faint music of it could be heard, with pleasure, anywhere in the small old house. All four Keaney babies had had the ringing cube, although by Zack's time its fur was matted and hardened.

In the attic now, their mother shook it again and again, tossed it and caught it in great loops of sweetly chiming sorrow; and at last held it against her cheek and wept for the tragedy of babies who grow up.

# Chapter Thirteen

During the days when his home was offered, hired out and rapidly dismantled, Roy lived another life in the strange new world below the trapdoor. On Friday morning, when after punching out increasingly urgent requests on the keypad of a second cash machine he found that he truly had no money, he stood for a while with his back leaning on the wall of the bank, legs shaking, lip trembling, and for the first time in two days was shocked almost into his right mind.

He at least had no illusions about the likelihood of Eden paying in his salary on Tuesday. What the *hell* had he done? Insulted Manderill, defamed the company, shot off his mouth about Marcus, broken his contract by ranting to reporters, stolen a sleeping bag, lost Alan's twenty-two-pound paddle ...

There were great issues, terrible issues about Helen and Zachary hovering around the edges of his mind. He pushed them back. For the moment, he told himself, it was the paddle which troubled him most. He had planned to take the money up to Eden, or at least to post it, because none of this, after all, was Alan's fault. Yes, he must focus on the paddle; a man must pay his debts. His mind began to slip away from him again, a comfortably tangled mess of knitting wool, as he pulled out this one strand and considered the problem of the paddle. If he could not get the money, he must find a replacement.

He wandered on through Trafalgar Square, and stopped again irresolute on the corner of Pall Mall, looking up the broad avenue towards Piccadilly. North of Piccadilly, he thought, lay a shop which had boat things in the window. Roy set off, with an uneven gait that made him thirty years older, and passers-by stepped sideways to avoid his shuffling progress. He had dropped the sleeping bag outside the bank, and the red jacket hung half off one shoulder. As he went, he coughed and shivered, hot and cold by turns, and sweat slicked his forehead to a pale, slimy shine.

When he stepped into the chandler's shop, between ranks of nursery-bright charts and books, the assistant strode forward to meet him. He was a commanding young man, themed to suit the shop in blue and white deck shoes and a yachting blazer.

'Can I help you, *sir?*' His tone was nicely poised between threat, since this was clearly some troublesome old wino, and politeness, since it was not entirely unknown for very rich yachtsmen to look very like troublesome old winos.

Roy blinked at him, and fell into a paroxysm of coughing. Finally he said, 'I need a paddle. For a canoe.'

'Kayak paddle, or Indian single?'

'About this long.' Roy held up his shaking hands like an angler.

'Single. Wood or fibreglass?'

'Wood – no, fibre— I don't know. A brown one. You could push a drawing pin into the blade, I remember that,' said Roy obscurely. 'It's for some sea scouts.'

The assistant moved away, pulled a paddle from a rack and walked back towards Roy. 'We don't have the fibreglass in, but this one is twenty-two pounds,' he said.

'That's the one!' said Roy joyfully. 'I'll take it!'

Holding the paddle in his right hand, from the pocket of his anorak he drew the bank card with his left, handing it over with a flourish. The assistant took it, and reached forward to swipe it through the slot of his machine. While his eyes were on the slot, Roy slid from the shop and began running up the road, panting, the paddle grasped in his hand like a javelin. The assistant gaped for a moment, then ran to the door. He saw Roy bolting up the road, and grimaced with indecision, hesitating to leave the ground floor of the shop unmanned lest this old loon should be a cunning diversion, a front for more ambitious thieves of electronics and watches and four-hundred-pound sets of offshore oilskins. He pushed the alarm bell and shouted up the stairs, then ran off in pursuit of the red anorak.

The delay cost him the quarry. At the corner with New Bond Street the pursuer finally gave up, and walked disconsolately back to face his manager and ring the police.

Roy meanwhile was doubled up in a doorway, shaking violently, racked by great tearing coughs. His head pounded, and despite the sweat which soaked right through his shirt to the underarms of his jacket, when he raised a trembling hand to his brow it was dry and burning. He sank to his knees, using the paddle to support him, arms wrapped round it. People stepped round him; when he tried to get up, he could not, and fell sideways instead, eyes closed, hair streaming in pepper-and-salt streaks on the pavement.

At last, far above his head, he heard voices.

'Up shit creek *with* a paddle, by the look of it.'

'Come on, mate. You can't lie there.'

He opened his eyes. Two policemen loomed impossibly high above him, their chequered hats blotting out the dazzle of the winter sky. He peered perversely at the bottoms of their trousers. Policemen's socks, he thought dimly, you never heard much about those. Were they uniform issue, or did they bring their own?

Long, long ago there had been clothes lists for his school, with 'socks navy blue NOT black' specified. Was it like that in the police? Squinting, he saw that one of the constables had navy socks and the other had air force blue. He smiled, and let himself drift. Then another bout of coughing racked him, and one of the voices said, 'Get him to an A and E, I think. Come on, mate. Up.'

Roy noticed, as they manhandled him to their car, that the younger one was the gentlest. He had an open, chubby moon face like a nice twelve-year-old boy. It was the older, narrow-faced policeman who hesitated by the car and said, 'Not going to be sick, is he? In the Panda? We could call an ambulance.'

'Ah, no,' said the younger, who sounded Irish. 'He'll be fine. He's got the flu, that's all. Come on, now,' for Roy was scrabbling anxiously, 'you can keep your paddle.'

'It's a potential weapon,' said the older man. 'Take it off him. Put it in the boot.'

'He's not a suspect, now,' protested the Irish boy. 'He's not a well man.'

'Well, you sit in the back with him then,' said the first policeman sourly. 'You and the bloody paddle and the vomit.'


While Roy was stretched out on three plastic chairs at the hospital, coughing and dozing and clutching his paddle, his youngest son was composing a letter:

Dear Shona,

wrote Zack, sitting at the homework desk in his bedroom,

You will be surprisd to hear from me your brother, but I want to know about Danny and Mum wont tell me. Dad has gone to live on a pavment for a bit, I heard them say. Doant worry about me but I seryously would like to know about Danny.

your brother
Zachary

The letter went with Zack to school on Monday, but as he was going to seal and post it he re-read it, and judged it babyish.

On Tuesday night, after his mother's revelation, he re-worked the whole composition.

Dear Shona,
You will be surprised to hear from me your brother.
Ass you know we are moveing out of the house (No.33) so please send your answer to No. 24 (the Darlings house).
I want to know about Danny and why he disapeard. He is my brother after all. Mum wont tell me anything and Dad has gone to live on a pavment for the moment, and I have to live at Mrs Darlings which is fine for now, but I am trying to organise knowing about my family so I know what genes I have got to cope with.
Mum is not staying at the Darlings, she is going off, don't know whare. Don't worry about me at all, I am growing up fine. But I do seryously want to know about Danny and things
Yours faithfully
Your brother
Zachary
PS I am cool about people being gay, if its that.

He posted it on Wednesday morning, and spent the rest of his spare time until Sunday stowing his childhood headquarters in a series of boxes in the small bedroom, and carefully selecting his marching gear for the campaign ahead. The computer and its games console must come, obviously; likewise a nucleus of favourite clothes, six or seven books, and Marvo the grey plush mouse, named after a cartoon magician and credited, during the years of his infancy, with wide-ranging supernatural powers. The rest he tossed into boxes and bags, surprised by how little he minded leaving any of it. You didn't, after all, need much stuff really. If the computer had been a laptop (Zack yearned for a laptop, it was almost his sole material ambition) he could have put it all in his rucksack and just walked out, down the road, like a turtle with its house on its back. The thought exhilarated him.

Roy, meanwhile, was seen in the casualty department by an overstretched exhausted nurse and equally exhausted houseman, diagnosed as having the flu, and left sitting up in an armchair just off the waiting area, since they had run out of trolleys.

'Have you got family we can ring?' the nurse had asked, and Roy had shaken his head firmly. 'A home where someone can keep an eye on you?'

Another head shake, and, 'I have to get this paddle to Alan Barton at Eden headquarters,' he said, or seemed to say, but it came out as 'Paddle Alanquarters' and the nurse pressed her lips together and went to tell the office to ring Social Services.

While the telephone was still ringing in the offices of that equally stretched and exhausted community resource, Roy suddenly felt a little better, and very light-headed, and pushed himself out of the armchair to stagger, unnoticed, towards the door, using his paddle as a walking stick.

'Care in the community,' sniffed a well-dressed woman bringing in a child with a suspected broken arm. 'Just look at it all! Britain two thousand!'

Nobody else saw Roy go out into the darkening street. A light rain was beginning to fall; the homebound crowds streamed by, intent on the coming weekend, leaving a hundred office doorways and urine-smelling alleys undisturbed for two days.

In one of these Roy Keaney collapsed, and lay until the small hours of Sunday morning. Of Monday he knew nothing at all; on Tuesday, about the time when Helen was negotiating with the Groschenbergs, he opened his eyes on brown, peeling shiny paintwork, two iron bedsteads and a high window through which thin sunlight filtered.

# Chapter Fourteen

'I didn't think it would be so hard,' said Danny dispiritedly. 'I thought we'd find him in one night, maybe two at most.'

'I know,' said Shona. 'How long is it now?'

Danny grimaced. 'It's Tuesday today. That's a week he's been out.'

'If he is out.'

'Well, you rang Mum, didn't you? When was that?'

'I got her on Sunday. She sounded spaced out. Not worried, just vague. Said Dad hadn't got back and she'd heard nothing. She said he was probably staying at Tony's or somewhere.'

'Did you ring Tony?'

'Shit!' said Shona, exasperated. 'I rang everybody. I sat in Julian Hemroyd's poxy little office and rang everyone I could think of. All the neighbours, all the old neighbours. Spent hours with the phone book ringing same-names who turned out to be strangers. Half of them didn't know what had happened, the other half were all agog from reading the papers. Nobody was any frigging use at all.' She thumped the table. 'This is stuff that Mum ought to be doing, but there's some kind of spring broken there. It does my head in. I probably ought to go and see her, but I can't face it.'

'Well, she doesn't know anything about the streets, does she?' said Danny judiciously. 'People don't know how quickly you can go right down. They vaguely think that anybody with a degree and a suit kind of automatically ends up in a proper bed with sheets. Since it's obviously our job now, should we do Missing Persons?'

'You cannot be serious. What good would that do? People disappear. You disappeared.'

Danny nodded, with a certain self-satisfied smirk. 'Indeed I did. But you found me OK. Did Mum say anything else?'

'She's got no money, the company's suing him for defamation or something, so she's letting the house. She was hoping for some Americans.'

'Where'll she go?'

'She didn't know. Sounded rather vague, actually, as if she didn't much care about that either. Suzy Darling is being wonderful, apparently.'

Danny's eyes softened. 'Ah, Mrs Darling. I loved that woman, you know. Didn't much like Dougie, bit of a thug, but I used to go round to tea at his house just to look at Mrs Darling. Lovely, lovely clothes. Soft, pastel, fluffy, cashmere . . . I used to stroke her arm. Remember how Mother was always in those stiff canvas smock things and jeans?'

'Well, Zack was little. She was probably enjoying giving up office clothes.'

'But Mrs Darling was just so *pretty*. And nice. Always gave us American cookies, the really expensive kind Mum refused to buy.'

'Yes, all right,' said Shona, suddenly feeling partisan about Helen. 'Suzy Darling has a lot more money than Mum ever had. And clothes.'

The two sipped silently at their tea for a moment. They were, as usual, in Ishmael's café; Ishmael himself regarded them with proprietorial curiosity, looking for echoes of Shona's broad, nose-ringed face in Danny's thin vivid one, but finding none.

He called over, 'You want more toast?'

'No thanks,' said Shona. 'I have to work.' She yawned. 'After all these nights, Christ knows how.'

'You could be one of those sleeping-beauty installations,' said Danny unsympathetically. 'Troll along to the Hemroyd Gallery with a mattress and just fall over and start snoring.'

'He'd sell me to some American speculator and I'd end up in a bank vault,' said Shona. 'You probably ought to go to work too, shouldn't you?'

'Nah,' said Danny, who was yawning too. 'I can go and see a couple of rehab cases then crash out all afternoon. Drugs counsellors don't work set hours, you know. And I've done my essays for this week.'

'It's not as if the rehab lot pay you much,' agreed Shona. She got up. 'So, tonight then? Charing Cross, ten o'clock?'

'I think we have to,' said Danny soberly. 'He has to be somewhere. If anything really bad had happened he would have turned up in a cell or a hospital. Actually, I still think it might have been him who they saw at Gower Street casualty on Friday, the one carrying the paddle.'

'But they said that was a really old crazy guy.'

'Dad might look that way by now,' said Danny bleakly. 'I've seen people go down faster than that. In the end it'll have to be the police.'

'Not yet, though,' said Shona quickly.

'No. Not yet.'


It was during that limbo time, with Roy disappeared and Helen numbly packing up the remains of the family home, that Roy and Helen's eldest son fell in love; and for the first time in his life began to entertain wild, unaccustomed thoughts of starting a home of his own.

Marcus had decided, after the hungover telephone confrontation with Eric Manderill, that discretion was the better part of valour. He had pushed aside the hollow unhappiness of the moment and reassured himself vigorously that he was too young and too brilliant to get bogged down in some lawsuit against Eden plc. A helpful anger had boosted this defiance half an hour later, when he was woken again by a fussy call from Eden's director of press relations, who insisted on reading him an agreed statement about his parting with the corporation and reminding him that within the terms of his earlier agreement he was not at liberty to depart from company policy regarding such statements.

Marcus merely snarled something and put the phone down. After a time he got up, pulled on his clothes and took a taxi back to his high empty Docklands flat. Here the three warm blue computer screens welcomed him, pulling him into a familiar world in which he was a king and emperor who swept aside contemptuous enemies with a twitch of his wrist. He left the answering machine on permanently, deleting inquiries from journalists with vicious little stabs of his forefinger and reflecting that it was time he got an agent, or at the very least an assistant. That was the problem of cyberspace; it enabled you to build empires entirely alone, to hold the whole plot in your own head and not be bothered with a workforce. Then abruptly, without warning, the cup spilled over and you found yourself having to mop up oceans of incoming hassle unaided.

He spent a lot of time online that week, deleting most of his e-mails unread and moving rapidly outward into his familiar Web world, clipping out ideas and designs with more precise little stabs and swoops of the mouse. He used his last powder but did not have the heart to go out and get more. Besides, his dealer might have seen the press and decide to leak a story about his habit. He did not eat for three days, which for him was not uncommon; he showered twice, and lived in pyjamas. When he slept he woke sweating, full of formless anger. Once Irena's voice came on the answering machine, the bad-tempered sexy growl almost unbalancing him, but he stabbed her to silence with his forefinger too, and went back into his screen.

On the fourth morning after he got back to the flat, there was an unfamiliar, insistent buzzing. Disorientated, Marcus peered at the computer, but the sound came again from behind him. It was several moments before he recognized the doorbell. Nobody ever called; that was not what the flat was for. Irena had a key, or had done until she threw it at him during their altercation in Soho. It was probably still there on the stained club carpet. Nobody rang Marcus's doorbell. He hesitated, then got up and crossed to the intercom.

'Yes?' His voice, unheard since the conversation with Manderill, had a grating unpleasant timbre. He cleared his throat. 'Yes? Who's there?'

'My name's Marie Hughes. I work at Eden headquarters—'

'So fuck off!' shouted Marcus. Ten seconds later, when he had reached his desk again, the buzzer went a third time. He flung himself across the room to disconnect it, but pushed the button to vent his fury first.

'Just go away!' he began. 'Talk to my lawyer—' but the small voice cut across him.

'It's not official. I have to see you about your mother.'

Marie, in her painstaking way, had worked out that given what he had done to his father, Roy's name was probably not the best one to invoke. A mother, on the other hand, always had a hold over a man. Her granny used to tell her that, with many a wink: *One day, dear, you'll have sons of your own, and you'll never really lose them, it's one of the perks.*

The tactic paid off; the intercom was silent for a moment and then Marcus's voice snapped, 'Come in then. Five minutes. Top floor.'

As she looked down at her hands in the lift, Marie saw that they were shaking. She had surprised herself with her determination. It had begun the day after she spoke to Helen, when Erika – who liked to play maternal doyenne to the younger PAs – had told her in the canteen about the full terms of Eden's letter to Roy.

'You don't want to get on the wrong side of them,' she said, with a tone of sententious warning. 'He'll have no money coming in at all now.'

Marie remembered Helen, up on the sunny heights of Hampstead, and shivered. 'What's his family s'posed to do?' she said plaintively. 'S' a bit hard.'

'He should have thought of that,' said Erika. 'Probably his wife works.'

Marie was silent. She knew that Helen did not work because after a couple of drinks in the office Roy would occasionally mention the fact with a somewhat unbecoming tone of resentment. Minutes later, when Erika was well off on another subject, the normally timid Marie suddenly interrupted her, hauling the topic back to her old boss.

'They could lose their home, though. What about that?'

'The Keaneys, you mean? Well, like I said, he should have thought of that. A man,' Erika pronounced firmly 'should be responsible that way.'

Marie bowed her head forward, so that her fair hair swung in a silky curtain. Her cheeks were flushed, not with embarrassment but anger. When she could master a casual tone again she said, 'Marcus Keaney – is it true he's left?'

'Yes,' said Erika, 'and he won't go short of money, for one.'

So Marie, a vague plan forming, had smiled and simpered down in the Human Resources office and thus illicitly acquired the home address of Marcus Keaney; and still without a very clear idea of what to say, she had set forth to right a wrong.

When the lift reached the top floor, it took all her resolution not to turn tail and flee. Marcus, however, was already glowering in the doorway of his flat, which behind him stretched menacingly dark and open, with the faint glow of a computer screen flickering on the side of his face.

'What'd you want?' he said, half blinded by the sunshine from the great floor-to-ceiling windows of the old warehouse.

Marie looked wildly up the corridor, but then steadied herself to step forward and look directly at the angry figure of the younger Mr Keaney.

Which, as it turned out, was the best thing she could possibly have done. The pouring sunlight fell on her, and Marcus – hungry, tired, surging with unacknowledged emotions – looked and was lost. He did not want at that moment to take her to bed, to show her off or flaunt her as a conquest. He did not even want to impress her and feed off adoration from her eyes. He only wanted to worship and protect her to the end of time. The *coup de foudre*, the arrow of Cupid, the ten-ton truck, every cliché of sudden foolish love struck cool, hard Marcus Keaney and he stared at little Marie Hughes like any Romeo at his Juliet.

*O, she doth teach the torches to burn bright!* He had never liked Shakespeare at school, but the words came almost to his lips before he mastered himself. Instead he said, in a high cracked voice he did not recognize, 'Yeah, won't you – come in?'

# Chapter Fifteen

Zachary had addressed the letter to his sister c/o the Hemroyd Gallery. Julian Hemroyd passed it on, with a certain amount of sighing, when she came in for her fourth session of monopolizing his phone and checking out hostels and police stations.

'*Just* think of me as an *accommodation address*,' he said to the big hunched figure at the desk.

Shona, impervious to heavy irony from lightweight sources, grunted, 'Yeah, I do, more or less,' and continued dialling.

The gallery owner stifled his irritation. He had publicized Shona Keaney's new and pleasingly blasphemous concept exhibition, and decided to defy her threats by murmuring, to favoured press contacts, certain oblique hints about her relationship to both Keaney the youthful cyber tycoon and Keaney the doorstep scourge of Eden. Now he was beginning to have a real fear that she might not bother to deliver any actual artworks to complete this potentially excellent commercial enterprise.

It was his fault; he had let her make too much money out of the shit sculptures, without noticing how little she spent on daily life. The fat bitch must be *coining* it if she had invested properly; perhaps this current indifference to her work was because she was, quite simply, no longer hungry enough. Certainly she seemed massively unconcerned by all his heavy hints about the need to photograph the work and set up press calls in advance. All she seemed to do was sit here morning after morning using his telephone, forcing him to open his post from a chair on the end of the desk, refusing all his playful invitations to a persuasive lunch and padding off alone to eat egg and chips at some scruff café.

He hovered for a moment, then gave up and went out into the front of the gallery to smile, glitteringly, at a couple of shocked tourists who were peering at a ten-foot totem pole studded with plaster casts of female genitalia wearing dentures.

Inside the office Shona finished her fruitless call, dropped the receiver on its cradle and reached, listlessly, for the envelope Hemroyd had pulled from his bundle of post. Seeing the unformed handwriting she straightened up, staring at it in astonishment, then slit the envelope deftly open to read her little brother's plea. Her face softened at his greeting and then split into a wide grin.

I want to know about Danny and why he disapeard. He is my brother after all. Mum wont tell me anything and Dad has gone to live on a pavment for the moment . . .

Shona chuckled with delight as she read on to the end.

. . . Don't worry about me at all, I am growing up fine. But I do seryously want to know about Danny and things

'Well, I'll be damned!' said Shona aloud. 'The Berlin Wall is coming down!'

Beyond the office door, in the gallery, Julian Hemroyd pricked up his ears. Berlin Wall rubble was, in his view, shamefully under-used in the art of topical-satirical installation.

At his desk, enraptured, Shona turned the paper over and read Zack's signature and coda:

PS I am cool about people being gay, if its that.

Shona jumped up, took the letter over to the window and read it again, then looked out with real happiness at the thin winter sunlight on the stalls of Camden Passage. The question of Roy, which had filled the foreground of her thoughts for over a week, was eclipsed by the brightness of this hope. Of all the Keaney children, she was the one best fitted to appreciate Zack's letter as the jailbreak it was. She, after all, had lived on at home for two years after Danny first slipped out through the door into that other world. She had watched the Berlin Wall of denial built by her parents out of tears and secrets, rows and compromises. She had heard it all.

'There must be something we can do.'

'There's nothing we can do. Perhaps we should accept it.'

'I never will accept it. If he expects to bring his degradation into this house . . .'

'It's his home. Whatever's happened.'

'It is not his home. It's our home, and Zachary's and Shona's. They've a right not to have this — perversion — shoved in their faces. So have we.'

'If we let go of Danny, we'll lose Shona. You know how she feels.'

'So we're going to run our lives, and the baby's life, on the whim of a teenage girl who can't even be bothered to pass a GCSE? Is that it?'

Now, watching motes of dust dance in the sunbeams flooding into Julian Hemroyd's back office, Shona heard the old voices again, but realized that they had lost their power to harm. She took a deep, relaxed breath and swung her arms. *I am growing up fine*, Zack had said. Well, he was too! A brave new shoot out of the old dungheap. Showed that parents couldn't rot you up totally, however hard they tried.

The letter released her, too, from the nagging guilt of having lost touch with his growing up. On every visit since she left, Shona had acquiesced tiredly with her mother's almost hysterical desire to prevent her having any private conversation with her little brother. She knew why: Helen did not trust her not to raise the memory of the missing twin. She had always thought that the boy must remember Danny, and must wonder why there were not two twins any more. But Helen had always flatly denied it.

'He has no memory of Danny at all. He wasn't even three. It's better that way. And Shonie, please, don't go on about it when your father's home. You know how he is.'

'He's wrong. You're wrong. You can't just blot people out.'

'I think we have to be the judges of that, darling. You've got your own life now.'

And so she had, through art college and after. She had led her own life, funded it herself by the fastest means possible, and abandoned her little brother on the far side of the wall. Now by a miracle he wanted to climb on top and see the view.

She could not wait to tell Danny. Suddenly tears spilt from Shona's eyes, and when Hemroyd poked his head back round the door to attempt another playful reminder about the wax exhibition, she was leaning her head on the window and gasping, laughing with hysterical happy sobs.

'Oh *dear*,' he said lamely. Julian simply hated women who cried. For no reason that he could understand, his private life was always full of them, and to have one in the sanctum of his gallery office was plain ghastly. 'Shall I make some *coffee*?'

The big young woman turned to him, her face alight and almost beautiful. 'Most creative idea you've ever had, Jules,' she said. 'Go for it.' She then, in full view of the astonished gallery owner, kissed the letter.

Busying himself with the kettle, Hemroyd allowed himself to speculate, with awe and foreboding, that Shona Keaney might actually have fallen in love. If she had, it was a bad omen for her work. In his experience, angry and controversial female artists lost all their edge once someone really loved them.

A few miles away, Roy was being propped up on lumpy, rather

smelly pillows by a thin black boy with a purple splodge in his hair and two small rather tarnished brass rings in his nose.

'Awri, mate?' this rough-hewn nurse inquired. 'Woss your name, anyway?'

Roy opened his mouth, but his throat was too sore to speak. Eventually he swallowed a mouthful of the lukewarm tea the boy was offering him, and managed a hoarse whisper. 'Doesn't matter.'

The boy grinned. 'You're like old Misery, aren't you? Nameless wonder.'

Roy looked around. A familiar drift of dull white hair straggled across the pillow two beds along.

'He's here?' he whispered. ''Straordinary – I dreamed about him. In the road.'

'He's in and out of here,' said the boy. 'Wanders off, like. Douglas did say he could go into the hostel full time, but he gets upset and, yeah, wanders off. Douglas might,' he added with an air of great magnanimity, 'get *you* a hostel place, right?'

'Where is this?' whispered Roy. 'Where am I?' He looked down at himself; he was naked to the waist, and the underpants he wore were not his own. Shivering despite the fusty warmth of the room, he pulled the sheet up over himself and noticed that it was more grey than white, and although it felt and smelt clean, that it had pale old stains on its frayed edges. 'It's not a hospital? Is it?'

'Nah,' said the boy. 'We got a doctor comes, though. He saw you. Said you didn't need to go to hospital. No beds there anyway. Flu epidemic.'

'How – how—' Roy was having difficulty getting words out.

The boy said bluntly, 'Douglas found you up St Margaret's alley in a pool of piss and stuff. Looked like you'd been sick, too. Lucky not to choke, he said, and hot as hell with fever. So you're here. We cleaned you up and put you in bed and you stayed out cold, more or less. But the doc said you was all right, just having the flu. You haveter watch for pneumonia, like, but you ain't got that.'

'What *is* it? This place?' Roy was tearful now, snivelling in front of this youth, revolted by himself.

'Shelter. Doug the Drug's. Whoops, man, I mustn't say that.'

'I'm not *on* drugs.'

'Misery ain't either, is he? More the drink, with him. Who comes in here is basically whoever Douglas says. And you're not 'zackly springin' around, are you, mate? You been on something. Drink, p'raps. I wouldn't argue with a nice soft bed. You hungry?'

But Roy was not. He lay propped against the lumpy pillows for a moment, then slid down the bed again and curled up, knees to his chest, sheet over his head.

'Suit yourself,' said the boy merrily as he left.


On Wednesday morning Helen left the half-packed disorder of No.33 and, with her yellow canvas holdall, walked up the road to the Ferris Home with snakes and ladders, Monopoly, Halma and the chessboard. The night before, as she carefully selected and checked the games, Suzy had exclaimed at this.

'You don't have to go! Surely you can miss one week!'

'Why?' said Helen, easing the brass hook of the folding chessboard shut. 'George and the others expect me. Wednesday is games day.'

'Yes, but—'

'Suzy,' said Helen, her eyes big and dark in a face which had grown visibly paler and thinner through the week, 'I have not been a huge success as a mother, or much to write home about as a wife—' she was going to add 'or a wage-earner, come to that' but tactfully refrained, since Suzy herself hadn't earned a penny for twenty years – 'but I happen to be a huge success at playing mah-jongg with the oldies at the Ferris Home. Build on success, they say, don't they?'

'Would you like me to stay here and sort out the kitchen things?' asked Suzy pleadingly.

'Yes please. Leave them everything except the most shamingly broken stuff, and the big flowery dish of my mother's. I'd quite like that kept safe, in the attic or somewhere. It's just about the last thing of hers that I've got.'

'I'll try and make some cupboard space,' said Suzy, brightening up at the prospect of a containable task. 'Americans always have special gadgets for waffles and things.'

'Thanks. You don't have to do all this.' Helen hefted her bag. 'Just stop when you've had enough. You've been wonderful.'

Suzy smiled, helplessly, and waved her unaccountable friend off up the road before turning back to the pans. After twenty minutes or so she pulled a mobile phone out of her jeans pocket – she was too punctilious to use Helen's – and rang James at work.

'Darling, did you have any luck?'

For James Darling, too, had been on Roy's track, urged on daily by his ever more worried and tearful wife. Now, across his big desk, his hands still turning over papers, he said into the speaker, 'No. None at all. My secretary's checked everything obvious. He could have gone abroad, like Stephen Fry after that play.'

'Sweetie, don't talk to me on that horrid echoey machine. Pick up the phone properly.'

James obeyed. 'That better? The thing is, sweetie, Helen doesn't seem to be too worried, so perhaps we should mind our own business. He's probably gone to France or something.'

'He has *no money*,' said Suzy. 'Helen told me all about it.'

'People have secret accounts,' said James vaguely. 'You're always reading about it in the papers. Fake disappearances, secret lives, all that.'

'Not Roy,' said Suzy with absolute certainty. 'He wouldn't

be organized enough for that sort of thing. James, I am worried sick.'

'Helen isn't,' said James again.

'I'm worried sick about that, too. I mean I'm worried because she doesn't seem to *care!*'

Dispirited, Suzy went back to Helen's cupboards and drawers, marvelling in spite of herself at the extraordinary tat and detritus that other people tolerate in such hidden kitchen places.

Helen's day at the Ferris Home began much as usual. George, who was thinking a great deal about his son, opted for a quiet game of chess with a new resident, Alan. Alan, at seventy-eight, was in the shocked and silently despairing state which overcame most new arrivals when they realized that they had, for the rest of their lives, exchanged home for a Home. Three ladies joined Helen for Monopoly, and Malcolm – a retired surgeon with painfully shaky hands – opted for Halma with almost bald Miss Grimsdale whose first name nobody knew, but who would occasionally reminisce in startling detail about working with Tito's partisans in the war ('We had to use torture, dear, there was no choice. Needs must when the devil drives').

Helen chose the boot as her counter, and found herself doing very badly indeed. She had a policy of never deliberately allowing even the most shaky or marginally demented of her companions to win, regarding that as a shameful affront to their dignity; she had pursued the same policy with their children, except occasionally with Danny when he was eight years old and cried easily. Today, however, there was no need for pretence. Both Helen's luck and her tactics were dreadful; her game was a series of unlucky throws, misjudged purchases, jail sentences (do not pass Go, do not collect £200) and diminishing stocks of money. Finally she was forced to sell her one house on the Old Kent Road to pay rent to sharp old Coral, who held

Mayfair, and bankrupted out of the game. It all felt strangely appropriate.

'Oh *dear*,' said the other ladies. 'Not your day, is it?' They continued to play to the death, with squeals of delight at their own ruthless hawkishness, and finally conceded victory to Coral.

As Helen packed up the game for lunch, Mrs Beazeley came over to their corner and said, 'Helen dear, would you mind leaving that to later and giving us a hand with the trays? Indira's left us in the lurch.'

Helen followed her towards the kitchen. 'She was a nice girl, I thought. The residents liked her.'

'They won't stay. If they will, they're not very bright. It is our main problem. They won't live in, though we've got the rooms at the top, and the area's so prosperous now that anybody who'll take this job has to travel, and with the fares so high ... well, it just goes round in circles. If *only* they'd live in.'

Helen, swiftly loading trays on the steel counter now, suddenly stopped what she was doing and said, 'What does a care assistant earn? If they do live in, I mean?'

Mrs Beazeley told her and Helen absorbed the shock. How could anybody say there were not two Britains? There must be a gap of mutual understanding, at the very least, if some people regularly settled for living all month on a figure which Suzy Darling or Amy Partlett spent on make-up, and which Helen herself would latterly have blown on ten metres of wallpaper.

'But it is full board,' said Mrs Beazeley defensively, reading her mind. 'So it's pocket money really.'

Helen began loading the trays again, straightening knives and forks with care and rejecting a series of soup spoons as inadequately clean. Mrs Beazeley worked alongside her. When they were ready to collect the plates from the cook and her lunchtime assistant, Helen straightened her collar and said diffidently, 'I'd take the job, for a while. Until you find someone.'

The manageress stared, aghast. 'But – you're—'

'Yes,' said Helen. 'I am. But I can still do the job.'

'It's not a volunteer place – it's very much full time. There's cleaning.'

'Obviously there is. How many days off a week?'

'One and a half,' said Mrs Beazeley automatically. 'By rota. As we've only five care assistants, that involves a lot of weekends and evenings. It is,' she added morosely, 'one of the main problems with the young girls. They want to go clubbing.'

'I don't,' said Helen. 'So do I get the job? Trial period?'

'Well, you're very local,' said Mrs Beazeley. She had collected her wits now, and supposed that some domestic financial upheaval or personal debt must have occurred, necessitating some extra money for the bills.

'No, you don't understand,' said Helen. The cook was filling plates now, and time seemed to press. 'I want the live-in job. I want a room here. The only thing I would ask is to have Wednesday as one of my days off, so I can still do the games day. I'd be here, but I couldn't be doing a full care assistant shift.'

Mrs Beazeley only said, 'Come and see me in the office when you've had your lunch.'

Strangely, the thing which upset her most about this otherwise tempting offer was the prospect of Helen – an educated woman, a middle-class Hampsteader, a *lady* – wearing the green nylon tabard of a care assistant.

# Chapter Sixteen

Tammy Groschenberg did not, in fact, have a collection of exotic American kitchen appliances. She had one box of familiar tools and children's favourite mugs, which she unpacked in ten minutes into the cupboards Suzy and Helen had cleared. Then she poked suspiciously at the controls of Helen's ancient Kenwood Mixer, gave up with a snort of amusement, and looked around with sunny approval at the rest of the kitchen.

She liked the way you could see trees from the back; dropping in on Saturday evening to check politely with her landlady that all was well, she had very much liked the way that from the top floor the branches of those back-garden trees were tinted by the orange sky glow of nocturnal London. She liked walking up the road towards the Heath and looking down at the city; she liked the dinginess of the Victorian brickwork, so satisfyingly ancient. Tammy was a firm believer in living in the style of whichever land you found yourself, and in the words of her distant mother in Ohio, was 'the fastest little settler in the West'.

'I haveta be,' she would say. 'If we're only someplace for six months, I gotta be a true-blue resident in six hours. That way I get a life.'

She would not by nature have chosen such a wandering fate, but accepted it with good humour as long as George gave her a free domestic rein and participated meekly – when he was at home – in whatever local social life she set up for the family. And she set it up fast. No sooner were Mary-Catherine and Mikey dropped at the primary school she had chosen, with a breezy instruction to 'Make friends, now! Ask them home and there'll be cookies!' than Tammy abandoned her unpacking to roam along the street in search of company.

Most houses looked unpromisingly empty. She frowned; maybe there weren't too many young moms at home. Too bad. Outside the Darlings' house, however, she brightened. The kitchen light was on in the basement, defying the overcast gloom of the day, and a light-haired woman was moving around down there. She was beating eggs, so she couldn't be a cleaner; could be a babysitter, thought Tammy, only she looked a bit too expensive for that. She rang the bell.

When Suzy came upstairs, wiping her hands on a teacloth, Tammy swung into her routine as soon as the door opened.

'Hi! I just moved in, seven doors down. We're from the USA, and this is an American custom.' She held out a neat brown bag of cookies. 'It's kinda like an insurance policy, for when I need to borrow a cup of sugar, right? I've got in first with my calorie contribution.'

Suzy looked at her, and recognized from Helen's description the brilliant white smile and the streaked urchin crop.

'You're from number thirty-three,' she said. 'And your name is Mrs, er, Grossen—'

'Groschenberg. Just Tammy, please. I have two kids, Mikey is seven and Mary-Catherine is six this week. I'm a homemaker and expert in spending George's money, which is handy because he has no time to do that, no time at all. Say, you must know Mrs Keaney?'

'Yes ...' Suzy hesitated. 'Well, come in. I'll make coffee and tell you about the area.'

'Yay!' said Tammy blithely, and stormed her first north London citadel.

Inside, she looked around with innocent pleasure, particularly at the string of onions on the kitchen ceiling. When Suzy – who was warming to this golden child every minute – told her that she bought them off a real French onion-seller who toured the area on a real bicycle, in a beret, Tammy was ecstatic.

'There was a lot of stuff like that, farmers coming in to sell stuff, in St Petersburg', she said. 'I thought I'd miss that. Now, I wanna know everything. Is it true there is a girls-only swimming hole on Hampstead Heath? Where you can skinnydip? And do you know Glenda Jackson? I just loved *Elizabeth R!* Can anybody join the Hampstead Theatre? I was coming up in a cab and he said that it was a club!' She rattled ahead, exclaiming at Suzy's answers, and eventually came back to the subject of her landlady.

'We are just so thrilled with the house, and we feel so lucky to find it – a real family home, Mrs Keaney must just hate having to leave it. These guys and their jobs, huh? Does yours travel?'

'We had a year in Frankfurt,' said Suzy. 'But that's the only time we've had to live outside London.' She hesitated. The door had slammed upstairs: Zack was home from school. He must have decided to go out at lunchtime, as a few of them did. She listened to see whether he would go straight upstairs to his top floor or come down to find food; she had no idea whether Tammy would recognize the boy or not. Suzy was bad at such moments; she hated lying, even by omission, and bit her lip.

Seeing her hesitation, Tammy ran her hand through her beautifully striped hair and said, 'Hey, I'm taking up your day. Throw me out.'

'No,' said Suzy. 'I'm going to tell you something I shouldn't, because in the end the truth is easier. If I lie, I can never remember the lie afterwards and get in an awful muddle.'

Tammy nodded with complete understanding, and listened while Suzy explained about the Keaneys. She clucked to hear of Helen's financial troubles and flight to Suzy's top floor, but when it came to the fact that Roy was still missing, the American girl's eyes opened wide in dismay.

'Hey! So he comes home from his lost weekend and he finds a whole new *family* in his home?'

'That's why I thought I should tell you,' said Suzy miserably. 'Helen didn't seem bothered, just smiled vaguely and said that was life. I did get her to have the lock changed, because it just wasn't fair on the tenants – on you, I mean – otherwise.'

'Gee,' said Tammy. 'Thanks.' And Suzy's approval of her new neighbour was complete when she heard the visitor's tone: not a trace of gee-thanks irony in it, only genuine, if bewildered, gratitude. After a moment's consideration, though, the bewilderment and mild shock left young Mrs Groschenberg's face and she said cheerfully, 'Anyway, what the heck. He's a nice guy, you say?'

'Very nice. James's best friend, really, though they haven't much in common in their work.'

'Well,' said Tammy. 'So Roy shows up, we give him a stiff – noggin, as you say – and point him up the road to you? OK?'

'Yes. That would be best. Then I can tell him where Helen is.'

'She's not here? With her kid?'

'No,' said Suzy, delivering the final shock of the story in a tone of pained regret. 'She's taken a living-in job as a care assistant at the old people's home up the road. The one with the castle tower on top.'

'She's a *maid*?' Tammy was aghast. 'Suzanne, I just feel so *dreadful* – I mean, coming and taking her house just because George can sign cheques – oh, hey, that's not right.'

'Don't,' said Suzy tiredly. 'We all feel dreadful too. Everyone who knows her. But the thing is, Tammy, when she told me about it she looked really happy. She said it would be like going home to her own parents. They died, you know.'

'Jeez! And the boy?'

'He couldn't go there with her. It's a really small room in

the attics they get, the live-in assistants. It would be completely impossible to have a child there. He's best off here with me.'

'How old is he? You said, like, nearly eleven?'

'I know,' said Suzy, even more wearily, 'but what can anybody do? She's made her mind up.'

'So his home's been taken over by me and my kids, and his dad's on the run somewhere, and his mother's gone off to be a maid and left him with her friend – this is, like, really dirtbowl stuff.'

'I suppose so,' said Suzy slowly. 'I suppose half the world lives like that, really – always have. Hand to mouth, families split up, everyone just getting by any way that they can.' She finished her coffee. 'Perhaps the unusual way to live is the way we do, with everything on tap and only builders and schools to grumble about. I'm going to get that boy downstairs and feed him something hot.'

'I'll vamoose,' said Tammy. 'Hey, come round, will you? Be friends?'

'Of course,' said Suzy, charmed.


The turrets and castellations of the Ferris Hill Home were a monument to the baronial pretensions of one Geo. T. Colliwell, 1810–1872, noted manufacturer of dubious opiates for the noisier infant. He was locally rumoured to have become an addict himself in his later years; one guidebook asserted that he suffered hallucinations and eventually expired of an overdose of Mother Maconochie's Patent Quieting Syrup, for every London village loves its legends. Certainly the architecture of the Home itself was enough to give credence to the idea of hallucinations; there were even, amid the square towers and pointed spires, two fair approximations in striped brickwork of the onion domes of Moscow.

Up among these red-brick battlements, too winding of access and weird of shape to accommodate elderly paying residents, lay five small bedrooms designed for the maids, cook and boot boy serving the Colliwell household. Now Mrs Beazeley allocated them to her live-in care workers, whenever any could be found to put up with them. Thus the Doras and Janes of 1890 were replaced a century later by Indiras and Winsomes, Martinas and Ivanas from the far-flung relics of Empire and the war zones of middle Europe.

When Helen Keaney first climbed the dusty stairs, exclaiming at the arrow-slits in the brickwork and the loud cheeping of the birds down the chimneys, only three of these bedrooms were occupied. Mrs Archer the cook used one during the week, returning thankfully to Streatham on Friday night when a contract meals service took over. Janice from Brixton lived in, reluctantly, until she was 'sorted out' with her boyfriend; and silent Marjan from Kosovo, with the grief of a whole people in her deep black eyes, slept in the third.

'They're good workers, them and the Croatians,' confided Mrs Beazeley as she ushered Helen into a wedge-shaped room with a grimy window and an iron bed. 'Only round here, the moment they get into the local Balkan network they're off to be nannies. It doesn't pay any better, and as often as not they work ridiculous hours, but they seem to like being in private houses.'

Helen looked around with perverse satisfaction at the plain poverty of the room, its lack of demands.

'Well, I feel rather the opposite,' she said. 'This will suit me fine for the moment.'

'Is your son . . .' began Mrs Beazeley, cringing at her own folly in raising the subject. Now she had got over the shock of visualizing clever Mrs Keaney in a servile nylon tabard, she did not want to lose the chance of her services.

Helen said easily, 'He's staying with a friend. It's handier for his studies.' She had, without lying, given the impression that Zack was rather older.

'Well, if that's all right. Students do like their independence, don't they? Only of course I *have* to have a rule about young men upstairs because of my young girls, they take advantage terribly otherwise.' Her sallow cheeks coloured and she dropped her eyes; an uncommon sight.

'No,' said Helen, making it easy for her. 'He won't be visiting me here. I'll see him in my time off. As you say, the young are so busy these days with their own lives . . .' She said it with an easy laugh, wondering why she did not feel treacherous. Probably because it had been true before; from the age of fourteen Marcus had made it clear that home was the last place, the least cool place in the world, to be; nor had the twins been prone to linger.

'Well,' said Mrs Beazeley. 'The bathroom is shared, and is at the end of the corridor. You may need to thump the geyser a little to get a response. I'm afraid I have never managed to get the company to put this floor on the main heating circuit.' The Ferris was one of a chain of retirement homes, and in the matron-manager's tenure had in fact changed ownership three times. Oldie-farming, as the current holding company's chairman referred to it, was not quite as lucrative as had originally been hoped; local authorities were deplorably stingy. Before she left Helen alone, Mrs Beazeley hesitated and once more, with heroic concern, risked her new treasure, 'You're all right? Quite sure this is the place for you?'

'Sure,' said Helen.


It was that night that Roy first saw Douglas. A tall, cadaverous man came into the dormitory where he lay in an uneasy tangled half-sleep, obscurely distressed by the fast shallow breathing of old Misery. He had lain here for he did not know how many days, tended with flippant kindness by the black boy and sometimes by a big, jelly-like girl with a deafening laugh. Still weak on his legs, he had gone no further than the cracked toilet and basin that led off the cold passageway outside, and made no sense of the tiled corridor that stretched away in diminishing perspective, or the odd shoutings and muffled television sounds that filtered through the walls. He had slept a great deal.

Now he did not want to sleep, and lay awake much of the nights, wondering. The mysterious Douglas, he had been told, 'normally worked nights' and was rarely visible by day. Now, through half-closed eyes, Roy watched him move gently towards the old man's bed and lay a hand on his hair; the breathing seemed to quieten.

Roy pressed his eyes shut. The tall form came towards him, and he sensed rather than saw the figure bend, and look at him with close attention. He peered through his lashes, still breathing as deeply as a sleeper, and saw the man holding up a small square of paper, and looking from it back to Roy's face. Then a hand descended, cool and gentle as snow, on his forehead, brushed aside a wisp of hair, and was gone. For a few minutes after the man had left Roy opened his eyes and looked wonderingly at the cracked cream paint of the ceiling; then he slept.

# Chapter Seventeen

'I think I've got him,' said Father Douglas Cantrip to Danny. 'In fact, I think I've had him for over a week. Sorry I didn't find out sooner. The newspaper picture was misleading, because of course the face was so animated and wild; looking at him as he is now, it was the old snapshot you gave me that clicked.'

'Can I have it back?' said Danny quickly, and took it, stashing it in an inside pocket with care. 'Thanks. Where is he? Is he OK?'

'In the sick bay, and yes, I think he is. Bad dose of flu, according to the doctor, and suspected amnesia. Myself, I suspect *not* amnesia. Or a very voluntary version.'

Danny nodded with an air of complete understanding. 'Shame-shock, we used to call it at the refuge. A lot of kids did it. "No, I wasn't on the game, no, I don't remember nuffink, must have tripped on the pavement" sort of thing.'

'Our hostel chaps are generally older, and they don't care so much any more. Well, anyway, he's all yours.'

'Were you going to move him into the hostel?'

'I don't know,' said the priest, running his hand through his wispy hair. 'I haven't talked to him myself — thought a middle-class voice might make things worse for him, the way he's been. But Zipper and Nelly say he's very quiet, very depressed, rolled in on himself, as Nelly puts it. I don't like putting them in the hostel if they're like that. If you can't exchange a few words or the offer of a fag, some of the lads do turn nasty. When I was in the prison service' — for the speaker, long before ordination, had been one of the eminent prison governors of his day — 'we used quite often to put the ones who got that way into single cells just for their own protection.'

'No single cell luxury when you're on the streets,' said Danny drily.

'No,' agreed Father Douglas. 'Perhaps that's why so many of them are so anxious to get back inside.'

Danny took the photograph out again and looked at it. 'So, basically, he's all mine and Shona's?'

'I've done what I can, for now,' said the priest. 'He can have another couple of nights, but all it will take is a couple of ODs to be sent round from casualty and I'll be in real trouble with that sick bay. Zipper reckons he's fine physically. Weak, but taking soup and bread. I think he'd be better leaving us, quite apart from the risk that he catches something off Misery while he's so weak.'

'Nits, most likely,' said Danny. 'Well, right you are. I'd better talk to Shona. Give me a day or two.'

'Have courage,' said the priest soberly. He rested his hand on Danny's shoulder for a moment, light and cool. 'All shall be well, and all manner of thing shall be well.'

'All manner of things would have to change quite drastically,' said Danny bitterly, 'before my father thought all was well concerning me.'

'Courage,' said the priest again.


Shona walked up to Suzy Darling's. She made a big looming figure in the dusk, its silhouette strangely topped by her star-burst spikes of hair. Even in this self-consciously *haut bohème* region she drew covert curious glances for her big boots and facial metalwork. As she passed No. 33 she glanced in, and saw a tubby little man with receding ginger hair standing at the sideboard pouring himself a drink; just so had her father stood at Christmas. She gave a cluck of amusement, then sobered as she glanced up to Zack's bedroom window, where light poured through his striped curtains and, presumably, some new child bounced on the bed. The uprooting of her parents seemed to Shona an entirely desirable deracination. The mud that clung to their roots was old, exhausted of all nutrition, poisoned even; the risk was worth taking. Zack, on the other hand, had already been moved on once from his babyhood home. He could be, of all of them, the one to suffer worst from this upheaval.

She looked up, troubled for a moment, and then closed her fingers over the folded, much-read letter in her pocket. Zack would be all right. Zack was coming on nicely. Already, days away from his eleventh birthday, he had made a difference. To Danny, in particular; Danny had cried over the letter, sitting in Ishmael's café, and said, 'He wants to know about me. Oh Shonie, do you think that if he knew the lot, he'd still be what he calls *cool* about it?'

'Why not?'

'You know why not. People aren't.'

'I heard a lovely expression once,' Shona said, 'from some famous physicist talking about teaching children scientific concepts like relativity and black holes. He said that there were very few things that children couldn't understand if you could only find "a courteous translation". I really liked that. *Courteous*. Sort of related to things they can hook up with. A familiar marked path into new territory.'

'Sounds like spin-doctoring to me,' said Danny, and grinned, fine arched eyebrows rising. But Shona saw there was gratitude and a new, almost relaxed look of happiness on her twin's face at that moment; and since she loved Danny more than any other human being, she was very grateful indeed to Zachary.

Now she rang the Darlings' doorbell with a flourish, and

greeted James Darling – shirtsleeved, drink in hand – with a blithe, 'Hi! Remember me? I'm Shona.'

James blinked. He had not seen her at Christmas, had not seen her, indeed, since her spiky, scowling image had been all over the newspapers, hands aloft and plastered with excrement, at the time of her shock exhibition in the Hemroyd Gallery ('The stink of decadence reached as far as the Angel' – *Daily Mail*). He held out a hand automatically, a well-drilled man of business, but when the full memory of that exhibition returned, it took every ounce of his politeness and resolution not to snatch it back. But the hand Shona put out to shake was soft, white and spotlessly clean, and the moment passed.

'Well, er, come in,' said James hospitably. 'Suzy will be glad to see you. Were you looking for Helena or Douglas? They're not home just now.'

'Nope,' said Shona. 'I dropped in to see Zack.'

'Ah ...' James, in the relaxation of his evening gin and vermouth, had actually forgotten that Zack was in the house. When Helen had left, after only one night, to take up her abode at the Ferris Home, James had been shocked at the fact that Zack was not going with her; his habitual reflex to being shocked by women's behaviour was to put the whole matter from his mind as fast as possible. When his secretary's researches drew a blank about Roy, he had managed much the same trick. A man had his job, money to earn, his own life to manage. If you took on the weird troubles of the whole world you would get nowhere. But when one of the weirdest figures actually turned up on your doorstep, there was only one thing to do. Offer it a drink.

'Drink?' he said now. 'Name your poison.'

'I wouldn't mind a whisky,' said Shona. 'Is Zack in, though?'

'Tell you what,' said James in a flash of inspiration, 'I reckon he's upstairs with Suzy. Take your drink up there, if you like.'

He held it out to her; Shona closed her big hand round the glass and smiled thanks; then she padded off upstairs, and James, with the air of one reprieved, sank into his armchair and reached for the TV remote control.

Suzy was indeed upstairs, offering to help Zack with homework. Zack, who had no particular intention of doing any that night, was just fending her off – he was not used to maternal fussing – when Shona appeared in the open doorway of the top bedroom.

'Hi, kid,' she said, and he stared, round-eyed with surprise.

'Shona!' said Suzy. She, too, had not seen her much for years, but her woman's eye cut through the bizarre presentation and saw again the moody, arty schoolgirl, Danny's twin, her friend Helen's frequent despair. She stepped forward, and with kindly resolution hugged her. 'Come to see Zack! Oh, that is nice!'

And, indeed, Suzy was enchanted by this heart-warming evidence of some residual family feeling in the exploded Keaney family. But there was one thing to clear up.

'Your mum,' she said awkwardly, 'isn't here. You know she's doing a live-in job for the moment?'

'Mum? Working?' said Shona. 'Gosh, what a throwback. I remember when I was twelve and Zacky was born, her saying she was never going to a bloody office again.'

'Well, not an office. She's, um, in the caring profession.'

'She's up at the Ferris Home, serving food and hosing down the oldies,' said Zack brutally. 'She says at least it's money. You know Dad's gone to live on pavements, and there's rich Yanks in our house, so I'm being a foundling at the Darlings. Left on the doorstep in a basket.'

It took Shona a moment or two to get rid of the twittering Suzy, who was attempting to soften these items of news into something she regarded as bearable. When Suzy had gone downstairs, insisting that Shona stay to supper and refocusing her mind on frozen shepherd's pie, Shona closed the door, sat on the bed and said, 'Thanks for writing. Danny was thrilled.'

'So you know what happened to Danny? Where he is?'

'Y-yes,' said Shona. 'Now, listen up. We've got a while

before Mrs Darling calls us for supper, and I am going to tell you everything there is to know about Danny. Then you can decide what you want to do. OK?'

'OK,' said Zack, and jumped onto the end of the bed away from her, sitting cross-legged on the pillow and regarding her with grave, deep-brown eyes. 'Shoot!'

That night, old Misery died. Roy was awake when it happened, around three in the morning. He slept too much by day, to escape his oppressive thoughts; at night, pockets of white wakefulness appeared when he would stare at the urban glow through the high barred window and trace the cracks on the shiny cream ceiling, incurious and resigned. What alerted him to the closeness of death was the change in the old man's breathing. The two were alone again in the room. Between them a pallid silent addict had come and gone, and his bed now lay stripped in the thin ghostly light from the street. Misery never spoke voluntarily by day, only mumbling mysteriously in his sleep; when Zipper or Nelly brought in his food he put his hands together, as if in prayer, and bowed his head to them in an incongruously Oriental gesture.

'Someone's taught 'im to do *namas kar*,' said Nelly once. 'I had a punter did that, Asian bloke.'

Now his breath began to clatter, and Roy, who had read of the death rattle but never heard it, was alert, sitting up in bed, wondering whether to do anything. Eventually he went to the door and called,

'Hello! I think there could be a problem . . .'

Nobody came; from the hostel rooms beyond the crumbling bathrooms and kitchens in this strange sad building came no sound beyond a distant, indeterminate low sobbing, interspersed with deep murmuring, though he could not tell whether both had the same source. Roy was afraid to explore. He turned back, went over to Misery's bed and bent over the old man. His eyes were shut, his face screwed up in a look, Roy thought, not of pain but of some crushing anxiety, a cosmic worry.

Instinctively he put his hand on the old man's head; the fine hair was surprisingly clean, no doubt washed and deloused by Nelly when he came in, and it was soft, like ravelled silk. The noisy breathing continued, and it seemed to Roy that the blood was draining from the old man's face even as he watched him. The familiar grog-blossom veins around his nose were paler every moment; like a sunrise, thought Roy wildly, turning into clear morning light. He could see quite well by the glow of the unknown street outside. In the pale glimmer, the old man, head tilted back on the pillow, was beginning to take on the severe beauty of a death mask. Then the breathing caught, snagged, and was silent; returned for a moment, then caught again, and did not return.

Roy was sitting with his hand on a dead man's head. So undramatic, so peaceful was this, his first clear sight of death, that his own breath seemed to stop. The inner voice from millennium night came back to him. *A new beginning. Freedom and light . . .*

Absurd. Roy did not believe in any afterlife, not for years, not since the dreariness of school hymns had been replaced by the twanging vitality of student rock and the worldly humanism of the intellectual life. Yet this old man with the suddenly beautiful alabaster face and silken hair did not seem to him a candidate for decay and oblivion; rather a knight on a tombstone, a figure that now belonged to some eternity of— yes, freedom and light. Misery, thought Roy, had escaped.

The door behind him opened, and the tall man came in.

'I'm sorry,' he said, in cultivated tones which seemed to Roy to come from another world, far from this grimy place of rest. 'I heard you call but I was with somebody very distressed. He's going to sleep now. Is it Misery? Has he gone?'

'I think so,' said Roy, struck by the absurdity of expressing even this much doubt. The man looked down, took the old man's wrist, and gently rolled one eye open. Roy looked away, shocked by even this small desecration. Lines from *King Lear* came to him:

Vex not his ghost: O! let him pass; he hates him
That would upon the rack of this tough world
Stretch him out longer.

'Yes,' said the priest. 'You're right. He's left us. God rest his soul.' He crossed himself, then gently folded Misery's old arms on his breast and pulled up the grey sheet. 'Do you mind if we don't move him before morning? Are you all right?'

'Yes,' said Roy. 'Let him rest.' He climbed back into his own bed and drew up his knees, fixing the newcomer with his eyes. 'Please, who are you?'

'I'm Douglas Cantrip. Father Douglas, if you are inclined to that sort of thing. I run this place.'

'What *is* this place?' asked Roy.

'A former small hospital, condemned by the local authority, repaired by volunteers and temporarily available as an overspill hostel for the London male homeless. It is officially part of a bigger charity, which need not trouble you for the moment; most of those who use it just call it Douglas's. Or, the Guv's.'

'Why the Guv's?'

'Because I was a prison governor for twenty years, before I left to be ordained. I didn't intend to do this sort of work at all; I intended to write books and look after an undemanding rural parish. Which I did, for two years. But to be honest with you, I missed my inmates. So I gravitated back to this work, where I was pretty sure to meet some of them or their friends, every now and then. Can you believe that?' The priest chuckled, and Roy felt his face move towards the unfamiliar shape of a smile.

'Was Misery one of them? Had he been in prison?'

'Yes. I've known him for nearly thirty years.'

'Will you tell me his story?' asked Roy, and thought immediately that this sounded like a child's request. He opened his mouth to modify it, but Father Douglas began, easily enough, sitting on the middle bed.

'His real name is Martin Bullamore,' he began. 'His father

was a distinguished orthopaedic surgeon in Manchester, who married beneath him. The wife ran off, and everything about her became some kind of shameful family secret. All the father's hopes and considerable determination focused on Martin, who was always told he would follow in his footsteps at medical school. This was back in the forties, and Martin would have been called up when he was eighteen, only his father pulled strings, so he told me. The boy was quite bitter about that. A lot of his friends died in the last few years of the war. Another cause of friction between them was that Martin didn't want to marry the partner's daughter. Or any girl.' Douglas paused, throwing a glance at Roy.

Eventually Roy asked, 'Was he gay? Homosexual?'

'Yes, he was. It wasn't an easy thing to be in the forties. According to him — back in the days when he used to talk — he did nothing about it until nineteen fifty-five, by which time he was married with two children. He wasn't much use as a doctor, by his own account, and didn't have much of a practice; his father still ruled his life even in his thirties, financing their house and laying down the law about the children's education. When Martin met a young man in the park, that was it. Remember, it was still illegal.'

'What happened?'

'He was arrested for indecency, and given a short sentence. His father cut him off. The wife had a nervous breakdown — no doubt assisted by the father-in-law — and was sectioned in an asylum, where she died. Old Bullamore had the children sent to boarding school and put with a great-aunt in the holidays. He believed that the "taint" was hereditary, and probably came to Martin through his libertine mother. Misery never found either of his children again, though he looked for over forty years.'

Douglas was silent for a moment, and Roy stared blindly at the wall, as if across an endless plain of human sorrow. Then the priest resumed.

'He found it hard to get work in the sixties, and scrambled

his brain with a lot of LSD; he turned into a pretty incompetent and disorganized dealer, but most of his sentences were short ones. I met him in Pentonville, through the prison chaplain who was worried that his mind was going, even then. Those hallucinogens were a pot of poison; half the demented of his generation owe their current state to Timothy Leary and company. But he had long lucid periods. I remember asking him what he wanted out of life, and he just said "to know that my children are not as miserable as I am". But he never achieved that. I helped him get work two or three times in the seventies, and always he blew it. I think he's been living on the streets for sixteen or seventeen years now, more and more scrambled. Zipper and Nelly say that the street kids called him "misery" because it was the only word they could make out.'

'It was a kid, a teenage boy I think, who told me that name. When I was . . .' Roy fell silent for a moment then finished with an attempt at smoothness, 'When I was buying him breakfast in a café. He stole my wallet. The café woman said it was to buy drugs.'

'Yes,' said Douglas. 'They do that all the time. But on the credit side, I can tell you that it was the street kids who kept the old man alive. He didn't have the wit to cover himself up or find a hostel when the temperature dropped; they used to bring him in here all the time, call him "Dad" and give him cigarettes. It was Zipper who brought him in this time, and came back himself into the bargain. He's another bolter.'

Seeing Roy's lost look, he explained further. 'Zipper is one of my volunteers. But he's a recovering heroin addict, and sometimes the methadone isn't enough any more and he has a crisis. He went out that day to score, and found Misery shaking all over in a doorway, and brought him back, and luckily I met the pair of them and headed Zip off from his errand. He was shaky and quite angry with me, but when you came in as well, it gave him something to be proud of, having both of you to manage. Nelly keeps an eye on him.'

'And who is — was — Nelly?'

Douglas looked at Roy carefully, then said, 'Do you truly want to know?'

'Yes.'

'She's been selling herself on the streets since she ran away from the children's home at twelve. She'd been raped there. She's now twenty-two and has announced that she's found God at the Baptist mission. She's HIV positive. It's all right, you're quite safe, she knows how to be careful.'

Roy closed his eyes. Unbidden, the image of Misery's grave, dead alabaster face floated before him. He opened them again on the sight of the tall restful man sitting on the next bed. He noticed how Douglas was dressed: old grey suit trousers which looked as if they had seen more than one charity shop, a ragged-sleeved beige sweater, and a frayed but good cotton shirt beneath it. He wore scuffed white trainers, yet despite this outfit you could never, thought Roy, have taken him for anything other than a gentleman born, a professional man.

'So now — you,' said Douglas, without changing his tone. 'Would you like to tell me your name?'

Roy was silent for a long time, staring up at the glimmering window.

'No,' he said at last. 'I have not done my name much honour lately.'

'Do you have somewhere to go when you leave here?'

'Nowhere that's possible.'

'Let me put it another way. Do you have responsibilities which you may need help in going back to carry out?'

Roy was not prepared for this question. Against his will he blurted, 'I have a wife. And son.'

'Can you go to them?'

'What good could I do them now? I'm on the beach, aren't I? I'm here.'

'You still have yourself. That's what they'll be missing. You.'

For an answer, Roy rolled over and turned his back on the living man and the dead one, curling his knees up to his chest, pulling the sheet over his head. Father Douglas watched him for a moment or two, then pulled the blanket over the shivering form, tucked in the sides and softly left the room.

# Chapter Eighteen

Surprisingly fast, a new pattern formed Helen's life. She woke at six thirty, negotiated a hot wash from the erratic gas geyser, and rapidly dressed, gazing out at the birds which hopped and squabbled on the rooftops in the first light of morning. The process of rousing and where necessary dressing the twenty-two residents took her and silent Marjan the best part of two hours. A handful of them needed no help at all, but most needed some assistance and seven or eight were nearing the point when Mrs Beazeley would, regretfully, tell their families that they must move to a home with 'full nursing care'.

Helen found it awkward to help those she knew socially from the games sessions, especially George and one-armed Henry. How could an old gentleman offer measured gallantries by day to a woman who sponged him in the morning? So she managed to leave them to gentle Marjan or, when she turned up on time, the rather less gentle Janice. Otherwise she found to her slight surprise that she liked performing these small services; the residents, even those she did not know at all, responded very quickly to her discretion and soft politeness.

'You don't have to give me my Mrs,' said Mrs Catchpole, painfully easing a withered arm into a knitted sleeve. 'Janice never does. Calls me dear, or old thing, or Mary when she can remember. Which isn't often, the amount she drinks the night before at those clubs of hers.'

'I just thought it would be politer, until we know one another,' said Helen, pulling the other sleeve round and stretching the cardigan to make it as easy as possible for the painful, stick-like arms.

'Well, it's quite nice really,' said Mrs Catchpole vaguely. 'Reminds me of when I was teaching. Oh, not for years now. The old life does float away, you know.'

'Did you have children?' asked Helen. She was asking a lot of questions during these morning sessions, and not merely out of kindness. There was a pressing need in her to know what happened in the second, final part of life. The part when children, husbands, friends, prosperity all drift away and leave you a withered leaf, at the paid mercy of rough-handed Janices. Perhaps, she sometimes thought, the reason she had so blindly blundered into this incongruous job was because only in such a setting could she begin to find out what the future might hold, and confront its terrors.

'I'm forty-eight,' she said once to Mr Dearborn, who had fought with Montgomery in the desert as a lance corporal in charge of a gun team. 'I ought to be getting ready to grow old too, oughtn't I?'

'No age at all!' snorted the old man. 'And only a fool gets ready for old age. Live a bit, girl! I'd show you how, if I could get out of this chair without breaking something!'

But Helen went on asking, and thinking about the years ahead and how they would always be separated from the years behind by the watershed of financial ruin. The thought perversely pleased her. At last, life was moving on, taking a shape she could speak of. Better to say, in old age, 'before we lost all our money' than to divide life into the time before and after you lost your children's allegiance. Besides, this was a kind of adventure: to live in a garret, work as a menial, drop out of the ratrace of polite middle-class society.

The day wore on, with meals to serve and physical needs to attend to; sometimes she found time to read to one of the near-blind residents, or to run out for batteries or lozenges to the shop on the corner. She tried to talk to Marjan but met only sad shakes of the head, and conversely tried to avoid hearing from Janice the details of how 'wasted' she had been the night before up at the Purple Pussycat in Acton.

At six, after eating high tea with the residents and washing it up, she was often free for a couple of hours, and generally walked down the road to the Darlings' to see Zack. He appeared preoccupied, but not hostile; a little distant and monosyllabic in conversation, as if he were focusing all his mental powers elsewhere. She spent more time talking to Suzy than to her son.

'Shona dropped in to see him, wasn't that nice?' said Suzy lightly. They were in the kitchen, almost like old times, drinking a glass of wine together. Helen was nonplussed and, thought her friend, a little wary.

'Were they – did they talk a lot alone?' she asked.

Suzy started at the oddness of the question. 'Well, I got out of the way – family, I thought. They both came down for supper.'

Helen's mouth turned down at the corners, so Suzy rushed to change the subject, albeit to another awkward one.

'Another thing – it's awful of me, I know, but I have to tell you that I have rather made friends with Tammy Groschenberg. She is such a *honey*—' Suzy broke off and giggled at her own Americanism. 'No, really, she's terribly nice, she was quite mortified about you – I mean ...' Horror-struck, she glanced at Helen, but behind her now habitual pallor her friend seemed composed enough.

'You told her, didn't you?' said Helen. 'About the fake business trip.'

'Well, I—'

'I knew you would, Suzy. Don't worry.'

'I shouldn't have – it was unforgivable, really.'

'Nothing's unforgivable,' said Helen, and a sadness in her voice made Suzy, who could think of no other redress, refill her friend's glass with a slightly shaking hand.

The next night things were better; Suzy met her at the door with a broad smile and, 'Good news! Come in, sit down.'

'What?' said Helen, who had been shaken badly that day by the abrupt death at high tea of Mr Dearborn, erstwhile ornament of the Desert Rats.

'Roy's OK!' said Suzy. 'Shona rang. She said just to tell you that they'd had word from him and he's definitely OK.'

'And?'

'That was it, really. No details. But it's great news, you must be so relieved.'

'Must I?' said Helen. 'Well, I suppose I must. But to be honest, it just all seems like another life. I can't even remember the last real conversation I had with Roy. Our life together has sort of passed peacefully away.'

Mr Dearborn, she thought, had not been at all peaceful. She had not known that heart attacks were so dramatic, such jarring shocks in the banality of a winter's teatime. He had struggled for breath; Mrs Beazeley had been swift and efficient, a nurse to her fingertips, elbowing aside those like his peers and Helen who merely loved him.

Suzy broke into this train of thought, herself upset. 'Well, Zack was very pleased. He's gone out now. I told him to wait till you got home and he said no sweat, he just had someone to see.'

'Fine,' said Helen absently. 'Look, I won't wait though. I need to get back to the Ferris, everyone's a bit shaken up. We had a death.'

'You're off duty!'

'Doesn't matter. Love to Zack when he gets in.'

Suzy was so upset that she rang Tammy Groschenberg, who hurried round the very next morning with a self-help tract called

'Women who detach and the friends who won't let go', excerpted from a women's therapy forum website and printed off on the long-suffering George's home computer.

'I love you,' said Marcus Keaney to Marie Hughes for the tenth time of the meal. 'I've never, ever said that to anyone else, I love you.'

Marie stabbed at her fillet steak – something she had never eaten until Marcus began his siege of her – and said weakly, 'I didn't think any of this would happen.'

'Nor did I. But it has. Marie, Marie, you're so beautiful and – and kind, and – and I don't know what to say, I don't want to give you any of my stale old lines.'

His hair was no longer gelled back, but fell dark and soft across his face; she was almost more touched by this than by anything he said, because it was done for her. She had said, in that first terrifyingly intense visit to his bare smart flat, that she found him frightening. In a flash of brave anger she had said that he frightened people on purpose, with the shiny black clothes and the 'scary hair'.

She had not expected him to go out and buy a light jacket and cheerful yellow shirt – in which he looked slightly ridiculous to anybody who had ever seen him before – nor to abandon the hair gel and attempt a Hugh Grant floppy fringe. He pushed it out of his eyes now to look at her, soft and beseeching as a puppy.

'I love you. Just say you might love me. I'll give you the whole world.'

'I still don't really know anything about you,' stalled Marie, 'except that you made a lot of money with the Internet and that you do drugs and stuff and that you made Mr Manderill sack your dad. That's what Erika said, anyway.'

Marcus leaned towards her, trying to take her hands. 'I told you, I *told* you, when we went out the other night, before you made me take you home, I told you that I'll never touch coke again if you don't want me to, or even smoke. And I've said I'm sorry about that lark with my Dad at Eden.'

'Lark!' She was severe now, although a small treacherous part of humble Marie was not unwilling to have such sudden, unexpected power over such a man. 'It wasn't a lark. It drove him sort of crazy, like you saw, so he blew his whole redundancy deal and they're still going to chase him to write a letter about how he was wrong and then he *still* won't have any money. So that means your mum hasn't got any money either. That's awful! It's not a lark!'

'I said I'm sorry.' For a moment the old cool petulance returned to Marcus's manner, and seeing his lower lip jutting out, Marie thought surprisedly that he did actually look rather like Roy. 'Anyway, he will get his money, won't he? In the end?'

'No!' said Marie with some violence, pulling her hands out of his reach yet again. 'I told you! I made Erika show me the copy of the solicitor's letter and contract stuff. I can't ask her anything any more because I'm getting a really, really creepy feeling that she sort of fancies me. She pushes her tit over so it touches my head when I'm sitting at the desk.'

'Bitch! I'll kill her! Keep away!'

'Don't be silly,' said Marie with hauteur. She mopped up some sauce with the only potato she permitted herself. 'And don't change the subject. The point is, Marcus, what are we going to do for your dad?'

Marcus loved the monosyllable 'we'. He hugged and stroked it inwardly and stored it away to dream of. Aloud he only said, 'I'm out of Eden. You know that. No power.'

'Well, what about your mum, and the money?'

'She can have money. I'll pay the bloody mortgage, sell my shares in Eden straightaway, whatever. I'll lose a packet if I do, but I'll do it. Look, I told you, I'll be good if you want me to be good. Beautiful, beautiful Marie, say you'll come out with me again?'

Marie looked at him, her big, serious blue eyes weighing him up. She had come the other day on a mission to confront a feared enemy, and fled from a sighing pursuer; she had come back twice now at his insistence but still her sense of mission held.

'Did you mean that about your mother? Will you really, really do it soon?'

'Yes,' said Marcus. 'For you, I will.'

'Not just for me.' Marie was beginning to be embarrassed by the ease of this victory, for which after all she had promised no reward. 'You have to do it because it's right.'

'I don't know about right, and stuff,' said Marcus with an edge of bitterness. 'Perhaps I just wasn't brought up very well, or something. And I can't tell you lies and pretend I want to help her and Dad for their own sake. They don't rate me one bit. They never did. They wanted me to be some publisher in tweed jackets, like Dad, and they don't like me or want me as I am. They think I'm a waste of space.'

'They're still your parents,' said Marie implacably.

'Right. If you say so. I'll look after the money as far as I can. But not for them, for you. If that's what you want.'

She regarded him with a serious, level gaze. 'I want you to do the right thing. People ought to do the right thing.'

'I told you, I don't get that. It's another world as far as I'm concerned. But if it's any help I can say one thing that's absolutely true.'

She waited, a light eyebrow raised.

He leaned forward and fixed her with big serious eyes. 'I'll say this. Cross my heart, even if you blow me out right now, I'll make up the money Dad lost over the redundancy. I'll do it because you asked me, even if I never see you again. That's how serious I am. Watch me. I'll write a cheque, I'll give it to you to give him.'

Wonderingly, Marie looked at his handsome, contortedly anxious but suddenly young and vulnerable face. With a leap of her heart she realized that he meant it. She had made a difference to him. A sense of humble wonder filled her. *You weren't made this pretty for nothing, girl,* her grandmother used to say as she brushed the shining hair. *There's power in a beautiful girl, you be sure you use it right.*

'Shall we go round and tell her, then?' she said, and Marcus promptly whistled – very rudely, Marie thought – for the bill.


Tammy Groschenberg was very much enjoying her vicarious part in the Keaney family drama. While the children were at school she would drop in on Suzy for the latest news, and once or twice in the evening had met Amy Partlett, who scared her a little with her chill Inns of Court aloofness, and Rod Partlett, who was much more her cup of tea. In the few days since the discovery that Roy was apparently safe – although nobody knew where – the affair had taken on a more festive, less anxiously concerned, aspect. For Tammy it was the best possible introduction into the society of this small adopted piece of London; she was extravagantly grateful to the Keaneys for having this baroque disaster, and was particularly enjoying a certain drawer she had discovered low down in the living-room tallboy, full of albums and loose photographs of them all from babyhood to around twelve years old. She had identified Shona, as the only girl, but spent a great deal of time poring over the boys' pictures and trying to date them and guess which was which. One in particular puzzled her: it looked like a thin, more beautiful Shona, around twelve years old, with cropped hair, holding a puppy. Only all the pictures of Shona at that age showed her well-rounded, more snub in the nose, and with a cascade of beautiful hair. Perhaps, thought Tammy, she had had an illness, lost hair and weight alike and been rewarded in her convalescence with the dog. That must be it.

She also very much enjoyed pictures of Marcus, a strikingly handsome boy very like his father must have been; in the early pictures he was always close to Roy, in the late ones alone, or standing in reluctant proximity to the twins.

She was poring over these pictures after the children had gone to bed, when the doorbell rang. George was in Strasbourg. She hesitated, then put the chain on and part-opened the door.

Marcus – unmistakable from his pictures – stood at the door with a girl she did not recognize, whose streaming hair shone like a river of pale-gold coins under the streetlight. Her first thought was embarrassment that the photo drawer was open; she clearly could not let him in there.

'Oh,' said Marcus. 'Is my mother in?'

'Mrs Keaney, he means,' supplied Marie. This woman must be babysitting the little brother. 'This is Mrs Keaney's elder son.'

'Ah, you don't know ...' Tammy pushed the door shut, slid the chain off and opened it wide. 'Look, guys, you'd better come in and I'll explain. The house is let, see.'

'Let? This quickly?' Marcus did not quite believe her. Tammy went to the tallboy, kicked the bottom drawer shut rather hastily, and pulled out of the top drawer George's tidy folder labelled DOMICILE. She found the tenancy agreement and thrust it at Marcus. 'See?'

He studied it for a moment and gave it up. 'I see. So where have she and my brother gone?'

'Your brother's been living down the road at Mrs Darling's,' said Tammy, rather proud of her neighbourhood knowledge, 'and Mrs Keaney is staying at the Ferris Home.'

'But that's an old people's home!' said Marie, startled. 'She's not old. She's not ill, is she?'

'No, she works there,' said Tammy. 'Live-in maid and carer, kind of thing.'

'What about the poor little boy? Who's looking after him?' asked Marie, scandalized. 'Is he with his nan?'

The phone rang. Tammy shrugged apologetically said, 'Sorry, it could be George calling in,' and picked it up. She listened, said, 'Hey!' in a shocked way once or twice, and, 'Yeah, I will,' and then turned back to them.

'You'd better know it, I reckon,' she said. 'That was Suzy Darling. Zachary's staying with them but he didn't get home tonight, and just left a note saying not to worry. He took a backpack and some clothes. They think he mighta run away.'

Marie went white, and tears sprang to her eyes; she clutched Marcus's jacket involuntarily. They had never touched yet, on their brief spiky trysts, except when he took her hand in restaurants and she withdrew it. She had feared his touch, not knowing how it might affect her determination not to capitulate too easily to his wooing. Now he encircled her with a protective arm, and she did not resist. It felt right. His arm was warm. She struggled for a moment to remember how horrid he had been to Roy, and how fragile a confidence she had in his moral transformation.

'We'll go straight down there,' he was saying now. 'Poor little bastard. What on earth does he think he's doing? Christ, I bet he's run off to join the grisly twins.'

Marie, who had not so far entirely believed her swain's lurid account of his siblings, pulled a sleeve across her eyes to clear their wetness. In the process she dislodged the warm arm; without it, her mind cleared and she turned on him.

'See what you did to them all?' she said fiercely. 'You and your clever *larks!*'


Zachary took the Underground to Waterloo. This was no particular novelty, although like most Londoners from north of the Thames he had a faint, unspoken conviction that the low land south of the river was somehow foreign. But he had been in the area twice with his friend Sam, once to visit the IMAX cinema, and once for the aquarium.

It was not even particularly strange being on his own, although he did spend much of the trip studying the A to Z street map with some care to plan his route to Shona's studio, whose address he had got out of her on the night she visited. He balanced on the edge of the seat rather than take his backpack off, and once or twice nearly fell to the floor when the trains stopped. This made him giggle, and grin ruefully at amused spectators; on the whole it was a cheerful journey. He was moving on, entering another era in his life: the new age in which he knew about things and there were no dark cobwebbed corners.

At Waterloo he hesitated. There were too many different ways to walk, and he could not understand which way up the map was compared to real life. Eventually he worked it out, and started walking southward. It was rougher-edged down here, dirtier and noisier and less calmly aloof than the London he knew best; for a few minutes he felt seriously unnerved. Then he squared his shoulders and walked on, unnoticed, a small boy with a backpack on his way from school or cubs or homework club. The road seemed endless, but at last he found the turning he had marked on the map; it was not a proper road, though, more a sort of tunnel with narrow pavements, under the railway. Under the tracks. An expression came to him from nowhere in particular, overheard in some grown-up conversation or at some door: 'from the wrong side of the tracks'. They said 'wrong side of the blanket' too, sometimes, and always laughed in a despising sort of way.

He hung back; it was dark in there and creepy, and the street at the far end had scarcer lights than the main road. Then he hitched up his rucksack and walked into the dark. Danny, Shona told him, had lived on the streets for two years. Danny had been on the underside of London; Danny had had much worse things, awful things, to work out and solve, and had done it and come through it, Shona had said, 'like a phoenix'. Zack had liked that. They did the phoenix at his primary school, in a lovely term about imaginary animals, with the best teacher he ever had. It was a bird that got old and stale and sad, then jumped in the fire and came up new and shining gold. And different, he thought; no phoenix was ever exactly like the old phoenix, it couldn't be.

He reached the lights. One more turning. He walked fast up the shabby road, past boarded windows and threatening archways, and found the name. Etheridge Lane. Few of the doors had numbers, and some were nailed up; but at last he found number 27, in wild red paint, daubed, he thought, to look rather like blood in a horror film. It was, Zack considered, actually seriously cool to have such a weird way-out sister; a warm feeling came into him at the knowledge that she had answered his letter and come right up the great hill of London to find him. She would be dead pleased that he had returned the compliment. He banged on the door with confidence.

Shona was asleep. Someone was banging on the door. Hell! She threw off the hairy rug under which she habitually slept, and put bare feet to the cold boards of the studio. Her hard boots repelled her, and she had no slippers. Shivering, she climbed down the open rickety stairs past the garage which lay beneath her studio, and opened the door to her brother.

'Shit!' she said. 'What are you doing here?'

'I've moved out,' said Zack grandly. 'I've come to live with you and Danny, on the wrong side of the tracks.'

# Chapter Nineteen

'Hay-lo!' said Zipper, and threw a bundle down on Roy's bed. 'Here y'are. Gear.' He dropped a pair of shoes on the floor with a double thud, and then something wooden which fell with a rolling clatter on the bare boards next to them.

Roy, who had been in a deep morning sleep, sat up bewildered. The bundle consisted of clothes: the only thing he recognized was Helen's red anorak with the fur hood.

'They come from the store,' said the black boy. 'Nelly chose them. She's good at sizes.' He gave an obscene chuckle. 'She can size up any guy in half a second, right?'

Roy examined the clothes: corduroy trousers, worn but decent; a belt; a white nylon shirt; a dark blue sweater of some finger-tingling acrylic material.

'They're not mine,' he said stupidly.

'You wouldn't want yours, man,' replied the boy. 'Some stuff doesn't wash out too good, right? Stinks. An' you got oil on them too.' He bent, and picked up the wooden paddle which had made the unaccountable noise, leaning it on the end of the bed. 'Nice, this. Shiny, all new. Wossit for?'

'It's a canoe paddle. I thought I must have lost it. It belongs to someone else.'

'You was curled up with it when Douglas found you. He locked it in the safe in his office, an' your shoes. Nobody likes shoes from the hostel store. Other people always got really weird feet, right?'

'Right,' said Roy helplessly.

'An' if you gonna shave, there's stuff in the plastic bag.'

Roy felt his chin. His growth of beard, never strong, was surprisingly thick. How many days had it been? How strange was his state of consciousness, that he had not even noticed it?

The swing door squeaked open with the usual lack of ceremony, and Nelly came in backwards, pushing the door with her broad buttocks. She was carrying a tray. A bowl of baked beans steamed on it alongside the usual break-and-marge.

'Last bed meal,' she said. 'Special breakfast. You cured. God be praised.'

'Yes,' said Roy automatically. He did not feel cured at all; exploring his numbness he found neither hope nor dread. Outside were the streets, the hard pavements, the doorways and alleys that stretched across the great valley of London, far below the safe hill where he had lived so long. Alone among those streets, he knew now, he would perish. He did not have the finely tuned skills for survival of these young people; he was less tough than stout, devout, long-suffering Nelly or sharp, jokey Zipper. He was not up to it, he could not play this game. He was a blunderer, got himself robbed, slept in the wrong places. He would die before he learnt the skills that kept you alive in such a state. *Poor naked wretches, wheresoe'er you are ...*

Yet going back up the hill to Hampstead and home seemed inconceivable; his mind shied away from it. He knew that up beyond the streets, above the invisible trapdoor through which he had so angrily dived, there still lay the old world of family and friends and work and self-respect, unchanged. There were still levers up there that he had once known how to operate, scenery he knew how to shift. But somehow that trapdoor was high above him now, and the thought of struggling up to it and confronting the competent world again filled him with a dreadful weariness. He ate his bread-and-beans, drank his tea, and looked around the derelict old ward with fearful affection. This place, whatever it was, had sheltered him and asked no questions. If he could have died here like the old man, and had quiet Douglas pull the sheet up over him, it would have been a good death. But the bed where Misery had rattled into oblivion was stripped now, the centre one made up for the next inmate, and his own would be his no longer.

When he had dressed, an old instinct from an earlier life as a gentlemanly house-guest made him strip his bed, fold the two hairy blankets and leave sheets and pillowcase in a bundle; for, he supposed, Nelly to deal with. He felt a ridiculous urge to leave a tip. Ridiculous because he had no money any more, none at all.

At last he pushed the door open, and saw that the corridor was not empty now. It held half a dozen men, young and old, universally shabby except for one slim leather-clad figure with slicked-back hair who reminded him, with a jolt of feeling, of his son Marcus. Some sort of altercation surrounded this man, and suddenly the tall figure of Father Douglas burst out of a room at the end saying something loud and angry, something containing the word 'Out!'

The leather man seemed disposed to argue, but two of the others, at a nod from the priest, took him by the arms and propelled him through what Roy now saw was the street door. With a small shock he realized that through all these days of sleep and shivering, he had never known or wondered which storey he was lying on. The room he had revived in was the nearest possible place to nowhere.

When the man in leather was evicted, Douglas glanced along the corridor and saw Roy standing outside the sick bay door, dressed and holding his canoe paddle. He moved swiftly towards him, hand outstretched.

'Good to see you up,' he said. 'I meant to come along earlier, but as you can see, we had a situation.' Noting Roy's bewilderment he added, 'Dealers. Drug pushers. We're a magnet to them, and we daren't be, or they'll close us down. It's happened before.' He took Roy's arm firmly, making him feel instantly safe. Roy had not known how much, these past days, he had longed for human touch.

'If you come to the office now,' Douglas said, 'we'll see if there's anything more we can do for you.'

Roy allowed himself to be led along the passage, past doors propped open to reveal rooms full of rolled bedding and occasional camp cots, in a smell of staleness and disinfectant. Outside the peeling, battered office door, Douglas paused and again put his hand on Roy's arm. The men had dispersed; through the open front door Roy could see two or three of them chatting and smoking on the street outside. One looked very like the boy who had stolen his wallet. As they reached the office the priest said in a low voice:

'There is someone here for you. Someone who'd like to look after you while you get your strength back.'

Roy stiffened. All he could think of was Helen, and how impossible it was to see her, explain to her, or in any way 'talk things through' or be 'looked after' by her. His betrayal was too great, not only in what he had done but in the way he did not really care.

'No,' he said. 'No, I can't see my wife. I can't explain, it's just become impossible, impossible ...' He was shaking, almost crying. He wrenched his arm away from the priest's hand and immediately felt lost and unsafe. He fought a shameful urge to reach out and grasp the hand again. Leaning on the wall, his head on leprous plaster, he said, 'Truly, I can't see Helen now. Just let me out, I'll go, I won't be any trouble.'

'It isn't your wife,' said Douglas gently. Beyond the frosted window of the office door, Roy saw a shape walking to and fro, something nervous in the movement echoing his own terror. The priest touched his arm again. 'It's your daughter.'

The shape was too thin to be Shona. Roy's eyes widened as Douglas pulled the door open and propelled him inside, the firm hand steady on his shoulder. 'Your daughter, Danielle.'

Half a mile away Shona sat in Ishmael's café with Zack, treating him to eggs and bacon. The boy was a little bleary-eyed from a night sleeping across the foot of Shona's mattress, but there was a glint of triumph in his eye, and he had changed his T-shirt for the one his mother hated, the Bob Marley one with 'Won't you help me sing these songs of freedom?' blazoned under a heroic yellow silhouette of the singer. He felt like a freedom fighter this morning. He had jumped across the tracks.

Shona looked at him, and thought how much older he seemed this morning than she had ever seen him before. After ringing Suzy from a phone box to head off any police hunt, and delivering a homily to Zack on the unwisdom of setting out to visit people when you couldn't be sure they were in, she had let him stay the night. The decision was swung by the boy's pleading that it was his birthday in the morning, after all, and he should therefore get his way.

In any case, today of all days she was glad to have company. For the fourth time since they had ordered their breakfast, Shona twirled her knife on the plastic tabletop and said, 'God, I hope it's going all right. I hope Danny's all right.'

'H-h-she will be,' said Zack. 'I mean, Dad'll see that it's no big deal *really*, is it?'

'Maybe not when you're eleven,' said Shona crushingly. 'You'll learn what a big deal some people think it is. Oh shit, I hope it's all right. I wanted to go too, but Danny said no. She said it was her chance.'

She could hardly eat her breakfast, so Zack had the sausage and all the fried bread.

Roy's first thought, as he stood in stupefaction in the office doorway, was how beautiful Danny was. Like a far younger Helen, delicate boned, clear-skinned, with big gentle eyes and a graceful neck. The jaw had a slight hardness to it, a wrong line, which would perhaps have troubled an ignorant onlooker for a moment; the brows were black and heavy. The dark hair was twisted into a knot low down on the nape, and she was quietly dressed in a long, dark-green woollen skirt with some kind of ethnic embroidery round the hem, black tights, flat shoes, and a dark green sweater tucked into a leather belt. The effect might have been dowdy, but for a pink cashmere shawl twisted gracefully round her shoulders.

And across her breasts. The father's eyes widened in shock, then returned to the creature's pale face.

She was looking at him, the big eyes clouded; in them, before he dropped his eyes again in confusion, Roy saw at once his son and a stranger. In that moment a long nightmare died: a nightmare of white bloated features, garish teased-up wigs, spider-black eyelashes, comic falsies, bloody carmine lips.

'I'm sorry,' said Danny in a soft voice. A line ran through Roy's head: *Her voice was ever soft, gentle and low, an excellent thing in woman.* 'I didn't want to spring myself on you when you've been so ill. I was going to ring. But Douglas said it would be best to get it over with, face to face.'

Roy, his eyes still fixed on her, moved sideways, hand groping for the support of a chair. Finding one, he sat down. The paddle lay across his lap.

After a brief silence, Douglas said easily, 'Well, there you are. Danielle has a proposition for you, Roy. I could keep you in the hostel for a few days if you want but I doubt you'd like the company much. Rough diamonds, my boys here.'

'I've got a little flat,' said Danny. 'One bedroom and a sofa bed. It's near the university, at the top of a ratty building at the back of the British Museum. It's cheap because there's been some argument about ownership of the lease going for years now, so they can't redevelop it. Anyway, I'd like you to have it for a bit. I work a few hours a week at the drug rehab centre near Victoria; a friend down there can put me up for a while. I'll be out of your way unless you need something.'

Roy found a voice. 'I can't throw you out of your home—' then remembered that he had already done so, seven years earlier. His voice cracked into silence.

'I've already packed,' said Danny. 'The fridge is full. The heater's on. I can take you straight round there now. Honestly, Dad' – it was, Douglas saw from his discreet corner near the door, as hard for Danielle to say the word as for Roy to hear it – 'it's the best thing. Shona lives in a hideous pig mess in Bankside and, you probably don't know it yet, number thirty-three is let out. Americans. Mother thought it would be best, so Shona says. Apparently there's some stuff about money arrangements, and this solves it neatly for the moment.'

Roy paled, and the great spasm of guilt flowed over him at last, the tide which he had kept back with his wall of numbness.

'Where is she living? What have I done to Helen? Where's – Zachary?'

'Fine. Everyone's fine. Everything's fine. We can tell you when you're stronger. Come on. We'll get a taxi.'

In the taxi, they could not look directly at one another. Sometimes Danny stole glances at her father, shocked by his air of deterioration and desperation. He had shaved, but not very efficiently; his clothes hung on him, and his eyes seemed sunken and dead. She hoped it would be all right to leave him alone in the flat; the greatest fear was that he would walk out and vanish into the streets, for which he was so palpably ill-equipped. A sudden rush of love rose, almost choking her: *my father*. She wanted to kneel on the juddering floor of the cab, take his hands, beg forgiveness, explain why everything had been the way it was. Then the dead eyes, turning towards her, made her look away, feigning insouciance.

She gave a self-conscious little 'Ah!' as the cab drew into her street and said lightly, 'I'll show you how to work everything, but there'll be a mobile number you can get me on, obviously. It's not a bad little flat. Entryphone doesn't always work in reverse, which is a bore; but the landlord's said he'll fix it. By the way, would you like me to send that paddle round to whoever it belongs to? Douglas said you wanted to get it to someone, and I could easily drop it off for you.'

The flat was high among the Bloomsbury rooftops, under the eaves of what had lately been a cheapish boarding house frequented by foreign academics using the Reading Room. The lower rooms were rented as some kind of office on a short lease. A narrow stairway led to an upper landing, off which lay a pair of rooms with the locks boarded over, and a still narrower run of steps up to the old attic.

Here, above the seedy emptiness, lay Danny's flat. It consisted of a bedroom barely big enough for the single divan and a basin, its corner chopped out to provide a minute bathroom; and a larger sitting room with a folding sofa bed, two chairs, a battered drop-leaf table and an alcove neatly arranged as a kitchen. The walls were lined with books, a library improvised with bricks and planks; it gave the room a casual student look, but on closer inspection this faded when the observant eye saw that the planks had been carefully varnished and the bricks sealed against dustiness. There was a faded Afghan rug on the floor and a cheap Indian throw over the sofa, but nothing about the apartment was louche or perverse. Roy, weak from climbing the stairs, sat directly on the nearest armchair and in spite of himself breathed out in relief.

Danielle watched him for a moment, then fished in a skirt pocket – not a handbag, Roy was pathetically and absurdly

grateful at that moment that there was no handbag to face —
for a set of keys. She held it out.

'Keys. I've got a set but I shan't use them.'

Silently Roy took the keys; their hands did not touch.

Danny rattled on, 'The phone will be diverted to my mobile,
so you needn't worry about that, but you can use it to call out.
If you want incoming calls, switch the bell back on — like this
— and arrange with whoever it is to ring in a signal, two rings
and cut, two rings and cut, then you'll know it's for you, and
get it before the diversion kicks in.'

She fiddled with the phone, to set the divert. During the
process Roy heard the soft recorded voice of the answering
machine: 'Danny here. I'm out. Leave a message. Thanks. *Beep.*'

'You still — call yourself Danny, then?'

The strange young woman turned, and smiled a familiar
smile. 'Oh yes. I've always been Danny, all the way.'

For a moment Roy felt that he could have talked more; but
his landlady seemed determined to melt away as fast as possible,
rattling out directions with nervy energy.

'Supper's in the fridge, needs twenty minutes in the oven.
There's bread and some ham for lunch. There's a packet from
the Governor — I mean Father Douglas — in the bedroom. My
mobile number's there, and the number of Shona's gallery where
everyone leaves messages for her. She won't have a mobile, says it
only encourages people to annoy you when they're too far away
for you to hit them.'

Then Danny was gone, and Roy was alone under the eaves.
He went to the window and climbed unsteadily onto a chair to
look out. Like Helen, miles to the north of him at the Ferris
Home, he had a vista of tiles and chimneypots and London
sparrows. He stood there a long time, until it began to rain,
sending gouts of water wobbling down the sloping windowpanes
like tears.

*Poor naked wretches.* He was filled with a deep thankfulness not
to be on the street; and with a sense of wonder when, wandering

through to the bedroom, he found the parcel containing another set of old clothes, a washbag and shaving tackle, and a plain unmarked envelope containing two twenty-pound notes. He went back to the telephone, and began to dial the mobile number; but halfway through a great weariness came over him again, and he put the receiver back on its cradle and sat silent, staring at the wall of books and bricks, the kitchenette and the tearful window, with eyes that saw none of it.

# Chapter Twenty

Years after all this, when the little garret had long been gutted and remodelled and extended into an expensive roof terrace by strangers, Roy could still re-create it, detail perfect, merely by closing his eyes. The days he spent there had the intensity of a first home or a childhood bedroom; unobtrusive as it was, the flat's calm personality wrapped him round. There was consolation in the very floor, whose uneven but carefully cream-painted boards made the cheap African mats sing with colour, and security in the humble ingenuities of the tiny cupboards and the orange-box chest. There was optimism in that little flat: clear colours and clear spaces.

It was long afterwards, too, that he learnt how Danny, through days of care, had laboured to strip it of any personality that might distress her father; how books and pictures and even the meagre store of bed linen in the bedroom cupboard had been examined and edited, anything that might disturb him being ruthlessly culled into cardboard boxes under the sink. Yet however much the owner thought she had taken her imprint off the flat, still a quiet, authoritative personality pervaded it.

Once Roy's powers of observation unfroze, he began to look at the details. The kitchen was equipped cheaply enough, but with good coffee, a grinder, and housewifely rows of pulses and pasta in plastic sweet jars clearly begged from some corner shop. There was decent olive oil in a pottery jar with a spout. The china was cheap but cleanly white; the tiny awkward store cupboard in the corner equipped as a serious cook would want it, with jars of tomatoes in oil, anchovies, spices and sea salt. There was even half a string of onions; and in the fridge a wedge of Parmesan with a grater.

Roy saw these things, but did not cook. He did sleep in the bed, which was an elderly divan but stiffened between mattress and base with some kind of heavy khaki webbing; the sheets were old but clean, and the duvet and pillows covered in plain dark-blue cotton cases. There was nothing particularly feminine about the place, but nothing bachelorly, either. The books were the greatest surprise: row after row of serious Penguins, aged Everyman Library volumes from book barrows, art history and world classics, Dante and Donne, Beowulf and Machiavelli. There were unmatching but carefully grouped sets of Dickens, Thackeray, Orwell, Eliot; and a shelf of biography and autobiography arranged not by alphabetical author but by period and association, as if by a historian.

It was the bookshelf that drew Roy into properly inhabiting the flat, rather than hunching around nervously on its surfaces and taking his meals at the fly-blown cafés below. To browse such a collection was irresistible. Often when he pulled volumes out he found neat faint pencil notes in the margin; at first he thought these were accidental acquisitions in books picked up off barrows, but after a while he saw the same writing often enough to understand that their owner had the lonely reader's habit of writing private notes, holding virtual conversations with the books. In works of criticism more than once the faint pencil drew wriggles down the side and wrote 'wrong, wrong, wrong!' or 'Yes!' In fiction and poetry there were underscorings and exclamation marks and small intent scribblings of *cf-cormorant in P.L., ?bestiary* or *nb ?? Darwin imagery*. There was a programme for Shona's infamous exhibition at the Hemroyd, with exclamation marks against some of the artist's wilder claims in the commentary. There was even, to Roy's jolted surprise, a new and clean copy of a revisionist book on Aubrey Beardsley which he himself had both published and supplied the foreword for at the end of 1999. It bore the Eden sunburst logo on the spine; it must have been the first book after the sale of Handfast. He grimaced, but in this safe, lonely haven felt surprisingly little pain at the monstrous memories which swam, long-dreaded, to the surface.

On the third evening, sitting in Danny's chair with Danny's Shakespeare open on his lap and the rain still bouncing off the window, Roy turned to *King Lear* to check the words of the 'Poor naked wretches' speech which haunted him whenever the memory of grey pavements came back. *Looped and window'd raggedness* . . .

The play fell open near the end, with the King stone mad, wandering the countryside near Dover, led by Edgar. His eye slid down the page, drawn by heavy pencil marks. They ran alongside the King's rant against his daughters' iniquity and the decadence of all womankind:

Down from the waist they are Centaurs,
Though women all above:
But to the girdle do the Gods inherit,
Beneath is all the fiends':
There's hell, there's darkness, there's the sulphurous pit,
Burning, scalding, stench, consumption; fie, fie, fie! pah, pah!
Give me an ounce of civet, good apothecary, to sweeten my imagination; there's money for thee . . .

As he was staring at this, conflicting meanings jostling in his mind, the doorbell buzzed. Remembering Danny's warning, he did not attempt to speak down the aged plastic intercom but went down the flights of stairs to the door and opened it a crack, looking cautiously round. It was Douglas Cantrip, a tall shabby figure with a plastic carrier bag.

'Might I come in?' he said diffidently. 'Not if you're busy, of course.'

Roy appreciated the small absurd courtesy, and led the tall man up the stairs; he had to duck as he walked along the corridor under the eaves, and so easy was the movement that Roy understood that the visitor knew this place better than he did.

'It's a good little flat, isn't it?' said the priest chattily, to cover Roy's silence as they stood together in the sitting room. 'I'm proud to say we helped Danielle find it, four years back. She has a controlled rent for another year, while some case goes on about the lease on these houses. At the moment it still belongs to one of the companies that funds the Trust.'

Roy raised his eyebrows, and Douglas continued, 'Oh yes, business in the community, all that. You may as well know, if your sense of irony has had a chance to return, that the Governor's Shelter in the old hospital got eighty thousand pounds out of the Eden Corporation last year. You've been their guest. Nice, eh?'

And Roy laughed, and laughed, and almost choked; and the mild eye of the priest rested on him while the tension flowed out of his body.

At last Roy said, still wheezing with the effort of the laughter, 'Can I make you a cup of tea?'

'No,' said Douglas, and pulled a bottle of whisky out of his carrier. 'I think you need a drink. And before you ask, no, I'm not in the habit of plying clients with alcohol when they're just off the street. But you are not an alcoholic, I believe.'

'I've been acting like one,' said Roy, morose again, remembering the hazy moments at Eden, the fog and the fury of his protest, the bottle he had left rolling on the corridor carpet outside Alan's office.

'No. I wouldn't say you'd been behaving like a drunk. More like a man in shock.'

'It wasn't just about being sacked, you know.'

'I don't know any of it, not really,' said Douglas. 'Do you want to tell me? It might not do any good at all, but I'm a safe pair of ears.'

'I think I owe you something. Well, a lot,' said Roy slowly. He went to the kitchen cupboard and, without asking, poured two fingers of whisky into each tumbler and brought water in a chipped but prettily engraved glass jug.

'No,' said Douglas. 'Not me. I'm not the hero here. We took you in, we take hundreds in, it's what we do. But we'd only have given you a temporary hostel bed when you got better, and you'd have hated it, and probably walked back out onto the pavement for some privacy. That's what people like you always do. That's why chaps in your position are the hardest of all to help. You see, I don't have it in my power to offer you anything like this,' he gestured round the calm little room. 'Not easily or quickly, anyway. You have your children to thank. Your twins.'

'Do you know what happened to Danny? What we did, how we were?' asked Roy in a low voice.

'Danielle is an old friend. She was nearly seventeen when we first met. So yes, I suppose I heard most of it.'

The voice was neutral, and gave Roy the courage to carry on, his eyes fixed on the shelves of books behind his interlocutor's head.

'Do you mind if we say Danny?' he asked painfully. 'I still can't get my head round – the other way.'

'As you like. Danny is Danny to most of us, most of the time. It's unusual; normally transsexuals in both directions prefer a name that underlines the new gender, shouts it out at you. Even a Hilary or a Francis doesn't usually stay the same.'

'You know others?' Roy was childish in his astonishment, but Douglas only nodded.

'Yes, of course. A lot of them do turn up on my beat, prison or hostel. I'm sorry to say it. It shouldn't have to be that way, especially for the ones with Danny's gifts and qualities. But it's one of those cruel tricks that society plays on people who are outside the normal range. If you're thought of as a freak, you end up living with real freaks.'

Douglas paused, and sipped his whisky, then added with a tone of apology, 'Actually, in my trade it's not fashionable or politically correct to refer to *any* of the clients as freaks. I suppose I came into it too late to learn the right responses.' He smiled. 'But believe me, some *are* freaks. Moral freaks, I mean, people without a compass or a conscience, people with obsessions, people who gladly let sexuality swamp the rest of their personality until they become monsters. They're brothers, of course, and as a Christian I have to keep on reminding myself of that.' The priest sighed. 'But they're bloody difficult brothers to come to terms with, I don't mind telling you. And they're often dangerous, if not physically, then dangerous to your mental balance. Danny is nothing like that, but because of what she was she's had to make her life alongside moral freaks and sexual obsessives. She's lived with people who are a lot less morally serious and a lot less kind than she is.'

Roy was silent. Then the quietness of the room and of the priest made him lurch into confession.

'In my case,' he said at last, 'it wasn't a cruel trick of society that pushed Danny out into – whatever it's been. It was me. And Helen, too, but it was really me that pushed Helen over the edge, by talking about the harm it would do Zachary. I think without my attitude she'd have tried to keep him – her— at home.'

Douglas sipped his whisky and waited.

'So will you tell me something?' said Roy finally, looking hard at the books. 'Will you tell me how bad it was for Daniel? At first, I mean?'

'You should ask her yourself.'

'I can't. I have to be prepared. Please.'

The tall man hesitated, then said, 'Right. I suppose you're right. If you're going to be revolted, it's better you show it in front of me rather than Danny. She's more easily hurt than people think.'

He put down his drink, and began.

'Daniel – the boy Daniel – was one of those curious souls who know, very early on, that they have been born in the wrong body. They know they are women, and are embarrassed and baffled by their maleness. When puberty comes they feel as if they are imprisoned in some terrible shell that gets worse every day. I know a lot of people don't believe in sex-change surgery, and think it's self-indulgence or mental illness or a perversion of homosexual desire. I daresay it is, sometimes.'

He glanced at Roy, who sat motionless, as if afraid. Then he then went on, 'But I've come to believe in it as something that is one hundred per cent real. It just happens to some people – like genius, or musicality. It's a kind of mystery. Gender is not entirely the same as sex, you know. Transsexuals don't just do this thing so that they can have sex in a different way. It's to do with identity. The soul, if you like.'

Roy said in a tight voice, 'I've heard all this psychobabble. It doesn't prepare you for your son – wanting to mutilate . . .' He could not go on.

'No,' said Douglas. 'I see that. Especially perhaps a quarrel-some, clever sort of son, who throws it in your face.'

Roy glanced his gratitude, then looked down at his knotted hands in his lap and said, 'I don't want to go through the gender stuff, and the transsexual rights stuff. If you don't mind. Just tell me the worst. I've imagined it for years. We saw the edge of it when he was at home. Just bloody tell me!' He was almost shouting, and refilled his glass with an unsteady hand, gesturing with the bottle towards Douglas, who gave a slight shake of his head.

'Daniel – the boy Daniel – sold himself. Was a rent boy for a time. You know that.'

'Yes,' said Roy almost inaudibly. 'He came home after the first time and told us. I went crazy. Did he tell you that?'

'She, not he, did,' said Douglas, confusingly. 'By which I mean that the boy Daniel, who I first met seven years ago, never said a thing against his parents, and gave me to understand that leaving home was entirely voluntary, a running-away, rebellious, thing. It's only lately, since your trouble, that Danny's told me about the things you said.'

Roy threw up his hand. 'I don't want you to say them.'

'I won't. You were shocked, literally in shock. You had other problems with your elder son. Shona can't have been that easy either, bless her.'

'It's no excuse.'

'It's an explanation, which is nearly as good for our purposes. Anyway, to be brutal about it Danny was turning tricks on the street for two months or so before we met. I remember this cheeky little rouged creature, sharp little face, that mop of black hair. He looked younger than sixteen.'

Roy's face was buried in his hands now.

The priest went on, 'I didn't scoop him up like some charity case, you know. It wasn't like that; nobody rescued Danny. He came to me. He came to the shelter in an awful week when Adam, another rent boy fresh out of a children's home, got carved up and sexually mutilated by a client.' Douglas picked up his glass again at this point, and took a drink. His hand, steady until now, shook in a slight momentary spasm of memory, and his eyes darkened. Then more calmly he continued.

'Danny came into the office and told me the name and address of the man who carved Adam. They all knew, the boys who worked the arcades at Piccadilly. None of them would go to the police. Anyway, your Danny had picked up the guy the next night' – it was Roy's turn to shudder now – 'and managed to get away from his hotel room with a wallet with ID and prints, and a folding cutthroat razor with the same prints, and Adam's blood on it. He was quite the detective, had all the evidence all beautifully organized in plastic bags.'

Roy opened his mouth to speak, then closed it. In his mind's eye he saw a small boy lying on his stomach on a bunk in some distant holiday cottage, rapt by *Emil and the Detectives*. How few years had gone by, he thought in horror, how short a time before the dreaming child was 'quite the detective' himself in an unimaginably horrible world.

'They got the man,' continued Douglas, 'and convicted him of indecent assault and grievous bodily harm. He was quite a well-known solicitor. Endredy. You might remember reading about the case.'

Roy was staring beyond the priest now, towards the bookshelves; there was a modern paperback copy of *Emil*, he had seen it. With a stab of pain he suddenly visualized the living room bookshelf at 33 Ferris Hill Road, and knew that the old copy, the yellow-jacketed family copy, was still there. So Danny had left, at sixteen, without his favourite book, and had played detective himself in this lethal and repulsive game. Tears pricked Roy's eyes. Not for the assured, new Danielle, not yet; but for his lost son.

Douglas was looking at him curiously, so Roy answered, 'Yes – maybe. Did Danny give evidence?'

'Yes. His identity was protected. After that he was a bit of a hero among the young gay community. Their lives are pretty brutal, for all the camp bravado they put on, and they hate these predators. But I got to know Danny pretty well during the run-up to the trial, because it was important he stayed off the streets for the sake of his own credibility as a witness. So we had him helping out in the hostel sick bay. A bit like Zipper, who's there now helping Nelly. That was the time when Danny told me how it really was. In the middle of the night, after we'd been cleaning up a tramp together, he told me that he was really a girl.'

'You believed him?'

'Yes. He had it all worked out. He used to curl up in the office chair in the evenings, reading my Shakespeare. He – she – talked about disguise, and cross-dressing, and ambiguity, and how there must always have been people who had the disorder. Very bright. But the money for the treatment and for getting a decent life were always going to be the problem. In fact, there were a lot of problems. And Danny has always been an impressively efficient problem solver.'

'Are you saying that he went back on the street?'

'I am saying,' said Douglas, 'that the boy did whatever it took to raise money. It's better that you shouldn't have any illusions about that. Danny won't want to tell you about it, because it's been over for a long time; and Shona's too loyal, and it may be that you ought never to tell your wife at all. Let me be the *deus ex machina*, or the go-between. If you're going to be reconciled to your daughter, I have to tell you frankly that Danny had, and to some extent still has, some friends you wouldn't like at all. People you wouldn't want to walk down the street with.'

'Freaks?' said Roy harshly. 'Why? Why still now? With this,' he gestured round the calm, civilized, monkish little flat. 'Is Danny still a—'

Douglas lifted a hand. He had heard a lot about this father of his young friend, and had been enjoined to patience. He remembered Danny saying, *He's not streetwise, don't load it on him, please, Douglas, you're the only one I'd trust, but I'm scared ... if anybody can find a way, you can.*

'Look,' said the priest now. 'I tried to explain. That's why I started with what you call the psychobabble. It's a hard world when you're born ambiguous. There are middle-class, educated, adult transsexuals who manage the whole business in a dignified, medical, intellectual sort of way. You read about them in the papers sometimes: respectable policemen who become policewomen, academics in Oxford colleges who suddenly reappear under the name of Annette and resume their places at High Table. That's fine. That's how it should be, for people like Danny who have refined sensibilities. But if there's no money and no support, especially if they're young and determined – well, there's a world that welcomes them.'

'Abuses them,' said Roy in a low voice. 'Corrupts them.'

'That too,' said Douglas steadily. 'But I tell you that in that world, among the gay and lesbian prostitutes, the transvestites, the men halfway to womanhood and the women travelling the other way, the SM set and the bondage queens and the auto-eroticists and the pimps and the voyeurs – I tell you, in that world Danny coped and flourished. Intellectually, emotionally, every way.'

'As a tart?' Roy's voice was harsh, almost squeaky.

Douglas shook his head. 'To be honest, I don't think there were many partners involved. In the end there was one old man, an Egyptian, rather a sweet old boy in his way, always swathed in Harrods furs. He took up the halfway Danny and accepted what she said she was. I think there was a good bit of financial support. Danny did three A levels at evening class, and worked in cafés. Soon after the Adam case, she got started on the medication and began dressing as a girl full-time. Three years ago, when she was twenty-one, she left this flat one morning for Victoria station and took the train to Brighton.'

'Is that where it happens?'

'It's a private clinic. Most of the treatment had been at Charing Cross, which is where most of them go. I think the Egyptian friend paid for Brighton.'

Roy sat motionless, trying not to think of Brighton.

Douglas concluded after a pause, 'It was exceptionally smooth and successful. No post-op complications, and the hormonal treatment is a new, very low dose. You have to admit, Danielle does not present any abnormal appearance. She got into her history of art course as a woman; to everyone except the passport authorities and Somerset House she is a woman. She's "out" to her friends, obviously; she doesn't need to be out to anybody else until she chooses to be. She takes it person by person, on a private level.'

'And the Egyptian?'

'He died last year. I think,' said Douglas, 'that it was then that Danielle started really longing to go home and make it up with you and her mother.' There was an unexplored question in his tone.

Roy said, 'Shona told Helen that, at Christmas. We always knew Danny was alive, through Shona. She seems to have been in touch all the time. It meant we didn't have to think about *how* he might be living.'

'Shona's been a rock to Danny, always. I sometimes think she's even cultivated that farouche image to keep her twin company, to be as freaky in her way as Danny was. Did you know she went down to Brighton?'

'I knew nothing,' said Roy bleakly. 'I haven't wanted to know. We chose to be numb to the whole thing. We told our friends Danny was studying in America, and changed the subject.'

'What are you going to do now?'

'I have no idea. I still find it – unspeakable.' The words rolled back to him: *there's hell, there's darkness, there's the sulphurous pit, burning, scalding, stench, consumption . . .*

Douglas looked at him with some sadness. 'An ounce of civet, good apothecary,' he said, startlingly, 'to sweeten your imagination. Danny used to say that was all you'd need. King Lear, you know?'

Roy nodded, stupefied at having his thoughts read.

'But I told her that she had to remember that civet was a very, very rare and expensive perfume in the sixteenth century. An ounce would cost a king's ransom. Like in *Macbeth* – "all the perfumes of Arabia will not sweeten this little hand . . ." I told her it wouldn't be easy.'

'And you're right, it's no good,' said Roy. 'Even though I'm here, taking Danny's home, sponging, accepting how wrong we were to throw our son out and let him lead this kind of life – in spite of all that stuff, it's just no good. The whole thing gives me nightmares. Helen used to scream about knives, in the night. We had to put it all away from us, push it away with both hands, or go under.'

Douglas' sad, steady gaze did not falter. 'Let time pass,' he said. 'There's no hurry, not for anything. Years go by, and the bad feelings wear away and make it easier to see the good ones.'

He changed his tone to a brisker one and pulled out a folded paper from his pocket, laying it on the little table as he stood up. 'Oh, by the way, you probably don't know the system. You're entitled to earnings-related benefit. Or just the basic income support, if you want fewer questions asked. Fill in the form and I'll take you down there in the morning. It's an income. Let time pass.'

# Chapter Twenty-one

Shona's exhibition was due to open in a week. She worked all hours, making up for the long nights and sleepy days she and Danny had spent while Roy was missing. The work was beginning to bore her; she could not even be bothered to spit at the wet wax of the pictures, but flicked water at them from the corner of a flannel, as she and Danny used to do in bathroom battles when they were six.

The work looked fine, she thought – good enough for Julian anyway – and she had written the really important bit, the impassioned and pretentious statement for the catalogue, weeks ago. It would do; it would be her last Hemroyd exhibition, and her good riddance to that world. In the suddenly bright days, she longed to be out of doors, sketching. Sometimes she even startled herself by thinking again of paint; not smeary showy impasto but watercolour perhaps, something delicate and understated to express the mournfulness of the streets she had tramped in the dawn, and their fuggy treacherous appeal at dusk.

She wanted, she thought, to depict the way streets looked when you were too bleakly miserable to go home; and the same streets in the cold dawn hours when you fear it is too late ever to do so again. Meanwhile she flicked water at wax grotesqueries and scrawled blasphemous challenges across them, yawning.

Danny would appear at the studio and sit reading or talking.

She often did this, but now there was an edge to it. The normally serene Danny, thought Shona with surprise, was nagging.

'You could go and see him. See how he's getting on. See what he's thinking.'

'No,' Shona would say. 'For God's sake, give it a few more days. He knows where to get you, and you left the gallery number so he can leave messages for me. Let him be. Let him settle. Douglas will keep an eye on him.'

'I was really careful,' said Danielle for the tenth time that morning. 'I boxed up anything that might upset him, not that there is much. But you know, Brighton stuff, old prescription records, letters from friends. Yusuf's picture, I took that down. I got rid of all the gender-change books, the medical stuff, the Chevalier d'Eon, April Ashley, Morris – even the literary ones that might be anybody's. I brought all my Oscar Wilde away with me, in case he felt uncomfortable with it.'

'For God's sake!' exploded Shona, ramming her knuckles into soft wax and wondering whether to outline them with some theatrical fake blood she had bought in Covent Garden. 'Your flat is lovely. It's the only place that ever makes me want to do the domestic thing. He's lucky to be there, and you've done everything to rescue him. If he's going to accept you and swallow the whole camel, then he's not going to strain at a couple of gnats like old clinic bills, let alone photos of poor old Yusuf in his Harrods mink.'

'I just want it to be ... I just want Dad to think I've done all right,' said Danny, and promptly burst into tears.

Shona put down her tools and came over to the bucket on which her twin was perched, throwing a warm clumsy arm round her shoulders.

'Come on,' she said 'You're just tired. I wish you didn't have to stay at Lillianne's. It isn't good for you, I bet you're not sleeping.'

'Well, right,' said Danielle, drying the brief tears. 'It's a bit of a noisy gaff, especially at night. There are quite a few midnight rows. But the girls are being really sweet. Especially as I'd backed off so much lately. I thought they'd think I was a snobby cow – a boring old bluestocking, Jo-Jo called me once – but as soon as I arrived, it was all hugs and tequila slammers and wanting cosy sessions over the Ann Summers catalogue.'

Shona snorted. 'Girls, phwah! Of course they're being nice, the poisonous old poofs. They just *lerve* having you back,' she said. 'I wish you didn't have to be there, though. There'll be trouble. Can't you stay with one of your straight friends from college?'

'All paired off,' said Danny gloomily. 'You know, the bit where they hover round you in the morning just dying to plump up the sofa cushions and make the little nest bright again. Say what you like about the transvestite scene, they're easygoing about who's in the house. I went into Lillianne's bathroom the other night and got the fright of my life, this guy with false boobs and a beard asleep in the bath with a basque on.'

'Bloody uncomfortable, wearing a basque in a hard bath.' Shona was momentarily diverted, and even allowed herself to wonder whether she could sell the idea to Julian Hemroyd as a living installation. 'Didn't the boning stick into him, where he had his bum on the hard enamel?'

'Oh, there was a duvet under him. My duvet. That's what I was looking for, only I didn't fancy it any more, so I nicked a blanket from Jo-Jo.'

'Could you ever, ever go on the game again?' asked Shona, who by now was back at the easel, flicking bloodstains at the wax. It was the kind of question she could only ask Danny when she had her back turned on her. There were more similarities between Shona and her father than either would have liked to hear enumerated.

'No,' said Danny with equanimity. 'I'd rather be a waitress.' And, fully recognizing the meaning of the turned back, 'It's nearly six years now, Shonie. It never went on for long. I hated it, specially after Adam got cut. And Yusuf never touched me. You know that was different.'

'I know,' said Shona. 'Sugar daddy. Decorative job. But it still freaks me out that you had to do it at all. And Lillianne and her mates freak me out really badly, because they love it, it's a power buzz to them. And I bet they think you ought to be doing it for money, because that's a big victory thing – "Yeah, look, I'm as good as a woman, better, because I get *paid* for being a woman." I hate Lillianne. I wish you weren't staying there.'

'Call yourself a fearless cutting-edge artist,' said Danny without rancour. 'You're practically Mary Whitehouse underneath, aren't you? Hey, who's that? If it's your slimy pal Hemroyd, I'm out of here.'

But the studio door scraped open to reveal Zachary, schoolbag on his shoulder, beaming.

'Hi!' he said expansively in his still high voice.

'Oh, for God's sake!' exploded Shona. 'Not bloody well again!'

This was now the third time that Zachary had crossed the tracks and turned up uninvited; the first time he had slept over, on the mattress, after Shona rang Suzy to reassure her; on the last occasion she had marched him straight back to the Darlings' that night, with instructions never, ever to turn up unannounced again. Now she stood arms akimbo, glaring at her little brother and trying to block his view of Danielle standing in the shadows under the skylight.

'You are meant to be at school!'

'It's Saturday!'

'Oh,' said Shona, momentarily taken aback. 'Well, anyway, you ought to ring before you swan in. Do Mum and Mrs Darling know you're down here?'

'Mum works Saturdays now. And Sundays, when they ask her. She likes it up there better than anywhere, she's totally into oldies. And Mrs Darling doesn't know. She thinks I play in a football team.'

'Zacky, you're only eleven. You can't wander all over London by yourself all the time. And it isn't always convenient.'

The boy's eyes had gone beyond her broad form now, and spotted Danny sitting still in the corner. His eyes widened.

'Hey, is that – are you . . . you look like . . .'

The slight figure rose, and stepped forward from the shadows. Shona, after a brief protective raising of her hand, dropped it and stayed silent for their meeting.

'Yes. I am Danny,' said the low, melodious voice. 'Danielle, born your big brother, now at your service in the role of sister.' A mock bow, a smile, a flicker of anxiety around the mouth.

Zachary looked at her carefully. 'You're actually, sort of – yeah, ordinary,' he said. 'I thought . . .'

'You thought I'd have red lips and a big blonde wig and something frilly on?' said Danny, who was in jeans and a yellow shirt. She smiled. 'Hey, it is good to see you. You were just a sprat when I left home. I'm sorry I lost touch with you and never wrote, but things were difficult. Being born wrong and having to put it right is hard work. It's lucky it doesn't happen often.'

Zachary crossed the floor and held out a hand. 'Cool to see you, too.'

After this neither knew quite what to say, so Shona said resignedly, 'You can stay this afternoon, Zacky, but you go home before dark.'

'It's really, really easy on the Northern Line,' said Zack airily. 'I don't even need to change. That's why I made the plan.'

'What plan?'

'I can come and live with you, down here, and still get to school on time and everything. It'll be cool.'

The twins exchanged horrified glances.

Zack pressed on, 'I can't stay with Mrs Darling. She's not family.'

'But there's Mum.'

'No, there isn't. She doesn't even come round every day, and when she does she talks to Mrs Darling and Mrs Groschenberg. And there isn't a house for us any more, and Mum doesn't want one. I heard her saying that things are perfect as they are, and she's found a way to live that suits her. And Mrs Darling tries to be nice to me, and she *is* nice, but Mr Darling thinks it's weird me being there. They had a big argument after Marcus was there the other night, and I list— I just accidentally overheard Mr Darling saying something about how it was like I'd been dumped on the doorstep in a *basket.*'

'You said you were a foundling. It was your joke. I was there.'

'It wasn't a joke when Mr Darling said it.'

Despite his determined poise, Shona could see that Zack was growing upset. Helpless, she glanced at Danny, who said, 'I know what you mean, Zack. Staying with people where you don't belong can be a bit of a bummer.'

'They're kind,' said Zack, 'but they don't *want* me. They're *sorry* for me, right?'

'And Shona's not sorry for you at all. You drive her nuts and stop her working.'

'But she's my sister, right? So she's in the family. She's sort of *got* to let me live with her.'

There was a silence. Then Danny went across to Zack, took him by the shoulders and turned him towards Shona.

'This boy,' she said dramatically, 'has got a more robust grasp of the idea of kinship than any other Keaney has shown for years. I think we should applaud it. He teaches us our family duty. Like in Robert Frost: "Home is the place where when you have to go there, they have to take you in."'

'What?' said Shona. 'You think I should let him live *here?*' She indicated the bare boards, crumbling plaster and ragged mattress. 'It isn't even legal for *me* to sleep here.'

'Certainly not. But it's time you got a flat. Don't bother with the council, rent one. You've got heaps of money salted away, and you're so not-fussy that you'd find something easily.

Especially round here, or in the Borough. As long as it's Northern Line, for school. Go on, Shonie. Be a big sister. I could come and sleep on your sofa too, and get out of Lillianne's.'

'This is *ridiculous*,' said Shona, but with diminishing conviction. 'He's a child. He ought to be in – in a house. With someone to – I don't know, go to parents' evenings and have tea parties and all that.'

'It was parents' evening last week,' said Zack. 'And Mum didn't come, because some old bloke died at the Home and she was busy. And I don't want tea parties, everyone goes to McDonald's now and I can fix that up myself. And Dad's gone away, though Mrs Darling says he's safe now and not pavementing. Please. Please! I'd rather come and live with you than with Marcus and soppy Marie.'

'Who the hell is Soppy Marie?' asked Shona wildly. 'Oh, for God's sake, let's get down to Ishmael's and have some lunch, and we'll go through all this stuff step by step.'

At Ishmael's, Zack was in high spirits, greeting the proprietor like an old friend. 'This is my other sister Danny,' he said, 'who used to be my brother when I was little, but she changed. Cool, yeah? We're going to all live together.'

'Fine, fine! Good to see you!' beamed Ishmael, and amazement lit his dark eyes as they rested with dawning comprehension on the unconscious figure of Danielle, who was scanning the laminated menu searching, without much hope, for the least greasy item.

'I tell you one thing,' said Danny at last, resignedly putting the menu down. 'It's about bloody time you learnt to fry your own breakfast, twin, then Zack and I could have muesli and live longer.'

'You don't live longer on muesli,' snarled Shona. 'It only seems that way.'

'That is such an *old* joke,' said Zachary, contentedly cocky. 'Danny, can I have fish and chips?'

'Yes. While we wait, go two doors down to the right, into Hammocks the estate agents, and ask for the flat rental list. Say it's for your sister who's a student, that'll get the price range. Go!' And to Shona Danny added, 'We have to get on with it. I just feel it's right. Poor little brat. It isn't fair if we just let him stay up there, and he might even end up in council care if things don't get any better.'

Shona nodded, helpless, and fiddled with the gold ring pierced through her upper lip. For the first time in ages she felt irritated by its presence.

Downriver and far, far upmarket from Ishmael's, Marie and Marcus sat behind a wide plate-glass window looking out at the wintry glitter of the Thames. Their waiter brought salad and grilled haloumi cheese; Marcus waited for him to be out of earshot and pulled from the pocket of his new pale linen jacket a jeweller's box. He had, until that morning, never been inside a jeweller's in his life, still less looked with interest at ornate Victorian settings.

He put the box in front of Marie. 'Please,' he said, 'open it, put it on, say you'll marry me.'

The curtain of gold hair fell over her face as she bent to look at the big ruby, with its corona of tiny diamonds. Her eyes filled with treacherous tears.

'It's lovely,' she said. 'It's lovely and old-fashioned. It's just what I love, things like this. My gran says I'm a real old-fashioned girl. It's not like anything I would have thought you'd buy. I don't know what to say.'

'It proves I love you,' said Marcus. 'Because my first reaction was that it looks like a bloody great jam tart. But then I saw it with your eyes and I bought it and now I think it's beautiful because you're so beautiful. So *now* will you marry me?'

Marie looked up at him, tilting her pretty little chin combatively, giving him a long, considering stare. She looked at his dark eyes, remembered the warmth of his arm, and then forced herself to remember also the aspects of his nature which had first made her confront him. In a flash of insight she saw how it would be all their lives: how she would have to be his conscience as well as her own, and how she would have to maintain her hold over him if she were to keep him safe from his own streaks of bitter destructiveness. She thought of her grandmother. *Use it to do some good.* Then she smiled.

'It's a dirty job all right,' she said, 'but someone's got to do it. Yeah. I'll marry you. But no more horribleness to people, all right? 'Cos that upsets me, and if I was your wife it would be my fault too, and everyone would hate both of us, not just you. I like people to be nice.'

There were tears in Marcus's eyes now, as he reached his hand softly across the table and took hers. 'I will be nice. I totally promise. Marie . . .'

The waiter, who had felt the rough edge of young Keaney's tongue often and had watched him sparring with successive imperiously sultry escorts, gave a low whistle when he saw the young man's face, and said to his colleague as they loaded the sweet trolley, 'Get them! Beauty and the Beast!'

'I think it's *sweet*,' said the other waiter. 'Shall we ring the *Standard* diary?'

'Nah, give them time. We need her name. They'll never give us fifty quid just for Marcus Meets Mystery Blonde. Bit like Dog Eats Bone.'

Tammy Groschenberg was still very much enjoying her vicarious contact with the Keaney drama. When Zack had first run away she had stayed with Suzy until the call came; afterwards she had contrived to drop in often enough to keep herself posted on his subsequent escapes. Suzy was glad to have her to talk to. Amy Partlett, who dropped in sometimes in the evening, was scornful of the whole arrangement.

'You're just encouraging Helen and Roy not to take responsibility. It's a false kindness, I saw a lot of this when I was doing matrimonial work. A friend or a sister or a matriarchal granny steps in, minds the kids, and the couple just spin off in their own directions because there's nothing to anchor them any more.'

'So I should let him go into *care* or something? With the *council?*' Suzy would protest, fiercely. 'How could you say that!'

'It would wake Helen up. She's behaving appallingly.'

Privately, Suzy thought the same, but the form of Helen's appalling behaviour was so unexpected that it took the wind from her sails, and even silenced James. If she had run off with a man, or even a woman, that would clearly have been deplorable but everyone would have understood, as it were, the grammar of the situation. But as it was, Helen worked long dedicated hours at the Ferris Hill Home for ridiculously low wages, and gave it much of her off-duty time as well. To Helen's friends it was merely inexplicable; to Mrs Beazeley a delirious, unbelievable joy. The matron-manager felt with delight that she had gained both a skivvy and a permanent keen volunteer.

When Helen came to the Darlings' she talked constantly and enthusiastically about the improvements that could be made to the residents' morale by word games and something she called Reminiscence Therapy; she spent some of her meagre resources buying collections of old London postcards for them all to discuss in the dayroom, and had persuaded James to give the Home his old computer instead of junking it, so they could learn about surfing the Net. It had taken James all evening to set it up with its own Internet service and address, assisted by Zack in one of his rare fits of enthusiasm; James found himself, haplessly, giving his own credit card number to pay for the connection. But Helen was triumphant.

'Mariette Hawkley managed to e-mail her grandson in Australia today!' she said to Suzy one evening, after a cursory greeting to her own son. 'She'll probably get an answer tomorrow. Imagine what that means!'

'Families *are* important,' said Suzy tightly. 'Talking of which, Zack seems unsettled—'

'Oh, I think he's fine,' Helen had said, unbothered. 'Probably got a lot of homework. It's so good of you having him.'

So Suzy gave up, rather than start a quarrel. She did not even dare ask Helen how long she intended this strange arrangement to go on; and certainly could not interest her in the mounting pile of post which Tammy Groschenberg brought round, much of it with bank or legal logos on the outside. Even when she had told Helen that Roy was safely found, and recovering from flu in a friend's apartment – Shona's suggested version – Helen had not bothered to ask any details or shown the slightest desire to visit him. She had just said, 'Good,' and fallen to talking about the Home again.

So when Suzy let off steam it was to Tammy, who would perch bright-eyed on the corner of a worktop going, 'Say!' and 'Oh my word!' and 'Honey!' in a satisfactorily sympathetic way.

'I am at my wits' end,' Suzy was saying that Saturday lunchtime when Zack was contentedly eating fish and chips with his sisters. 'Shona had to bring him back the other night, that's three times he's run away to her awful studio wherever it is, Elephant and Castle or somewhere – and I think he's probably there today. I rang the school and he isn't *in* any football team, and they were very sniffy about Helen not being at parents' evening.'

'Oh my word!' said Tammy, glancing across to where her own Mary-Catherine and Mikey were playing with Dougie Darling's old wooden railway set. Suzy never threw toys away, but stored them in the devout hope of grandchildren to come. 'Have you spoken with Helen about this? Really openly, sharing your fears?'

'Oh, um, yes,' said Suzy, rather shiftily. 'It isn't easy.' Sometimes her British nature recoiled quite strongly from Tammy's guileless American faith in the healing power of talk.

'She must be feeling a great personal burden of guilt about

the financial situation,' persisted Tammy. 'Sometimes that results in denial.'

'I'm just afraid that James might crack and say something rude,' said Suzy. 'He says he's got an awful suspicion that we're being expected to virtually *adopt* Zachary.'

'Is that something you ever might consider?' asked Tammy, putting the tips of her fingers together to form a tent, like a counsellor might in a movie.

Suzy stared at her. 'No!' she said. 'I like the boy of course, and Helen is my friend, and maybe if he was three or four and there'd been a disaster ... but he's so self-possessed, and he doesn't want to be mothered, and – no, no, we couldn't!'

Nonetheless, the thought upset her for the rest of the day. When Zachary came back, bribed by Shona with a firm promise that she would look at flats over the weekend, Suzy was quite short with him. The boy appeared not to notice, but went upstairs whistling, more blithe than she had ever seen him.

# Chapter Twenty-two

Julian Hemroyd liked to open exhibitions on a Thursday, in the hope of news coverage on the Friday, thoughtful arty reviews on Saturday, and ritual tabloid outrage and episcopal condemnations in the Sunday papers. On Monday, therefore, he was not best pleased to arrive at the gallery office to find the menacing bulk of Shona Keaney hunched over his desk, having been let in by his craven assistant Jane. Jane herself was sitting at the gallery counter, addressing press releases. She looked up apologetically.

'What is *she* doing here? Why isn't she finishing off the waxes?' hissed Hemroyd.

'She did say,' bleated Jane, 'that the exhibition's ready. She needed to ring some people, and you let her do it before, so . . .'

Her employer stamped into his office. He was about to start remonstrating with his artist when her appearance silenced him. Not only was she dressed in a strangely conventional Marks & Spencer navy blazer and pink T-shirt, but her hair had been taken out of its plaits and formed an odd frizz around her face. Worst of all, the gilt nose studs, lip ring, and eyebrow pin had all gone, leaving only fading red marks and, in the case of the eyebrow, a shiny pink Elastoplast. She looked, he thought wildly, like a district nurse with a skin problem on her way to a welfare conference.

In that moment of blank horror all Julian could think of was the number of picture editors who had promised to send photographers to the opening of her 'Blood Sabbath' exhibition on Thursday morning. Could the studs and rings, he wondered, be put back in?

'I won't be a mo,' said the horribly conventional figure at the desk. 'Just finalizing my new flat. You have to move quickly, the way London is.'

'New flat?' said Hemroyd, who was nothing if not cowardly about personal confrontation. 'Nice. Where?'

'At the very, very top of an old tenement. I was a bit reluctant to move, but the light is stunning. It means I can give up the studio, now I'm not doing any more big pieces.'

A horrid suspicion entered the gallery owner's head. 'No more sculpture? No more installations?'

'No. I'm going to draw, and work in pastel and watercolour. Figurative all the way. A whole new direction. Forward into the past, I say.'

'But the Hemroyd Gallery doesn't usually—'

'That's the other thing,' said Shona. 'It's been fun, but this is the end of the road. After this exhibition – it's ready, by the way, don't sweat – I shan't be selling or exhibiting for at least eighteen months, and then it'll be in a different part of the art market altogether. And I'm giving up the masterclasses. Thanks to you, I can afford a creative sabbatical.'

'Well ... well ... so this exhibition is going to be a bit of a swansong. We must, er, make something of that,' said Hemroyd. Fury heaved in his stomach, but his smooth face masked its churning. 'For the launch,' he continued ingratiatingly as she turned back to her notepad, 'I had been thinking of a photo opportunity in the old church down the road, with you under the stained-glass windows with a brick, sort of ironic ...' His voice faded. The way she looked this morning, a picture of Shona with a brick in a church would suggest only a keen member of the Mother's Union promoting the rebuilding fund. How dare she drop the punk look, now, just when he needed her to be at her very worst behaved!

But she was more treacherous even than that.

'No,' said Shona. 'I meant to mention about photos. The work's finished, and you've got the catalogue notes; but no personal publicity. I'm going to be looking after my little brother for a while, and I don't want him embarrassed at school. Apparently he got teased quite a lot over the shit exhibition. Anyway, since I'm changing direction it's better that I disappear, the sooner the better. I might exhibit under a new name next time.'

Hemroyd considered. *Reclusive artist . . . a vision of terrifying post-Christian change speaking through the bleak melted eloquence of candle wax and blood . . .* Maybe he could suggest a nervous breakdown brought on by the sheer intensity of her creativity.

No, it wouldn't do. He must have pictures. Damn the girl! Aloud he said, 'Oh . . . is that your last word on the subject, sweetie?'

'Yes,' said Shona. 'I'm glad you grasp that, Julian.'

They looked at one another with pure hate; the hate that can only arise between two commercial allies whose profit-time has finally run out.


Danny saw the flat on Monday evening, when Shona had signed the lease. The stairs were formidable, but the view and the light were enough reward. There was a matchbox of a bedroom for Zack, a studio bedsitter for Shona, and an L-shaped kitchen-diner with enough room for a sofabed to unfurl occasionally in the sitting part of the L. It bore signs of recently evicted and none-too-careful tenants, but it would do. Shona could afford the rent from the tax-free income on shares which she had, with unexpected canniness, bought when her first work set the London chattering classes aflame. For the rest, she would do some teaching and, she said airily, 'draw every damn benefit that the kid entitles me to'.

Danny roamed around, opening crooked cupboard doors and testing the windows for leaks. 'This is just so weird,' she said approvingly. 'The Keaneys, all scattered across the rooftops of London. Dad's up under the rafters in my flat, Mum is – according to Zack – living in some sort of Victorian garret at the Ferris Home, and now you're going to be perched up here.'

'So *you* can now get out of Lillianne's fetid basement. You can't be the only underground member of the Flying Keaneys.'

'Yes,' said Danny with a shudder. 'I think you're right. You should have heard the racket last night. Jo-Jo had some kind of fight; he's off his face most nights. Screaming the odds, sobbing, scratching when you try to get him to bed.' She held out a forearm with long, angry red marks. 'I wouldn't mind a week or so here on the sofa, but I'm starting to miss my books a lot. Oh please, Shonie, go and see Dad. I've shot my bolt, I can't go and see him if he doesn't ask. But if he still never wants to see me again, then I'll just cut my losses and have my flat back, and we'll have to find him somewhere else to go.'

Shona looked at Danielle and said sympathetically, 'You're losing heart, aren't you?' She was wearing jeans and a pale blue sweater instead of her usual wildly flapping dungarees and donkey jacket; her twin noted with interest that Shona was not, in fact, as large as she had always seemed to be. The hair was growing too; and that was a definitely ornamental feminine-type belt. Goodness, thought Danny with an unexpected moment of laughter that nearly choked her, what we could be seeing here is the *second* Keaney sibling to abandon masculine attire and get dragged up. Next stop, Marcus in a tutu.

Marcus was on her mind for once, because the three of them had discussed him avidly over their Saturday lunch. Zack painted a portrait of the relationship with Soppy Marie, as he disgustedly called her, which had stupefied both Shona and Danny.

'But he's such a *confirmed* callous bastard. You mean he

came round again and offered to help Mum and Dad? With money?'

'I told you. Marie made him. She said it was family duty, and people had to look after each other. She got brought up by a granny or something when her mother ran off, so she knows all that stuff.'

'But Marcus *offered*? He went to see the *Darlings*?'

The pair of them had marvelled while Zack ate his food and much of theirs. The boy thought they were making altogether too much of it; in his brief experience, grown-ups were always changing their minds about their relatives. It was what they did. Look at Dad, swanning off without even saying goodbye; or Mum, one minute flapping around designing bathrooms and going on about how you had to have good wallpaper if it was going to last twenty years, and then without warning bogging off to live in an attic in a wrinkly-home and letting some Americans with big teeth move in. Or the whole thing about Danny, leaving home at sixteen just because he said he was a girl really. Now Marcus had changed his spots as well. So what? Zack had expressed these views loudly when he grew bored of their discussion, and the twins had teased him greatly for his pains.

Now Danny was dragged back from thoughts of Marcus, and of Zack's comfortingly phlegmatic reaction to emotional drama, by Shona's repeating the question.

'Are you losing hope already? I always thought Dad would come round and see sense. I still think he will. And if he does, Mum will. And if he doesn't, we'll start from the other end by going to see Mum. In a sense, them splitting up is good. They reinforced each other in being so stubborn about you. Divide and rule.'

Danny reverted to her theme. 'Dad hasn't rung. Douglas hasn't rung. What's going on up there?'

'Douglas will ring if there's anything to ring about. Meanwhile, for God's sake let's rent a van and go to IKEA for some furniture.'

Danny brightened at this practical thought. 'Why spend money renting? You can buy a whole row of cupboards for what it costs to rent a van. We'll use Lillianne's.'

'It's full of S and M gear and black velveteen mattresses, isn't it?'

'No!' said Danny crushingly. 'That was years ago. She's a partner in this interior decorating thing now — she could do this place up for you dead cheap—'

'Absolutely bloody not,' said Shona. 'White paint and bland Swedish chairs only. I'm not having Zack live in some postmodern ironic brothel theme, full of MDF screens with lace-edged grope holes bored through them.'

'Talking of which,' said Danny smoothly, 'is innocent little Zack coming to your opening on Thursday? "Blood Sabbath", is it?'

'No,' said Shona, irritated. 'He's seen the stuff, and I've explained that it's pretentious crap but that it's the last lot, and it helps pay the rent. He knows the score.'

'He'll come, you know. He'll run away from school and come. He's rather proud of you these days.'

'Let him try. Insubordinate brat!'

The twins, their spirits lifted by the prospect of a bit of home furnishing, talked on. By the time they locked up the rented flat and walked back to the studio, they were both cheerful. They went to sleep, head to tail on Shona's big mattress like when they were children, in the jaunty conviction that the Roy business would work out fine in the end. It was optimism, after all, that had kept them going through the worst parts of their twenty-three shared years.

Julian Hemroyd had a meeting on Tuesday morning with a freelance searcher after stories, a friend from his heyday in public relations. This friend, a pale-eyed disdainful young man called Clement, often fulfilled the role of unattributable go-between when there was sensitive information to be fed to journalists about one of the gallery's artists. It was Clem who had leaked Maurizio Greer's old conviction in Australia for handling child pornography, just in time to sell the last few lingering papier-mâché figurines on the back of the scandal. Julian had been outwardly horrified by the publicity, and sent Maurizio a graceful note and a bunch of flowers. It was Clem who had helped Julian to punish the bondage artist Emma Steerby for breaking her contract with Hemroyd's by passing to the *Daily Mail* the humiliating fact that she still took an allowance of one thousand pounds a month from her father the bishop. Julian had pretended to be deeply shocked by this story too.

Now he said to Clem, 'You know the chap who lay in the doorway of Eden Corp, shouting the odds from a cardboard box or whatever? The sacked chap, Roy Keaney? Sacked by his own son, the whiz kid?'

'Oh, vaguely. Two-day wonder, never heard anything more of it. That creep Manderill is quite clever at stopping scandals. Didn't the whiz kid leave the company himself anyway?'

'Yes. Well, the man on the pavement, he's Shona Keaney's father.'

Clem was unimpressed. Fathers were little help to him in his trade. He had expected a great deal more mileage out of Emma Steerby's episcopal parent than he got. It seemed that these days, incongruous parentage was not enough to grip the public imagination. In an age where nobody paid much attention to what their father wanted them to do, it was becoming commonplace for the offspring even of bishops to turn out extravagantly louche.

He sniffed and waved a dismissive hand in the air. 'Might be worth a par in the diaries, that's all.'

'There were good pictures of the guy ranting in his sleeping bag.'

'Wino pictures ... I dunno.'

'But obviously, her brother's the whiz kid, that's another thing.'

'Yeah, but he's gone quiet, too. I'm sorry, Jules, I'll do my best but it's not quite the business.'

'She's got another brother. She said she was going to look after him for a bit. That's why she won't do new pictures.'

'So is the other brother weird?'

'Dunno. She said he was a kid.'

'All right. I'll ask one of my boys to look around a bit. But if it's just some sad-fuck worthy business about her minding the kid because the mother's sick or something, nobody'll touch it. The PCC gets very shirty about kids and privacy. But I'll ask, there might be something funny – child art prodigy or whatever. Where does Ms Keaney hang out? Who does she eat with?'

Julian shuddered theatrically. 'Greasy spoon cafés nobody's ever heard of. There's a Turkish one near her studio, down past Waterloo. She tried to get me to have lunch there once, but it was too horrible. Ismails, or Mohammed's, or something. She said it was her regular.'

'Okeydoke. But I can't promise anything. Perhaps if they all have sex with fried eggs, or something, that might amuse the *Sun*. But *Sun* punters don't buy expensive artworks, do they?'

'No,' said Hemroyd. 'But the others'll pick it up if it's shocking enough. You know my motto. Kick up enough dust, and some of it's bound to be gold dust.'

The 'boy' sent down to the café by Clem was an ambitious young man who dreamed of a billet on a broadsheet diary column. He was uninspired by the errand, and fastidiously repelled by Ishmael's tea slopped in the saucer. But when he asked, for form's sake, about the brother Shona had taken up with, Ishmael had things to tell him which brightened up his day considerably.

Later that night this talented boy rang his employer and did credit to his expensive public-school education by saying the single word: 'Eureka!'

# Chapter Twenty-three

After several long, healing days and quiet evenings with Douglas and the whisky bottle, Roy made a decision and rang Danny's mobile.

Shona confused him by answering it; her voice was not 'gentle and low, an excellent thing in woman', but more on the lines of a nautical foghorn.

'Dad. Good. News for you: Zachary's going to stay with me for a bit. Mum says OK, but I suppose you've got a say in it. I've got a flat, it's on the Northern Line, he can get to school in half an hour. And you won't be beholden to James and Suzy Darling.'

Roy, having nerved himself for Danny, was unnerved again by this blast of practicality, and indeed by the mention of Zack. His guilt about this youngest, often forgotten son was so great that he had not yet even examined it himself. He had lived through these last days very deep in the past. Although Douglas had not returned to the subject of Danny's last seven years, they had wound themselves through all Roy's thinking and especially through his reading: the bones of Daniel-Danielle's history were fleshed out into personality by the very choice of books on the shelves, by scribbled notes down margins and the pages where each volume — fiction, philosophy, poetry, devotion — most fell open.

Moreover he had thought more steadily and deeply during these past days than at any time since he was a student himself. As an adult – as a man of letters, a publisher – Roy had believed himself to be in the more thoughtful sector of humanity. He often quoted the line about the importance of leading an 'examined life'. Now, however, he saw how much the small preoccupations of daily life had swamped and adulterated real thought: the house, the garden, health, children, the journey to work, finances, deals, working lunches, clashing personalities, newspapers, television, rumours, gossip, e-mails, letters, social awkwardness, social ambition . . . In this cacophony, how could you ever think?

Over and over, his thoughts came back to the mysterious theme of personality: of the soul, the essence beyond the physical, the enduring invisible core of the human animal. Were souls male and female? Or were the very concepts of male and female too low and biological to affect pure spirit? What had genitalia to do with conscience, worship, aspiration? Or perhaps – here the battered row of angelology took his eye – could it be that the earthy physical characteristics we call male and female were just a reflection of higher, bodiless archetypes: masculine and feminine, Ares and Aphrodite, Mars and Venus, Yin and Yang? If so, could you truly be born with a feminine essence trapped in a biologically male body, or vice versa? And if that happened, how could you live?

Well, you could live all right. Find a *modus vivendi*, reject the social demands of your biological gender, be a tomboy or a pansy, embrace homosexual loves, even cross-dress. That way you got dandies and exquisite fops on the one side, dungaree'd clumpers like Shona on the other. Roy was struck, reflecting on it for the first time, by Father Douglas's theory that Shona's alarming lack of femininity might have been a pose all these years, a deliberate mirror image of her twin's dilemma. Did she dabble in excrement and set out to shock and upset people simply in order to make Danny's journey a less lonely one?

At the thought his eyes filled with tears for her: his little Shonie, the cuddly baby girl with arms ever upstretched, who lay in his lap sucking her thumb, or swirled up her skirts with three-year-old sauciness to display the matching knickers. She must have been ten or eleven before she abruptly rejected dresses for jeans, cut her hair off ragged with the kitchen scissors, and began to shock on purpose. Was it for Danny?

And where was Danny in those memories? A solemn small boy, always reading; a wistful figure, Roy thought now with surprised new perception, a boy who hung back in company, nervous of bigger boys, but then became suddenly impassioned about something quite unexpected – a visit to the National Portrait Gallery, a new story, a book, a teacher who had opened some intellectual gateway. Did he cuddle Danny enough? Did Helen? Or did something hold them back all his life, some wrongness which they could not put a name to?

He could not remember. Apart from odd fleeting visions of the boy outstretched, ignoring holiday sun for *Emil and the Detectives* or a Narnia book, any happy memories Roy might have had were blocked by the one looming moment.

It was two days after Marcus discarded Balliol and parental influence, sneering defiance and contempt at his father. It was a bad, bad week. But how fair was it, after all, to expect a fifteen-year-old to be sensitive to the fact that his parents were having troubles elsewhere? Could Daniel have begun to understand how much Marcus's rejection meant to Roy, and how terrible it was to Helen that her husband and son were at odds? And on their part, would they have listened more closely and sympathetically to Daniel if he had sprung his shock at a better moment?

Roy could not know what might have been. He could only remember, with awful clarity, what was. The parents had been sitting in the kitchen with a glass of wine, agonizing together about Marcus's future; Daniel had come downstairs wearing his sister's school skirt and announced his intention of changing sex.

'I'm a girl. I've been a girl since I was born. I've read things about it in the library. I can't have the operation for a few years legally, but I can start hormones more or less now, or when I'm sixteen. It's better if I live as a girl straightaway.'

Danny's voice, Roy remembered with a wince, was breaking; the speech went from growl to squeak. He had two spots, one on his nose and one on his chin; he had lately begun to stroke his chin uncertainly, as boys do when they sense the coming stubble of adolescence. At the time these things had irritated him, as they had before with Marcus; Roy, never entirely secure in his own physical appearance, had found that the gawky gracelessness of adolescent boys seemed to drag him backward to unlikeable periods of his own life. Daniel's entrance in a pleated grey skirt, tights and blouse inflated the father's habitual unease into stormy rage; all the rage which Marcus had escaped by drawling his defiance on the phone and ringing off.

Then Helen had wept. Between the father's anger and the mother's tears, Daniel had – Roy saw now – kept a remarkably steady head, trying in a rapid gabble to explain all that he had learned about transsexual nature and its remedy. Perhaps he spoke in too much detail of the remedy, and with too much enthusiasm; after all, the boy must have been researching it furtively in the borough library for years. The timing, too, was explicable: he must have been driven to new levels of desperate passion as each new fetter of masculinity hung itself on him – the encroaching stubble, the unruly member, the growling voice.

Perhaps the trouble was that Danny had thought about it alone for so long, and explored the subject so much that in his childishness he forgot to allow for what the shock would mean to parents asked to confront it all at once. The treatments which, to him, seemed like a necessary scouring clean of his body from the accretions of masculinity, a God-given escape route from his dilemma, were to his parents nothing but grotesque horrors. Certainly he had spoken that day with horrid familiarity of drugs and hormones, testicle removal and the conversion of penis to vaginal walls.

Well, well, thought Roy. It was partly their fault. He and Helen had always believed, or so they thought, in openness about the body and proper biological terms. Daniel was only speaking a language he thought would engage them, and trying to prove his credentials as a genuine transsexual rather than some pervert or prankster. He had said, 'I'm not Boy George, you know, it's not some gay pose thing,' and plunged back into explanation; and all of this with his spots and his growl and his pleated school skirt. No wonder, thought Roy bitterly, that this memory eclipsed all the others, and had in its turn been blotted out by years of denial. The tragicomic horror of it was not to be borne.

Or perhaps it was the guilt that made him draw the curtain over it for so long. They should have gone with Danny to a psychiatrist, asked for assessment, sympathized with the feelings at least, acknowledged the possibility that he was right. They should not have shouted and wept. There should not have been tight, difficult weeks of saying nothing, weeks when Shona in turn, in gallant sympathy, became silently rebellious in every small thing.

Finally on the list of his self-indictments Roy accepted that when Danny came home from a foray to the West End with his defiant boast of having sold himself, in Shona's school uniform, there should have been at the very least an attempt to claw back parental responsibility. He was only just sixteen. It was a criminal offence. He was standing on the edge of an unspeakable abyss. Their son could have been dead, or drug-addicted, within months. After the first terrible evening, Father Douglas had not talked any more about the life of the street boys, but Roy had visited them in nightmares every night since.

It was any parent's duty to drag a child back from such a fate, but the Keaneys had not risen to their duty. Helen had clutched Zachary and sobbed over and over again that he must never know about it, and Roy had told Daniel, in cold tones he could hear in his head today, that unless he returned instantly and absolutely to the normal state of a decent schoolboy and never mentioned any of his filthy ideas again to anybody, he could get out.

So Danny had gone back to the streets, back to the friends Douglas mentioned – the man who called himself Lillianne, the little Adam who was castrated by some madman, all the hidden horrors of the West End arcades. And Roy and Helen had remained safe up on their northern hill with Zachary and the shocked, angry Shona, pretending all was well. They had paid the price, Roy thought, in seven years of increasing numbness and despair. He had really believed, poor sap! that he never thought much about his vanished second son. He had run with the herd, focusing all his semi-comic displays of paternal irritation and resigned disapproval on the waywardness of Marcus and Shona.

Now, in the high, quiet little flat above Bloomsbury, Roy saw that not a day had passed in which he and Helen were not, in a great way or a small one, crippled by the history of Daniel.

So today he had telephoned, to take a first tentative step back into the maze and search for its heart, and his. Hearing Shona's voice paralysed him momentarily, reminding him of Zack and Helen and the financial and domestic impasse into which, emotionally blind and maimed, he had stumbled, dragging them all behind him.

Helplessly he said, 'I rang to speak to Danny.'

'Good,' said Shona. 'She's out, buying sheets. Would it be better if I just told her to come round?'

'Yes. Er, if she would.' Roy put the phone down, and looked around the little flat. Soon the invisible Danny who haunted it, and him, night and day, would be joined by the real one. His child. He could say that, and said it aloud. 'My child.' Not son, not daughter. Just child, with the right which all children have, to be acknowledged.

✳    ✳    ✳

Shona put down Danny's mobile and smiled, her heart hammering. It was happening. At last, at last, it was happening. The thaw was coming, the springtime. Things would move, the family unfreeze; the dice would roll, the players start to journey once more across the chequered board to win and lose, laugh and curse.

When she heard Danny's light step on the stairs she ran to the banister outside her door and shouted, 'Dad rang! For you! Wants you round there! And Dan, he said it, he said *she!*'

# Chapter Twenty-four

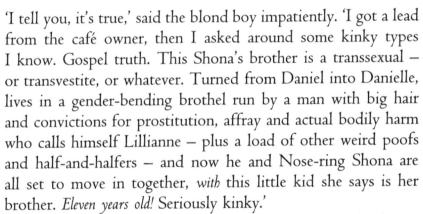

'I tell you, it's true,' said the blond boy impatiently. 'I got a lead from the café owner, then I asked around some kinky types I know. Gospel truth. This Shona's brother is a transsexual – or transvestite, or whatever. Turned from Daniel into Danielle, lives in a gender-bending brothel run by a man with big hair and convictions for prostitution, affray and actual bodily harm who calls himself Lillianne – plus a load of other weird poofs and half-and-halfers – and now he and Nose-ring Shona are all set to move in together, *with* this little kid she says is her brother. *Eleven years old!* Seriously kinky.'

Clem considered, pursing his little mouth. 'It's a lot better than just the old guy on the pavement being her father,' he said judiciously. 'But actually even the old-guy story just got better, because there was a rumour going round yesterday about the son, Marcus Keaney, the whiz kid who threw him out of Eden.'

'What?'

'New mystery girlfriend. Ring in box passed across table at the Riverbank. Virtually down on one knee. Hearts and flowers. The old girlfriend was that Russian witch Irena Sodoff, or whatever she's called. She's bloody good copy herself. The *Mirror* rang her and she didn't even know about the new girl. It was quite funny.'

'So,' the younger man frowned, counting Keaneys on his

fingers, 'is the Marcus guy on speakers with the gender-bender and the shit-carver? Or are they on the mad old ranter's side? And where's the mother in all this?'

'A family at war,' said Clem reflectively. 'A parable of today's fractured society . . . sackings, streetwalkers, society blondes and sexual ambiguity . . .'

'And in the middle of it all this little kid – with his face bleeped out, obviously.'

'But he'd be identified automatically if we're identifying the family.'

'Public interest. For his own protection. We Had No Option But To Lay Bare All The Facts To A Concerned Public. The Corruption Behind The Trendy Art Establishment.'

'Yeah,' said Clem. 'I like it. And any paper would get away with it, no question, if the guy really is a sex-change tart and the boy really is eleven. The only thing is,' he frowned, 'Julian Hemroyd might think it's a bit near the knuckle. I'm not sure whether it'll actually sell any artworks.'

'Truth must out,' said the young man piously, rubbing two fingers together. 'What do we need most, Julian Hemroyd or good stories?'

'A fair point, crudely made. Tell you what, if you can organize a pic of the transsexual guy in a skirt, preferably kissing off a punter, we'll do it. That'll make it OK about the kid.'

'Magic.'


Danny was due to move her bags out of Lillianne's basement and into Shona's flat; she had folded skirts, jeans and sweaters in her methodical way and was intending to go straight back and pack them while that unruly household was still safely asleep. But the message from her father made her dump the parcel of bedclothes she had just chosen for Zack and run straight down to the bus stop, long dark skirt flying, hair escaping its pins to ripple over her collar as she swung herself aboard a moving bus. It got stuck in traffic on Kingsway, so she jumped off again and ran up the road. When she got to the familiar doorway, she was thoroughly out of breath, and sat on the bottom step for a moment, wheezing.

'Why do I – *whoo!* – care so much?' she said aloud. 'Why on earth? Everyone else my age – *huff* – doesn't give a damn about parents.'

A passing woman with a leather music case, beaky and academic, looked down kindly at the breathless figure on the step. Students! she thought. The same all down the ages. The thin girl looked up at her and smiled. 'Sorry. Talking to myself.'

Danny relished these tiny, easy encounters; it was why she did her household shopping in the smallest and most personal of market stalls and corner shops. She loved the gentle, friendly anonymity of the city, and the triumph of being just another young woman with a straw basket, making small talk about not squashing the raspberries. She had learnt, through the years of gradual transformation, to spot the moment when someone suspected that she was not a woman born; these days it hardly ever happened. Danny thought to herself happily that she was one of the lucky ones; short of stature, slight of build, clear of skin, she had the option of being discreet and anonymous. Just a young woman, no more or less.

After a moment she got up, and rang the bell. Rather to her surprise the entryphone spoke: 'Come on up!'

'You've fixed it!'

'It was only a loose wire,' said the disembodied paternal voice. 'Douglas and I tracked it out to the corridor.'

Men, thought Danny, are good at such things. I never was. The thought was a balm to her. She climbed the stairs two at a time and found her father on the landing, silhouetted against the skylight. Awkwardly, he led her in.

'I feel terrible, welcoming you to your own flat. You should have kept some keys, at least.' He had been indescribably touched, at the end of their last meeting, that as she left she had changed her mind, and put her own set of keys down by the phone without comment. He had not noticed it until she was gone.

'I wanted you to feel safe,' said Danny now. 'I never feel safe unless I've got both sets of keys.'

He made her tea, and offered biscuits; their eyes did not quite meet. Then Roy crossed over to the high window and, with his back to his child, said, 'I wanted to say sorry. And I wanted to say that I think I understand better than I did.'

'I'm sorry too. Seven years on, I've got a better idea about how hard the whole bit is for people to take. I've learned to break it much more slowly, and skip the biology lesson. Even so, it's lost me friends at college once or twice. I rushed you.'

'That was no excuse. You were a child. If we'd got you help, from home ... if you'd been able to stay safe at home ...' Roy could not go on. He turned, though, and looked directly at Danielle. Those quiet, thoughtful dark eyes, he thought, had seen things he never would, not outside some perverse *Grand Guignol* cinema film or late-night television shock show. That slight figure had walked upright through horrors, and he had sent her there.

Danny did not deny it. Roy could not have borne it if she had made light of her exile.

'Yes,' she said. 'I think about that often. Some Hampstead shrink, a referral to the Charing Cross unit ... a few weeks recovering in my own bed, not at Yusuf's or Lillianne's.' She sighed, then grinned. 'But I suppose if I *had* stayed safe up the hill, I wouldn't have met a lot of people who've become friends. I would have thought they were just sad, disgusting freaks. Perhaps it's been for the best. A mind-broadening experience.'

Roy tried not to wince, but a coldness crept into him at the mention of the friends. *But to the girdle ... burning, scalding, stench, consumption ...*

As steadily as he could, he said, 'Douglas told me about Adam, and what you did.'

'Well, there you are.' A spark of amusement lit the sombre dark eyes, and Danny's face was transformed by the smile. 'Maybe they would never have got the guy at all if you'd kept me safe at home. Maybe I was sent. Endredy is still inside, I'm happy to say. So it's all right, Dad. You threw me in, but I swam.'

A momentary illusion shook Danny then; for a moment she thought her father was going to move towards her, arms outstretched, and hug her. She closed her eyes for a moment to embrace the chimera, but when she opened them Roy was still by the window, still awkward.

He said, 'Yes, you stayed afloat. You did well. You look well.' And Danny had to be satisfied, for the moment, with that.

They sat down, drank their tea, and spoke of Shona, of Zachary and of Helen's strange purdah in the Ferris Home. Roy was still slow, strangely baffled and unfocused, on the subject of his wife and youngest son.

'Does Helen know that I'm here? That you and I ...?'

'No,' said Danny. 'Shona didn't want to rock the boat by saying that I'd be around Zack as well. Mum might have freaked and refused to let him come – and God knows she's got nowhere to put him. He's gone completely on strike about staying at the Darlings'. So Shona just told Suzy to pass on the messages that you were safe and staying with a friend. She also mentioned that I was fine as well, and doing a degree at UCL. Suzy was a bit surprised by that, because it turns out that you and Mum always told the neighbours I was studying abroad.'

Roy looked down at his hands, awkwardly.

'Perhaps,' said Danny mischievously, 'she misheard. Perhaps you said I *was* a broad.' At Roy's involuntarily outraged expression she dared to laugh, and said lightly, 'There I am. Annoying my dad again.'

He smiled; and Danny reflected that if you could not have family embraces, you could at least have family teasing. She had grown used, these past years, to making do with whatever came her way.

Neither of them felt ready to raise the subject of Roy's giving back the flat. They spoke of books, and of Danny's university course. But as she was leaving, her father said, without knowing why, 'May I ask, what was the picture that normally hangs over the gas fire?' There was a paler rectangle on the worn cream paint of the wall, and a bare hook. In the hurry of tidying up, Danny had forgotten to put up something else in the space.

Danny hesitated for only a fraction of a second before saying, 'Yusuf. A friend who died last year.'

'Douglas mentioned him. A good friend, he thought.'

'A kind of surrogate father. When I met him he was a seventy-eight-year old asthmatic, impotent, gentle romantic. I was a stroppy kid in transition.'

Roy, who knew that their meeting today had not been all that Danielle deserved, felt rebuked by the words 'a kind of surrogate father'. To punish himself he forced out a question he had resolved not to ask.

'Was he in love with you?'

'He used to say that he loved the idea I had, of the woman that I would be. Ideal woman, sort of thing. He gave me that book,' she pointed to the Yeats poems Roy had been reading earlier, one of the few expensive editions on the shelves. 'You know the one? The pilgrim soul in you, the sorrows of your changing face. I told you he was a romantic.'

'But he died?'

'He always was dying. Ever since I first met him and moved into his flat for a while. He had a tumour, and he knew all about it and never told me. He saw me through my first operation and then died. And if you're wondering, no, he didn't leave me his money. That went quite correctly to his family back in Egypt. He left me one thousand pounds and his big mink coat, which I dare not wear outdoors for fear of having paint thrown on me.'

'Where is it?' asked Roy, for the sake of saying something. He was tired now, his head throbbing; he wanted to lie down.

'It's in a locked tin chest on the landing cupboard, together with his picture and anything else I thought might freak out a nicely brought-up chap from Ferris Hill Road,' said Danny, with a crooked grin. 'Don't even think about any of it, Dad. Start from where we are, right?'

'Right,' said Roy. 'Yes, you're right.'


Up in Ferris Hill Road, Zack was packed and ready. Suzy Darling flapped around him, anxious and ineffective, listening out for the doorbell.

'Your mother said she'd be round by five,' she said. 'Oh, dear, I do wish she would hurry. Shona will be here for you soon, and you ought to see your mum.'

'She's probably got a crisis at the Home,' said Zack. 'Look, I'll be at school every day, I'll probably drop in here or the Home, won't I?'

'Yes, but . . .' Suzy could not go on. Her whole picture of family life was being wrenched and skewed by these pernicious Keaneys. Certainly it was good of Shona to get a new flat especially to look after her little brother, and certainly Shona with her peculiar way of earning a living didn't seem to be tied down by long working hours like her own Dougie and Helena. But it surely couldn't be right for the boy to live down in the teeming, roaring, seedy morass of Shona's south London when he could be up here, in the cool fresh air by the Heath, with *nice* people. Proper parents . . .

She took a grip on herself. 'Yes,' she said more firmly. 'You must come and see us often. Have your tea here whenever you want. You've always got a room here if you want to be near your friends for a party or – or – football.'

In the end Helen and Shona arrived at almost the same time. Zack sat on Suzy's kitchen table, legs swinging, while the three women held a stilted conversation. Helen produced a wad of money.

'I meant to give you something for Zack's keep – I'm sorry it's cash but the account's still frozen,' she began.

Suzy was horrified, as if a guest had casually asked for the bill at the dinner table. 'No, no, no ... I couldn't possibly – perhaps Shona ...'

'Oh yes,' said Shona, reaching out a large, capable hand. 'I shall dole it out as pocket money.'

'Yippee!' said Zack.

'In very small quantities, tied closely to household duties,' Shona finished, glaring at him. 'But you need some too.' She proffered half the bundle of notes back to her mother.

'No, it's amazing how little you need when you're getting full board. I'm putting the whole of the rent into the bank, so even the overdraft might come down soon. I thought at first that these care-home girls were *woefully* underpaid, but now I'm not so sure.'

'Your amusements are probably rather cheaper than clubbing and having to impress boys,' said Shona tartly. 'And you've already got enough clothes, I suppose.'

Incredibly to Suzy, Shona and Helen then began a political argument about the immorality of low-paid care workers (Shona) and the warped selfish values of modern youth (Helen). When she could stand it no longer their hostess said, 'Well, Zachary had better get off south with you, Shona. He'll have unpacking to do, and homework, won't you, Zack?'

'Homework, *not*,' said the boy. 'Are we going out for a pizza with Danny, like you said?'

Shona froze. Helen, however, either did not hear or pretended not to.

'I need to get back anyway,' she said. 'There's a new resident who says he hasn't played canasta for ten years. He's homesick, poor old chap, because his sister's too demented for the Ferris so she's in another home. I said I'd give him a game.' She gathered up her bag and said to her son, 'Be good, darling. See you at the weekend, perhaps?'

Zack glanced from his mother – distraite, hurrying away from him – to the reassuring form of Shona, at whom he found it far easier to look now that the studs and nose ring had gone and the places almost healed. He squared his shoulders and smiled.

'OK. 'Bye. See you.'

Shona took his bags, he hefted the box with the computer in it; together they set off down the cold street to the Underground as Helen walked off in the other direction to the turreted Home.

When they were all gone, Suzy, quite uncharacteristically, had a very large gin and French, and then another. She was later found by James stretched out on the sofa fast asleep, not having even started the supper.

# Chapter Twenty-five

The opening of 'Blood Sabbath' was a success; the air of the gallery was heavy with incense and lit by great wax candles after a frenzy of ecclesiastical set-dressing by Julian. He had even found some real church censers to dangle, spewing sacred smoke, from the steel ceiling beams. This achieved an eerie, claustrophobic atmosphere through which the daubed and spat-upon wax canvases loomed like a bad dream, aggravated by the desperate sneezing of those guests who could not quite take the sweet fragrant clouds of incense.

Shona herself made only the briefest of appearances and was startlingly rude to three art critics; but since two of them thoroughly hated the third, they overlooked her remarks to them in favour of joyfully reporting the discomfiture of their Sunday colleague. A sour-faced young woman reputed to be a scout for Saatchi bought two pictures in the first five minutes, which created a pleasing frisson. Julian's dispirited assistant went around trying to stick red spots to the frames, but the spilt wax caused them to keep falling off. Julian completely forgot about his conversation with Clem, and went around informing everybody with an air of pained hauteur that really creative work had no need of tawdry hype, but would always find a way into the art history books. He also took the opportunity to introduce two of his newer sculpture protégés to the press, and to mention that Shona Keaney had come to the end of this particular strand in her work and was going on 'a long retreat, probably in Wales'.

'A religious retreat?' asked a boyish reporter he had not met before, and who had been singularly impervious to the last ten minutes' worth of art jargon. 'Like, with nuns?'

'No ... more of a search for the, mmm, inner child,' said Julian, rather wildly because he had glimpsed the fourth of the truly important critics staring rather morosely at a crucifix done in bloodstained fist marks and captioned *stilltoday, stilldying, pinochet*. The title was not, in fact, Shona's; he had hastily added it himself.

'Inner child, eh?' said the man, scribbling.

Hemroyd, with a muttered apology, shouldered his way off through the crowd to enlighten the critic.


So after that, the watchers had nearly everything they needed. Only the photograph was missing now. The patient vigil of Ernie Archer, snapper to the stars, went unrewarded until Saturday. But on that afternoon, around half past three with good winter sunshine still lighting the street to perfection, a cheerful Danny arrived at last at Lillianne's tall peeling house in Pimlico to collect her bags.

She was still in good spirits from her visit to Roy the day before, and from a long giggly evening playing Cluedo with her sister and brother. She found Lillianne and Jo-Jo in correspondingly rip-roaring form after an afternoon out upsetting shopwalkers in Harvey Nichols.

Ernie Archer, armed with a Polaroid provided by one of Clem's contacts, recognized Danny instantly and snapped her from across the road as she let herself into the basement flat. Then, being a perfectionist, he moved in closer and waited a while in case she came out again. He had been severely disappointed by the subject's dowdy dress sense, and hoped wistfully that she was planning to go inside and change into something shinier and tighter.

He was rewarded for his patience. Before long a massive, heavily rouged creature muscled like a rugby fullback but with blonde candyfloss wig and tight sequinned dress emerged from the front door, shrieking with laughter. Behind her – or him – came a busty person in leggings and a furry fake leopardskin top, with equally incredible carrot-coloured curls. Each carried a bag. The small figure between them, with the fullback's arm draped in comradely fashion over her shoulder, was Danny, laughingly protesting. 'Hello, *darling* world,' said the leopardskin person, who sounded drunk. The carroty wig was slipping forward over one eye. 'Ooh, look, *paparazzi*, Lil. We're the Tar-ra-ra Palmer Tomkinsons, the It girls of the twenty-first century. Mwaah!'

'No, behave. Honestly.' Danny shushed the creature, then gave it a reproving peck on the cheek and raised a hand in decorous farewell.

Not that it would look like that in the picture, thought Ernie Archer as his shutter fired with a harsh artillery rattle. In the picture it would look like a pretty good snog. The drag artists' exuberance prevented them, it seemed, from minding the camera. Ernie thought that the dark one, the target, glanced towards the noise for one startled moment; but he could not be sure.

When she got back with her luggage, Danielle saw that Shona had bought a table and six folding chairs. They were of pale, clean pine, and Zachary was unfolding them ceremoniously round the table.

'That's a *lot* of chairs,' she said to him, kicking her bags into the corner of the already crowded little flat. 'Why?'

'It was my idea. In case Mum and Dad and Marcus came to supper. We could cook tacos. I can do that on my own.'

'What about Soppy Marie?' asked Danny idly, to conceal how touched she was at the boy's thought. 'Where does she sit?'

'On Marcus's knee, by the sound of things,' said Shona, emerging from the tiny bathroom. 'Zack insisted on this dinner party set-up. I was trying to work out when we were all last round the same table. I reckon September nineteen ninety-three, just before Marcus went up to Oxford. I remember a rather scratchy game of Monopoly when Mum stormed off to bed and Zacky kept coming downstairs and trying to join in and squishing the piles of money around.'

'Marcus was never back home after that, was he?' said Danny. 'Not while I was there, anyway.'

'Well, you went at the beginning of November. I remember, because it was so cold and wet and I was scared you were out on the streets in the rain.'

'And then I rang you at Christmas, and they were out.'

'And after that you vanished again, and then you rang and said I could get in touch through Douglas.'

'Do you remember when we met Marcus, in that club?'

'And how he insisted on being so cool about your dress and that weird wig you used to have? Oh, shit!' Shona laughed. 'I suppose it's one thing about being a poser, you can *never* show surprise!'

Zachary listened. It pleased him when the twins half-forgot his presence and went off into these riffs of shared memory; it filled the hollows and cracks of ignorance in his own knowledge of his family. Last night he had lain for the first time in his new bed, in the matchbox of a room high above the roaring traffic, and wondered which of his three siblings he was going to be most like. He hoped not Marcus, even though Marcus was rich and had lots of computers. Marcus, they had admitted to him, had not even bothered to find out where Danny was all that time. He, Zack, had done better. The thought warmed him.

For Shona he had a cautious, amused respect which was turning into something more; for Danny an awed admiration. Not because of the sex change; that was one weird thing, and both the twins had impressed on him its rarity and irrelevance to his own future. The admiration was because Danny had gone away; away from Mum and Dad without even a big sister to go to. It was awesome to Zack that this runaway brother had survived and got along fine, and got a flat and A levels and gone to university and organized a whole life, starting from only five years older than he was now. He, Zachary, had them both to look after him and even so there were moments of alarming bleakness about this new life. His duvet cover was stiff and scratchy; the pillow smelt oddly chemical. He had not really packed enough clothes. There was school stuff which he had forgotten still at No. 33, with the Americans; he was in a certain amount of trouble about this already, and had not told school about any of it. Being at Mrs Darling's had been annoying and boring and embarrassing, but it had still been the same sort of thing as being at home. The same sort of house, the same sort of breakfast. He wondered how he would wake up in time to get the Tube to school on Monday. Shona slept in till after nine o'clock, and he had no idea what time Danny got up. And the flat was ever so small for three.

It was Danny who voiced his thoughts, perching on one of the new chairs at the table which took up more of the small kitchen than was comfortable.

'Seriously, Shona, we can't all three fit in here for long. Not unless we start using your big room to live in, and then what about your work?'

'I'll manage. I've dragged the sofabed into there anyway, it won't open with this damn table here. You and I will just have to bunk up together.'

'Is your bed OK, Zacky?'

'Brilliant, thanks,' said the youngest Keaney. He was blinking, Danny saw, rather rapidly.


The photo of Danny at Lillianne's was too late for the Sunday paper which had bought the story; its newsdesk in any case had a laudable old-fashioned punctiliousness about filling in details, and preferred to get chapter and verse before launching its exclusives on a sleepy world. Accordingly it sent its own young man down to talk to Ishmael, and to make an undercover visit to one of Lillianne's famous Wednesday night parties. He arrived suitably dressed at the tall decrepit house in Pimlico, so famously convenient for Victoria coach station and its busloads of excitable party-lovers from Manchester. Danny was not there, but a long giggling flirtation with Jo-Jo, conducted at shouting volume over several karaoke Village People numbers, gleaned enough new material for the reporter's purposes.

Ishmael – utterly star-struck by his press visitors, and vaguely convinced that it was all to do with Shona's art – was equally helpful in directing him to the estate agent a few doors along who had rented the flat to the young Keaneys. Another flirtation, this time with the receptionist Denise over a drink in the pub opposite, confirmed the details and the involvement of the young boy. The discreet tape whirred as the girl, flushed and flattered, rattled on about the group. She had been given to understand that Shona, Danny and Zack were young Hollywood discoveries and their minder, spending time incognito in south London to perfect their accents for a new film. Her new friend, she heard, was a showbiz writer who knew a lot of film and modelling scouts and had wondered whether someone of the ravishing appearance of Denise might be involved in the movie too.

'The kid looked really excited, they were all going through the files together and having a laugh about all the stairs. It was ever so sweet, and they're doing really well with the accents, I'd hardly have known. It's not a very big flat, though, from the floorplan.'

'One big bedroom and a little room, you said. So they'll be a bit crowded?'

'Yeah, it seems funny when they're in films, dunnit?'

'Probably like method acting. You know, like Ralph Fiennes in that desert film.'

He was a generous boy, the reporter. He did not just pump people and leave them abruptly; that would have been bad manners. So he threw in a few made-up stories about movie stars to brighten up Denise's life, and bought her another drink before he left.

Roy ventured further and further from the flat during that week, walking miles from Bloomsbury into the East, loitering in St Paul's Cathedral and around the gardens by the Inns of Court, crossing the river bridges to and fro, threading his way through the glass monoliths of the City. He still avoided the West End, scene of his working life and his lonely descent, but otherwise he found during these long walks that the city could comfort, as well as threaten.

It was years since he had walked so aimlessly; years of running on tracks between his high northern home and the offices of Handfast or Eden, with odd visits to the theatre and lunchtime forays to a small, rarely changing set of restaurants when he was with an author or a contact. Great tracts of London's life had, he saw now, been hidden from him either by indifferent familiarity or because he never visited certain quarters except to roll through them in a taxi or beneath them on the Tube.

Now, at leisure all day long, he watched the knots of smokers on the pavement outside their buildings, and observed young men and women of the City spilling out of their offices into wine bars after work. Sometimes the scuttling clerks, with their narrow faces and dark clothes, made him think of their Dickensian forebears. So did the lawyers flapping their way to the Old Bailey, and the broad-bottomed, booming liverymen greeting one another by their worshipful old halls. Sometimes Fu Manchu was at his shoulder as he slipped down oddly unchanged alleyways to the broad glimmer of the Thames.

Like the hours of reading in Danny's flat, these walks took him back to a simpler time, the time after university when his mind was still unfolding and all things seemed possible; the time when he had first known Helen, before they had migrated to the city's northern heights and made their nest there. He tried to think of Helen, but a fog still came over part of his mind. Danny's account of her new life at the Ferris Home had shocked him, but not surprised him much; there was something strangely appropriate about her retreat into this elderly world.

She had missed her parents, he suddenly thought, much more than he had ever understood. His own had faded more slowly, indeed almost unnoticed by him; but one day, standing alone in the mist in some cramped ancient little City churchyard, he suddenly and vividly remembered the moment at his own father's funeral, during the singing of 'The Lord is my shepherd', when his wife had fallen into noisy raw sobs in the pew next to him. At the time he had been merely embarrassed and a little annoyed; she barely knew her father-in-law. It was inappropriate to carry on so. Now he thought that she must have been re-living her own parents' deaths ten years earlier.

He still did not want to see her. He had the fare, from his benefit money; could have got on the Tube and gone north to talk to her, or to the Darlings. He could not do it. Instead he took to crossing the river and searching for Shona's world. He found her studio beyond the railway tunnel, and stood outside, head flung back, wondering what went on behind the high grimy windows. The next evening he found his way to the new flat, and again stood outside, a shabby nondescript figure in need of a haircut, too shy to ring his own children's doorbell.

He looked after his own simple needs; began to cook omelettes and make salads in Danny's neat kitchen alcove, and to take the clothes which Father Douglas had given him to the launderette. One evening mid-week when Douglas was with him, sipping tea and talking books, Danny dropped in. Roy watched the two of them together, touched in spite of himself and filled with a shamed wonder that the child he had rejected so summarily from his own hearth had found the way to others who did not.

When Danny had left and he was alone again with Douglas, he said, 'Sh-she is quite a person, don't you think?'

'Yes,' said Douglas. 'Quite a person. You wouldn't think she had so much to go through, every day.'

'What?' asked Roy uncertainly.

'The coming out. Just now, when you were in the bathroom, she quickly told me that she'd come out to her new tutor at UCL. The old one left, and she was in a bit of a dilemma about the new woman, because she's a bit old-fashioned in a lot of ways. But she did it today, and it went OK. You saw how relieved she was. She's always happy when it goes well.'

'Does it sometimes not?'

'I'm afraid so. That's why she's so discreet. She says it's never a real friendship until she has broken the news, but that with some people she has a gut feeling it's better to have a second-division friendship and not mention it.'

'But everyone must know who knew him, I mean her, when ...'

'There aren't that many. I worry most about a particular chap called Lillianne, the transvestite king of the jungle. He's devoted to Danny, wouldn't dream of blowing the gaff on purpose, but accidentally anything could happen. A year ago she was approached through Lillianne by a chap from a television company making a documentary about transsexuals.'

'God, why?'

'He'd heard that Danny was one of the most straight types, and wanted to film her going through her day and talking about it. It was a good programme, a BBC religious department thing. I thought she should have done it, myself. Just put the cards on the table. I must confess that I even thought it might help get her parents back in touch. And she was terribly broke then, and they'd have paid.'

'But it didn't happen?'

'No. She was adamant. Said her life was private. Said that once you did telly, the papers would be giggling about you for years.'

'Does she ever get trouble now?'

'Don't think so. Lillianne swears he never gave her address to anyone.'


The dossier was complete by the time the reporters came to the flat on Saturday morning for the final quotes. It was politic to leave it this late before alerting the quarry, for a mid-week warning of what was to come often caused lawyers and injunctions to be summoned up.

Zack was alone, watching television, and would not push the button to let them in. He shouted down the intercom, 'I'm not supposed to let people in till my sisters get home, right? Shona's gone to the shops.'

They waited. When Shona arrived, the cameraman snapped her busily while the reporter struggled to recognize this frumpish but conventional figure from the pictures he had on the file.

'What d'you want? Put that fucking camera down or I'll smash it,' said Shona nastily, causing the photographer to jump back out of reach.

'We want to talk to you about your brother Daniel, his habits and associates, and your custody of a child called Zachary Keaney. Is Daniel with you?'

'My sister—' began Shona, but saw that she was trapped. 'Oh, piss off, you vultures. Piss off, or I'll kill you.' She kicked out, catching the reporter on the shin; the camera flashed and rattled again. Fumbling with the key, dragging her bursting carrier bags through the door, she summoned all her considerable strength to slam it. When the catch had caught, she leaned on the inside of the door looking up the grey stairs, and found that her legs were trembling.

They staked out the flat for two hours more, but the missing twin did not come home. She had been on her way from the British Library when her mobile rang with Shona's warning. By the time the newspaper's deadline loomed and the stakeout was abandoned, Danielle Keaney was sitting at the desk in Father Douglas's office at the shelter, sobbing inconsolably with her head on her arms while the priest, his face death-pale and grim, stood above her murmuring useless consolations.

# Chapter Twenty-six

Neither of the twins slept in more than fitful, nightmare snatches. Shona at the flat, Danny in the sick bay at the shelter, each lay awake in the small hours shaking at the thought of what the morning might bring. Twice in the darkness Shona almost got up to walk to Waterloo station and collect the papers early, but she was afraid that Zack might wake and find himself abandoned. So deep was her sense of doom that she began imagining still worse scenarios: of herself being mugged, run over, or blown up by a stray terrorist bomb while on this errand, and Zack left to wake up bewildered and encounter the dreaded day alone.

Hunched in her bed she struggled to persuade herself it would not be so bad. She tried to think that the story might not appear after all. But she had been too long in a publicity-seeking business not to know in her heart that it *would* appear, and that it would be at least partly her fault. The blow which was about to fall upon them all was a whiplash effect from the notoriety which she, with Julian Hemroyd's encouragement, had light-heartedly courted. She had done it to defy the lumpen bourgeoisie, to spit revenge in her parents' eye, to make money. She had thought, stupid simpleton, that scandal was a tap she could turn on and off at will. Now it was going to drown them all in humiliation.

She rolled over and lay spreadeagled, crucified, on her back; tears overflowed her eyes and ran back into her ears. Most of all she thought of Danny, and wished with all her heart that she had asked her to come home once evening fell. They should be together to face the worst.

At the shelter, meanwhile, Douglas had tried to persuade Danny to take a sleeping pill; she would not, but lay with hot unhappy eyes in the sick-bay, lit by the same street glow through the high barred window that her father had watched night after night. She remembered Jo-Jo shrieking 'paparazzi' with drunken glee, and how her stomach had briefly knotted when she saw the camera; but she had pushed it aside, dismissing it as part of their lives, not hers. Lillianne's establishment, after all, was often featured in Sunday papers of the naughty-vicar persuasion.

Now she knew what they had wanted, and without much difficulty could trace the steps by which she had become so hatefully newsworthy. It would presumably be Roy's revolt and Shona's exhibition which had made someone gossip to some reporter about the oddity of their family. Even so, the days had passed when a mere sex change, especially of a dowdy student like herself, was splashable news. What Shona had told her, in that brief panicky phone call, made it clear that it was Zachary's living at the flat which had given them the hook for their prurient story.

They should have thought of that; but the twins, thought Danny bitterly, had been so focused on doing what *was* right that they had forgotten about the need for it to *seem* right. They wanted Zack to be safe and happy and supported in his life by his blood family. They had forgotten that society does not smile on the cohabitation of children of eleven with sex freaks.

Come to that, they had forgotten that she *was* a freak to the middle England readership. A sex-changed former rent boy, no less. How could the Sunday readers know how far she had travelled from that old world? How could they guess that neither of the twins would dream of allowing their young brother to meet Lillianne and Jo-Jo and the rest of them? Shona would not even take him to the Hemroyd Gallery, and had taken out all her studs and rings and bought a horrid square blazer at Marks & Spencer out of homage to normality, all for Zack's sake.

But they couldn't know that. They wouldn't. And nor would Roy when he read it. His revulsion had never died, Danny knew that. He bravely held it in check, he tried not to shrink from her, but her big sad eyes saw how it was.

'He still can't take it. He still thinks first about what's under my clothes, about the things I've done and the people I've lived with. I'm still a monster, however hard he tries.' She had sobbed out this conviction to Douglas in the office during the long passionate storm of tears that evening. He had stroked her hair but not denied it. Douglas never lied. Danny rolled face downward on the bed which had been Misery's, and wept through the night as if her heart would break.

Down the corridor in the priest's office, the light burned late. He had gone out for the paper at midnight, identifying without difficulty the one which held the story. Handing over the coins under the sickly glow of a street lamp, he had seen it flagged above the title, a picture of Lillianne in full fig cut into closeness with a young boy whose face was in shadow and the words CHILD OF OUR TIMES?

Now it lay on his desk, spread open under the battered Anglepoise lamp. It was, if anything, worse than he had feared. Carefully, the piece made no direct accusation of abuse, but the implication glared from every line. There was a highly-coloured and dateless account of Danny's career as a rent boy, the relationship with a 'millionaire Arab playboy' and the sex-change surgery. There was a picture of her kissing Lillianne's bloated white cheek, with Jo-Jo making an obscene gesture behind them. Douglas had to admit that it was probably not, in point of fact, an obscene gesture, but Jo-Jo's outfits made most of her gestures susceptible to being captioned that way. There was a box inset with a lurid account of 'Wednesday night at Lili's' and the goings-on both visible and imagined. There was a library shot of Shona: topless, dreadlocked and smeared with dung at Hemroyd's northern gallery. There was the picture of Roy on the pavement with his fist raised and his face contorted. Zack himself was represented by a facially fuzzed-out picture of some child model a good two years younger. The newspaper concluded with a pious claim that they had 'laid all the evidence' before the Social Services in the London borough in question, and waited to see whether the 'trendy, PC establishment' there would do anything to protect this child from further corruption into the world of vice and coprophagic art.

The priest stared wearily at the pages. It was not, in fact, a major story. It was on the inside pages. Of those who read it, few would do more than cluck in comfortable disapproval. Everyone would forget it by Monday morning. Such exposés were rarely followed by daily papers unless genuinely public figures were involved. Social Services would probably investigate cursorily, but a happy schoolboy staying at his elder sister's with parental consent was not likely, given their more pressing concerns, to provoke them to any action.

All the same, Douglas was filled with fear, a cold dread for Danielle. The years of courage, he thought, had left her brittle. She smiled, she joked, she seemed to reach out sunnily towards the world; yet Roy had snapped suddenly and left his solid life in hopeless fragments, and Douglas thought that she was very like her father.

Soundlessly he crept along the cold tiled corridor and peered through the glazed top of the sick-bay door. Danny lay on her face, fully dressed, asleep on a damp pillow with her skirt crumpled up to show sparrow-thin legs. He edged into the room, pulled a blanket gently over the forlorn figure, and went back to his room to gather up his coat and the newspaper. Something had to be done, and done before the dawn broke.

# Chapter Twenty-seven

Shona fell asleep just before dawn, and slept heavily until eight; waking with a start she remembered what the day must bring, and swung from the bed with a cold dank feeling at the pit of her stomach. The sleep, though, had brought clarity and she knew that the first thing to do was find Danny and be with her when she confronted the newspaper. On big bare feet she went into Zack's slit of a room and found him naked, bedclothes and pyjamas flung to the floor, his chest red with an angry rash and his brow burning.

Anxiety displaced the earlier dread; her cool hand on his brow woke him and she said tensely, 'What's up, Zacky? You don't look well.' He raised his head, eyes wild, and immediately vomited, the small head hanging over the side of the bed as he retched.

'S-sorry,' he said at last. 'I'll clean it up ...' Trying to sit up, he wobbled so much that she was afraid he would fall out of bed. She threw an arm round the child and laid him back down, as gently as she could with the hammering anxieties inside her. The muscles in her forearm seemed to lock and twitch with tension. Zack's face was waxy, his brow clammy; he clenched his eyes tightly against the morning light. Shona had no experience of disease and little of children; she shook with terror at the responsibility she had so lightly taken on. She had read about meningitis and how you had to press the rash with a glass and see if it faded. They had no glasses, only garish IKEA plastic tumblers chosen by Zack. Danny, she thought wildly, Danny would be better, Danny had been a sick-bay orderly at Douglas's—

With a jolt she remembered about Danny and the newspaper. As her head spun with the complexity of the situation, Zack moaned, rolled sideways, and began once more to retch painfully. He was clutching her hand; Shona let him hold it until the spasm passed, and then eased her hand gently from his grasp and said, 'Lie still. Try and relax. I'm going to get an ambulance.'

When it came, forty-five terrifying minutes later, Shona saw that there were a couple of Sunday papers thrust beside the driver's seat. One of them was folded open at the page where Danny stood trapped in the flashlight between Lillianne and Jo-Jo. By then, she did not even care. Zack was moaning, thrashing, vomiting, hot-browed and hysterical. The only words they could understand were, 'Mum – I want Mum – where's Mum?'

Shona, white-faced, held his hand while the paramedic bent over him, and said, 'She's coming, she's coming, we'll fetch her,' and tried through her panic to remember Suzy Darling's telephone number.

Roy was with Father Douglas. Roused from his bed at 4 a.m. by the insistent buzzing of the entryphone, he had listened with puzzled docility to the priest's preamble, then read the newspaper article in silence while rain wept down the skylight and the cheap Chianti-bottle lamps threw pools of warm light onto Danny's African rugs.

After a while he folded the newspaper and said, 'Horrible.'

Douglas regarded him in silence. There was something different about the man, a resolution and clarity of eye that the priest had not seen before.

Roy said again, 'Horrible, horrible. Bastards. It's a modern version of the stocks, isn't it? Formulaic humiliation.'

'You do know why Danielle was caught there, leaving Lillianne's? Why she'd been staying there, in a house she hasn't visited for at least two years?'

'Because I'm here in her flat.'

'Yes. Lil is not so bad; he was a good friend to her in the bad times. He's a straightforward male prostitute and the flamboyant transvestism is purely for commercial reasons as far as I can see; but he was sympathetic to Danny always. Jo-Jo is a nasty piece of work, into everything kinky that's going, but not very happy; I can never make him out. But it's open house for friends there, and I suppose a free lodging was the point.'

'So having thrown my son out of his home onto the streets and into danger at sixteen, I've now managed to do it again?'

'Yes,' said Douglas. The two men glanced around at the invincible security and seclusion of the little flat. 'Yes, I doubt there'd have been a story if she'd just been a mousy Bloomsbury student.'

'I'm going to kill them,' said Roy unemotionally. 'I'm going to kill them *today*.'

'Wouldn't it be better,' said Douglas, 'to see Danny first, and tell her it's all right? She was in a bad state last night.'

'Obviously,' said Roy. He rubbed his stubbled chin. 'Yes, obviously. Poor kid, poor baby. Let me shave, and we'll be there when she wakes up.'


Danny woke up when it was still dark, from a nightmare about Zachary being eaten by a giant spider with a crab's shell. Memory swept over her and made her catch her breath; somehow during her sleep more of the consequences of the coming exposure had sunk in. What about Professor Dinevor, who had accepted the news of her nature with courteous caution? What would she think when she read about Lillianne's house, and saw the photograph, and learnt about the distant months of prostitution? In the brief panicky call to her mobile, Shona had repeated the reporter's words about 'habits and associates'. It was not hard to guess what that meant.

Professor Dinevor doesn't read the *Sunday Probe*, she told herself now; but instantly a mocking inner voice replied, yes, but she'll be shown it. Fellow students read it, Danny knew, with what they liked to pretend was a spirit of sophisticated irony. Shopkeepers had it on wire stands and glanced through it when trade was slack; market stallholders wrapped it round potatoes; Nelly and Zipper cackled over it together with the guys at the shelter, although Zipper could barely read. Middle-class homes saw it too, or were shown it by their cleaners. Suzy and James Darling would see the pictures and reports eventually, and a copy was bound to find its way into the Ferris Home for Helen's eye.

Everyone would know everything. That, on top of his curling disgust, would build a final and irrevocable wall between Danny and her father. It was over. She got out of bed, smoothed down her skirt, and used the cracked shabby bathroom. Ten minutes later, with hair drawn back in a severe knot, a thin young woman walked from the shelter into the quiet Sunday morning street. She walked towards the river, stopping at an early newsstand to buy a paper. The seller, jocular in the chilly morning, blowing on frozen fingers that poked through woolly gloves, tried to pass the time of day without success. This girl was taciturn. She bought her paper, opened it, stood reading the centre pages for a while, then crumpled it into a waste-bin and walked on rapidly towards the Embankment. The man shrugged; people were odd about Sunday papers, no doubt about it.

They had been at the hospital for half an hour, swept from casualty to cubicle and on to a ward, before Shona got a chance to telephone. Zack was all but unconscious, still groaning but surrounded by nurses and their reassuring paraphernalia; the doctor, who looked curiously at Shona's shocked youthful face and thought her too young to be decently the mother of a child of eleven, nonetheless congratulated her on the speed of her reaction.

'Almost certainly meningococcal. But you've got him here quickly, and his chances are excellent because of that.'

Now, marginally relieved by these words, Shona was dialling Hampstead with fumbling fingers.

'. . . 3689,' said the answering machine. 'James and Suzy. Speak after the bleep. Thanks. 'Byee!'

Shona rapped out a message, and found she had no more coins. She ran to the hospital shop, bought a bar of chocolate and returned to the phone. Eventually Directory Enquiries answered and gave her the number of the Ferris Home.

'I need to speak to Mrs Keaney. Urgently,' she said.

Mrs Beazeley's voice crackled scornfully down the line. 'I will give her a message. Unfortunately we are not able to allow staff to take personal calls in the office. She can call you back.'

'No she fucking *can't!*' yelled Shona. 'Look, her youngest son is seriously ill. Just get her to the phone, or I'll come up there and rip your head off!'

There was a clucking, but the telephone was laid down on a surface rather than cut off. After some minutes and another ten pence piece, Helen's voice came on the line. She was squeakily agitated.

'What is it? Who is this? Roy?'

'No. Shona. Zacky's ill. Meningitis. He should be OK, but he wants you. Get down here, OK? Now!'

Helen squeaked some more; Shona felt exasperation, as if she were the mother and this her hopeless teenager. She gave the details of the hospital and concluded, 'Look, just *come*. Just bloody *come*. Get a taxi.'

The telephone she was using was not at the main hospital entrance but nearer to the tea stall where she had got change;

behind her was the entrance to the accident and emergency department. An ambulance drew up as she turned away from the kiosk, and a paramedic got out and rapidly lowered the ramp. She heard him say, 'We've got a jumper. Not in for long, but very hypothermic. Luckily for her there was a copper on the floating police station under the bridge. They never seem to reckon with that being there. They think they're all on their own.'

It meant nothing to Shona, who was dialling the number of Danny's mobile. Not until, receiving no answer, she turned and saw beneath the stretcher coverings the draggled corner of a dark skirt with a stitched ethnic pattern round the hem.

'Gone,' said Douglas to Roy. His face was white, lined, suddenly very old under the neon light of the sick bay. 'I should have thought of that. I bet she's gone to get a paper. I really thought she'd sleep on, after all that crying.'

Roy took his arm. 'Where? Where would she go?'

Their thoughts ran parallel; she would not go to her flat to face Roy, nor to Lillianne's, nor to any friend they knew of. Her only bolthole must be Shona's new flat.

Douglas went to the wall of his office and unlocked a small safe, pulling out a roll of notes. 'I haven't taken a taxi in years,' he said. 'But come on.'

South of the river, Shona's doorbell went unanswered, so they rang all the others. Eventually a crone appeared from the bottom flat and said, with every appearance of satisfaction, 'There was an ambulance went, with the little boy. Half an hour past. He looked near to dying. I suppose we're lucky still to *have* ambulances, with the country in this state.'

Their cab to the hospital narrowly overtook another one, containing a dishevelled dark young man and a pale angel-faced blonde. They had been set on their way when, twenty minutes earlier, Suzy Darling had stumbled downstairs to hear the answering machine and immediately rung not only the Ferris

Home but Marcus in Docklands. As Suzy said to James, 'Who knows, they might suddenly need to go private, and he *is* the man with the plastic cards.'

So that was how all six Keaneys came to be under the same roof again, for the first time in seven years.

# Chapter Twenty-eight

Shona chased the stretcher into A & E, not quite believing what she saw. The half-heard voices jarred in her mind: ... *a jumper ... not long in, but very hypothermic.* The police had seen it happen; she knew about the floating police station under Charing Cross Bridge. One of her boyfriends had been in the river force, and had once taken her into the little pontoon hut and shown her their drawer full of photographs of fished-out corpses. They all looked weirdly alike, blank faces and lank hair bringing the variety of ages and races together in a horrid siblinghood. The policeman, a poetic spirit, had quoted Thomas Hood's poem about the Victorian drowned slattern:

> One more unfortunate
> Weary of breath
> Rashly importunate,
> Gone to her death!

They had speculated on what, in the age of sleeping pills and railway lines and high buildings, made people take this old-fashioned final route out of London life. Was it the dark water, some ancient instinct to find oblivion in the river Lethe? Did its flow and swirl hypnotize and comfort you at the final dreadful moment?

But never, never in a thousand years would she have expected it of Danny. Danny had survived so much for so long, had served seven years in the twilight and emerged bright-spirited into the sun. In the first awful year, a teenage Shona had lain awake terrified for her twin, but not lately, not for years, not since she had understood the thread of steely strength that ran through Danny's slight form. She had relied on it; too complacently, she thought now. She should never, ever have let Danny out of her sight ...

Running into A & E, looking wildly round as the stretcher vanished through curtains, she still barely believed the disaster. The place blurred before her, and she no longer knew which curtains, or felt sure of what she had seen. After a breathless moment she went to the desk and said, 'I think my sister – just came – in – recognized her skirt ...'

'Name?'

'Keaney—'

'A little boy called Keaney – but he's gone up to the ward.'

'I know. That's my brother.'

The girl looked up, confused and suspicious. The usual row of sleepy drunks and roughly bandaged dossers sat on plastic chairs, glaring resentfully at anybody who looked like jumping their queue. At the desk the receptionist continued tapping and peering at a computer and riffling through scrawled notes. Finally she said, 'Were they both in the same incident, then? Only I've just got the one Keaney, gone up to paeds—'

A policeman behind her coughed. 'Would that be the young lady we just brought in, with the coloured bits on her skirt? Only if you do have details, miss, we'd be obliged ...'

By the time Shona had explained, her mother and father were both standing in the doorway staring at each other wildly and wordlessly across the tall anxious figure of Father Douglas Cantrip.

'Helen, you're here – do you know what's happened?' began

Roy, but his daughter came over with a long stride and rapidly told them both. Helen, huge-eyed beneath her ragged dark crop, burst into tears and sat down.

'I can't – I can't ...' she began.

Roy said, 'Where is he?'

'Children's ward. We were lucky. He's in a side ward with all the tubes and stuff and a nurse watching him until they're sure he's stable. They said he was responding OK.'

'Where is it? Take us there.' It was still Roy talking, with a crispness none of them had heard for years. He took Helen's arm. Limply, she let him.

Shona hesitated, then said, 'I'll come up, and if he's OK I'll leave you two there. Let me just speak to Douglas.'

She murmured something rapidly to the tall man, who grimaced and looked round at the curtained cubicles. Roy's sharp ears caught the word 'Danny', and he stiffened, following the priest's gaze; but Helen was clutching distractingly at his arm, and he led her off towards the lift under Shona's direction.

When they reached the ward and received reassurances about Zack – whose colour was already less alarming – Roy left Helen to sit by the half-dozing boy and moved back to stand near the door with Shona. Out of the side of his mouth he said, 'What was that downstairs? You said something about Danny.'

'I'm pretty sure it's her. In casualty.'

'Why? How? I have to see her. The paper—'

'I know. Look, we can go down. I'll tell you on the way,' said Shona.

She went over to the bed where the limp, damp-faced child lay loosely holding his mother's hand. 'Zacky, we're going downstairs, Mum'll stay with you, OK?'

'Mummy's here,' said Helen, with a limp automatism that made Roy flinch. Zack blinked, screwing up his eyes against the light from the frosted window of the side ward.

The nurse said, 'Looks worse than it is. Really, he's doing well. Have the tubes out soon. We'll be fine now his mum's here.' She smiled brightly at Helen, who began to weep quietly.

Father and daughter made the journey back down to the casualty reception, walking fast and breathless down long corridors where their shoes squeaked in sympathetic agitation. When they got there, the policeman was emerging from behind some curtains.

He said, 'You were quite right, miss. The young lady's awake now, and we've confirmed her identity.' To the nurse hovering beside him he said, 'This young lady is Miss Keaney's sister. We've confirmed identification with another gentleman, Mr Cantrip. Clerical gentleman.' And to Shona again, 'Miss, the vicar said to tell you that he would be over by the machine getting a cup of tea, if anybody wanted him.'

'So you're Danielle's sister then? Well, you can see her now,' said the nurse brightly. 'She's just got to stay until we've done a chest X-ray, to see if there's a problem with water in the lungs.'

'I,' said Roy, 'am her father.' He hesitated. 'Do you mind, Shonie?'

'Be my guest,' she said. 'But I want to go in afterwards.'

So Roy stepped through the curtain without a backward glance, to take his pallid, damp-haired daughter in his arms.


There are no fairy tales, thought Shona much later, no pantomime endings with every demon quashed and every dame and misfit paired and squared. The nearest to the roseate happy ending came during the confused half-hour after Roy's embrace of Danny, with the appearance of Marcus and Marie, hand in hand, decently concerned about the sick child but wrapped in shining undentable happiness. The prince and princess, thought Shona drily, love's young dream, the pantomime finale. All they needed was a shower of rose petals and sequins from the polystyrene ceiling tiles of the A&E waiting area.

She and Roy were by then sitting on a plastic bench outside X-ray with Danny between then, her head nestled into her father's shoulder, his hand on her hair. When she saw her elder brother come through the swing doors, Shona jumped to her feet and hurried to intercept him.

'We heard about Zack from Mrs Darling,' he began. 'Hey, is that – over on the bench, is that who I think it is?'

'Yes,' said Shona repressively. 'River accident. Don't ask.'

'The little boy ...' began Marie anxiously.

'Zack's going to be all right,' said Shona. 'Look, Marcus, don't stir anything. I mean it.'

'He isn't here to be nasty,' said Marie with sublime confidence. 'Are you, Markie? Come on, let's say hello nicely to your dad.'

So, prompted by his fiancée, Marcus managed the awkwardness of the moment reasonably well. He grinned at Danny and made a double thumbs up, receiving a thin smile in return. Then he met his father's eye – not without difficulty – and said, 'Cheers, Dad. Good to see you. I was going to come round and say sorry about all that crap back at Eden, right? I owe you one. I was a bit of an arsehole, actually. Don't know what came over me. Can we talk about sorting something out?'

Roy, preoccupied with his daughters, had managed a stiff, surprised grimace of goodwill. He also stared in amazed recognition at the gentle beauty on his son's arm, received the startling news of their engagement and rather pointedly wished Marie luck.

Shona watched them all, still wary. It would have been difficult, she thought with a burst of inward amusement, to devise a more ridiculously British, pathologically underplayed script for a family catharsis. Mrs Groschenberg would not have liked it at all.

The happy pair hung around for a while, drinking machine

coffee, and then went up to the children's ward. Zachary, sitting up by lunchtime, extracted the promise of a laptop computer from his big brother in two minutes flat. So, Shona supposed, for him the fairy tale came closer than for most.

In the end Roy took Danny home to Bloomsbury in a taxi. Douglas shared it as far as the shelter so that he could give them a spare pillow and quilt from his winter emergency store. Before he left the hospital he spoke to Shona.

'You know where I am if you need me,' he said simply. 'Any of you.'

'I wish you'd speak to Mum,' said Shona uneasily. 'She's the one, really ... I mean, you worked wonders with Dad. Look at them.'

Douglas glanced towards Roy and Danny, still arm in arm and deep in conversation. Then, with a troubled air, he said, 'There's no magic, you know. It wasn't me who changed your father; it was himself.'

'But if Mum could talk to someone – she's gone so weird. The thing is, Zacky asked for her and I just felt so helpless ...' Shona could not go on. She had not cried for years, and did not want to begin.

Douglas laid a hand on her shoulder. 'Wait and see,' he said. 'Let time pass.' And as Shona dropped her eyes and fought the treacherous tears, his footsteps squeaked away towards the door and the waiting taxi.


Helen slept overnight in the parents' room at the hospital. By morning, however, with Zack well out of danger, she had become oddly fretful about getting back to her job. She rather shocked the nurses by talking distractedly of the need to hurry back and get the screen set up for the reminiscence therapy slide show.

So Shona, who had wearily gone back to the flat to sleep, arrived at the children's ward in the morning to find that her mother had just left. Her brother, on the other hand, was eating beans on toast and displaying self-conscious poise as he informed the nurse that he 'lived with his sister really' but that it was quite nice to see your mum for an hour or so when you felt ill and babyish.

'There's a note,' said the nurse to Shona, raising her eyebrows.

Shona sat heavily on the bed and unfolded a piece of paper with the hospital trust's logo at the top and Helen's loopy handwriting on it.

Dear Shona,

Please don't think too badly of me if I can't step backwards. I did my best for you all once, and it wasn't very good. Zack has told me how good you and Danny are being to him, and all about the flat. I think it's the right thing, and he's best staying with you and sometimes Suzy and we'll all be in touch, obviously. I look forward to meeting Danielle sometime.

I'm sorry. Things don't always end up tidily, do they?

Mum

Not even 'love, Mum', thought her daughter, folding the paper and putting it into her jeans pocket. After a while she attempted to talk to Zachary.

'Mum had to get back to work,' she began.

'I know,' said the boy. Then, 'Is Danny OK? One of the nurses said something—'

'Danny's with Dad,' said Shona. 'They're both absolutely fine.'

'They getting on again, then?'

'Yeah. Looks like it. Shall we have them down to supper?'

'Yeah. Is Dad going home to Hampstead then? Does he know the Yanks are in the house?'

'Zacky, I don't know what he and Mum will do,' said Shona truthfully. 'But when there's been a time like this, people don't always find it easy to go backwards to how things were.'

Zack, who had been concentrating on getting the last few baked beans onto his toast, looked up at her in surprise. 'I know *that*,' he said. 'I mean, *I* couldn't go back to living like we used to, when it was just us three in the house and I didn't know anyone in the family except Dad and Mum. That was *gross*.'

'Can we cope then, just you and me in the flat?' said Shona with unaccustomed hesitancy. 'Because I'd really like that.'

'Yeah. Me too,' said Zack. 'Can I get a different duvet? It's scratchy.'

'Sure,' said his big sister. 'It might be just that it's too new. Danny says you have to put them through a really hot wash to get the factory starch out.'


So it seemed, thought Shona, that they were still fragmented. Scattered across the London rooftops in pairs. Her and Zack, Danny and Roy, Marcus and Marie, and then Helen perched all alone above her nest of wrinkled gentility.

All the same, they had moved on. They had met and spoken civilly, proffered help and, under Marie's remorselessly sweet pressing, resolved to meet for a big family lunch once the two invalids were fit enough. Over Zachary's bed most of the adults had also, albeit without much meeting of eyes, managed to unite in brief dismissive deploring of the ways of the tabloid press.

Yes, the Keaneys were no longer frozen helplessly in separate squares. They could all throw their dice now and move on, each at his own pace. Sitting on the end of the hospital bed, Shona sighed and yawned while Zack plunged into the computer magazine she had bought him.

More than anything, she wanted to go quietly to her studio,

lay out her pencils and draw something. Rooftops and chimneys, she thought, stretching across a wide city landscape to a blurred infinity. A sunrise, perhaps.